D1504993

CHIMES AT MIDNIGHT

CHIMES AT MIDNIGHT

MICHAEL A. BLACK

FIVE STAR

A part of Gale, Cengage Learning

GALE
CENGAGE Learning·

Farmington Hills, Mich • San Francisco • New York • Waterville, Maine
Meriden, Conn • Mason, Ohio • Chicago

LIBRARY OF CONGRESS CATALOGING-IN-PUBLICATION DATA

Black, Michael A., 1949–
    Chimes at midnight / Michael A. Black. — First edition.
      pages cm
    ISBN 978-1-4328-2801-1 (hardcover) — ISBN 1-4328-2801-0 (hardcover)
      1. Murder—Investigation—Fiction. 2. Terrorism—Prevention—Fiction. I. Title.
    PS3602.L325C55 2014
    813'.6—dc23   2014003154

First Edition. First Printing: June 2014
Find us on Facebook– https://www.facebook.com/FiveStarCengage
Visit our website– http://www.gale.cengage.com/fivestar/
Contact Five Star™ Publishing at FiveStar@cengage.com

Printed in the United States of America
1 2 3 4 5 6 7 18 17 16 15 14

To the memory of Chief Donald Story, who served with honor, integrity, and professionalism.

ACKNOWLEDGMENTS

It's been said that writing a novel is sort of like running a marathon. I would certainly agree with that, but would also point out that like running a race you periodically need help from a lot of people along the way. I would like to thank the following individuals for their help and assistance with the writing of this book. *Chimes at Midnight* would not otherwise have been possible.

My sincere thanks to:

Lieutenant Dave Case, Chicago Police Department, who had my back on this one, convinced me to keep going when I wanted to quit, and helped me through the rough spots.

Detective Tonya Eskridge, Matteson Police Department, and Ms. Shauna Washington for their advice on volleyball and on the character of Felicia.

Detective Quintin Peterson, "Q," Washington, D.C. Metro Police Department (retired), for his insight, advice, and words of encouragement.

Ms. Deni Dietz, the peerless editor who worked tirelessly to make this novel better.

Lastly, I wish to add that *Chimes at Midnight* is a work of fiction and should only be considered as such. Anyone attempting to view it as anything other than a source of entertainment, such as a political commentary, is completely misreading my intentions. I would also like to express my unwavering respect and gratitude for all of those brave men and women with whom I've served, both in the military and in police work, and to those who continue to put their lives on the line every day to keep us all safe.

We have heard the chimes at midnight.

—*Henry IV, Part Two*, III:2

PROLOGUE

Mogadishu, Somalia ~ *October 4, 1993*
2345 hrs

The stale air in the room stank of sweat, body odor, and vomit. Private First Class Kevin McClain wondered if he was going to die quickly or from another slow, protracted torture session. He wondered if he was ever going to see his family again: his mom, his dad, his fiancée Lynn. He wondered if Spec Four Fisk, who was unconscious next to him, was going to make it.

McClain felt more sweat trickling down his side, surprised he could still feel anything. He'd stopped trying to work his hands and wrists to loosen his bonds. After hours of futility and the fading sensations in his arms, he'd given up. But maybe that was a benefit. He could barely feel the throbbing pain from the two fingernails on his right hand they'd ripped off earlier. His index and middle. At least he'd been able to give them the finger as they tore off the second one—a small measure of defiant comfort. Very small. He remembered them laughing.

Fisk moaned. More like an unconscious grunt. He didn't look good. The blood leaking from his wound looked darker now. Was that a bad sign? The assholes wouldn't even put a fresh dressing on the wound. But that wouldn't make any difference if they didn't get some help soon. McClain's whole body hurt from the crash and the beating they'd given him. Worse than he'd ever gotten in the ring. Maybe Fisk was the lucky one. He'd been unconscious the whole time, after they'd

11

been hit. From the looks of it, he didn't have much time left. The fucking skinnies couldn't torture a dead man. McClain wondered how long it would be before they were both being dragged naked through the streets.

He shifted, trying to ease the weight off his numb arms, tied behind his back. He estimated it was going on eight hours since they'd been separated from the platoon, but he couldn't be sure. Sporadic gunfire, sometimes heavy, followed by periods of silence—which he figured were enemy prayer times—had continued throughout the day. Was it still day? The damn windows of the hut had been boarded over. No light filtered in between the cracks. The room was dark. The single light bulb dangling on a cord from the ceiling was off. He knew they had electricity. He'd heard the droning of a portable generator. Probably stolen from some hospital after the U.N. installed it. But the darkness was a blessing—he couldn't see how totally fucked things were. Night or early morning, the only illumination came from the row of candles on the table along the wall. Candles—

The longer she stands, the shorter she grows.

The old nursery rhyme wound through McClain's memory. The candles were the closest thing he had to a clock. Several of them had been reduced to puddles of wax. That meant what? A couple hours at least.

The nursery verse should be changed. *The longer she stands, the less time we've got.*

He heard voices, and then the sound of a motor coming to life. The hut seemed to shake. They'd started the generator. The hanging light bulb suddenly went on and about thirty seconds later the curtain separating the other room whipped back. A figure paused in the doorway, the scariest-looking black man McClain had ever seen. The darkest, too. Not that his dark skin was scary. McClain had grown up on the south side of Chicago and was used to seeing blacks. He had fought black kids in the boxing ring, gone to school with gangbangers and thugs. But this guy took thuggery to a whole new level.

The dark man smiled, the uneven whiteness interrupted by several missing teeth. But his eyes, the so-called windows to the soul, looked inhuman, cold, empty. Without any trace of humanity or compassion. The asshole looked high, too. Probably from *khat.*

He turned and spoke to the guys behind him in that sing-songy language that must have been Somali. Two more guys came in and one pointed an AK-47 with a sawed-off stock at McClain's face while the other flipped him over and tugged on the ropes securing his wrists. The guy tossed McClain on his back again and he felt the pain shooting through his arms once more. The numbness came and went, like undulating needles, but at least it reminded him that his arms were still there. And still tied. McClain's constant twisting and pulling hadn't mattered. And now, even if he could get loose, he doubted he could move. He tried to flex his hands and fingers, but it was like they weren't connected anymore.

"Hey, G.I.," the dark man said. "You going to make a statement now. For my camera." His English had a foreign tincture to it, making "G.I." sound like "Shi-eye." French sounding.

If he told the asshole to fuck off, would they kill him quicker? He wished he knew how to say it in Somali. Still, a statement might buy him some time. Time for what? A longer torture session? He'd all but given up that the good guys would find him.

"You gonna say how nice we treating you," the dark man continued. He turned and spoke again in his native language and the two guys pulled McClain across the dirt floor and slammed his back against the wall. The flimsy metal shook but stayed in place.

Make them shoot me. Get this shit over with. Die sooner rather than later.

But the assholes would probably drag his naked body through the streets then. He hoped his mom and dad wouldn't see that. Lynn, either.

"Hey, G.I., you ready?"

McClain mustered all the strength he could. "Fuck you."

The dark man looked at the others and laughed. Then McClain saw a blur of motion and felt the kick to his side. He wondered if his ribs were broken.

What a lousy way to die.

The boot drove into his side again, sending more waves of pain through his body.

"You ready now?" the dark man asked, the grin stretching across his face. "Or you want more? We got plenty more if you want."

McClain tried to talk but his throat felt paralyzed. The other two skinnies grabbed him under his arms and stood him up. Then the dark man began pummeling him with body blows. McClain tried to tense his core, like he'd learned in the ring, but the constant barrage, some with fists, some with knees, soon had him aching each time he breathed. His legs deserted him and he sagged down, held semi-upright by the two assholes holding his arms. Finally, they let him settle onto his knees.

The dark man's face floated in front of him. A hand gripped his forehead and pulled his head back.

"This is our way," the dark man said. His breath stank. "We beat you till we get what we want." He paused and his eyes widened, a crazy expression twisting his face. McClain suddenly knew what the devil looked like. "Or maybe we just kill you friend." His boot tapped into Fisk's side. "What you think about *tat?*" He spoke in Somali again. The two guys let McClain crumple forward. He felt hands turn his head so he could see.

The other two skinnies rolled Fisk onto his back. The dressing McClain had put on the wound fell off and it leaked a stream of blood onto the dirty linoleum. The bastards began pulling down Fisk's pants.

"How 'bout we have some fun with him first?" the dark man said. "We show you what we gonna do to you next."

Oh, God, what are they going to do?

Poor Fisk was probably beyond caring, but McClain knew this was for *his* benefit. They were trying to break him quicker. And they were succeeding.

McClain considered the throbbing pain in his side, then figured what the fuck, why die slow? He nodded toward his captors. The dark man's smile widened as he leaned over.

McClain summoned all the strength he had and spat at the dark face. He wanted to tear the asshole's head off. The dark man merely brushed him away as he would a child and said something in the foreign tongue again. One of the skinnies pulled off Fisk's underwear, exposing his shriveled genitals. The guy turned and smiled at McClain, then reached into his pocket and took out a knife, wiping the blade on his pants.

Oh, God! McClain closed his eyes.

The dark man grabbed McClain's face and peeled back his eyelids.

"No, you watch, G.I.," he said, his breath a wind from hell. "You know what we gonna do now? You next."

The other skinny kept wiping the blade back and forth, back and forth.

The dark man leaned close, his voice a soft whisper in McClain's ear. "You can stop it, G.I. You can save you friend. And you self."

McClain tried to close his eyes, but the fingers dug into his lids, pinning them open. The blade kept going back and forth, back and forth, gleaming silver in the garish light till it somehow looked white hot.

The dark man whispered again. "You want to be a man, or half a man?"

The guy held the blade in front of McClain's face. He'd never seen such a shiny knife.

"Come on," the dark man said. "Save you friend. Save you self. We just want you to make a little statement. We tell you what to say."

McClain panted, couldn't catch his breath, and in his gut knew he was ready to give in. He couldn't stand the sight of the knife anymore. The thought of its razor-sharp blade cutting into his flesh . . . yeah, he was ready. What would it hurt? A statement. It would be okay. Everybody'd understand, wouldn't they?

His breath suddenly came back to him. How could they break him this easily? He was a ranger. An airborne ranger. Fuck these assholes.

The heavy whisper in his ear: "You ready, G.I.?"

McClain managed to shake his head. It hurt to move. Wouldn't it be better to give up and die?

The skinny with the knife grabbed Fisk's dick and stretched it out, holding the blade against it. The dark man spoke in Somali again, then turned to McClain. His smile looked like the rictus of death.

"We do his balls first, then we feed them to you," the dark man said, his voice a guttural roar now. "Tat what you want?"

McClain saw the blade gleaming in the light. He couldn't let it happen. He just couldn't.

"Okay," he said. His voice sounded like a hollow whisper. Like it belonged to someone else outside his body. Like it wasn't really him.

If I can keep that voice talking, he thought, *we can all get through this.*

They left him lying on his side in the corner of the room as they watched the playback on the camcorder. The voice McClain heard, denouncing his country and saying how the U.S. was wrong being in Somalia, sounded like it didn't belong to him. But he knew it did. How could he have done it? But what choice did he have? He began to sob. He thought about his Uncle Walter, U.S. Navy. Shot down over Viet Nam in 1970. Died in captivity as a POW. "Those bastards tried to break him, but they couldn't," McClain's father used to say over and over. "So they killed him. He was a man. A real man."

What would Dad say now? What's he going to say when he sees that video?

More laughter from the other room. The curtain slid back.

"You do good, G.I.," the dark man said, popping his head through the opening. "You do real good."

"Movie star," another one said. He said something in Somali. It sounded ominous.

McClain couldn't look up. He waited for the darkness to return. He knew they were going to kill him. He hoped it would be quick. For him and for Fisk. They let the curtain fall back into place, hiding their movements.

He exhaled, silently relieved that he'd been granted a few more minutes. But the reality of the situation, of what he'd done, hovered over him like the skinny's gleaming knife blade. What would his folks think? What would Lynn think?

He forced himself to open his eyes and look around. Fisk had lost so much blood he couldn't last much longer. McClain began to feel an odd sense of detachment and figured he was going into shock.

Won't be long now. What a lousy place to die.

He closed his eyes.

He felt a boot on the side of his face, grinding his head down into the dirty linoleum.

"Maybe we have some fun with you now," he heard the dark man say.

Oh, God, this time he had nothing to trade. It wouldn't be quick.

He felt dust in his mouth and tried to cough. He struggled to clear his eyes but all he could see was the motley curtain hanging in the doorway. The curtain rustled slightly, pulling to one side, and through the crack McClain saw another black face. This one was striped like a tiger, with black camo and a gold tooth in front. The face had a pair of night-vision goggles upon its forehead. The man flipped the glasses down and McClain heard the generator sputter and stop. Then the room went dark, except for the solitary candles still flickering on the far wall.

McClain blinked as the darkness enveloped him. Then he heard a muffled series of shots. Sound-suppressed shots—the kind the Delta boys used.

Oh, God, could it be?

He dared not hope, yet hope was all he had.

The pressure on his face stopped. Someone collapsed on top of him. Flashlight and laser beams illuminated the inside of the room. McClain stared into the open, dead eyes of the dark man, whose face was on the floor a few feet away. McClain spat at the dead face, his bloody spittle running down over the still-open eyes.

"Hey, you got some grit, boy," the tiger-striped face said in the semi-darkness. McClain felt himself being rolled over and then his wrists were suddenly free. "We're friendlies. They got any more here besides you and him?"

It took McClain a few seconds to understand the words and what they meant. Was it really over? Or could this be some kind of elaborate ruse?

"Hey, I asked you a question, soldier."

"Just me and him," McClain managed to say. He felt his lips curling into a smile. "Thanks for coming."

"Hey, we ain't out of the briar patch yet," Tiger Face said. The gold tooth flashed. "Come on."

McClain felt himself being lifted. Lifted so easily that he felt like a small child being picked up after falling in the playground.

"Doc, get here," Tiger Face said. "This other one looks pretty bad."

The curtain flipped open and two more men came in. One was slender. Waspish-looking. He moved past McClain and knelt next to Fisk, checking him over. The other guy was big and burly. His face was painted in the same manner as the other two, but it looked craggy. Even in the shadows McClain could tell this one was older than the other two. Forties maybe, but he looked like he was cast out of iron. Especially his hands, which had the look of power in them. McClain tried to keep his balance as their eyes locked. It was too dark to see much more than the shadows on the man's face as Tiger Face helped McClain through the door. Two more guys in camo BDUs were hunched over the camcorder.

"Take a look at this," one of them said. He was young. The tiger stripes stretched over high cheekbones and his eyes had an Asian cast.

The craggy man barked out orders. "Take it with. We're on a timetable here. Get a stretcher for the one in there." He pointed to the other room. "He good to go, Doc?"

"Yes, sir."

Tiger Face pushed McClain against the wall and paused. "We cool?"

Somebody outside grunted. Tiger Face pushed McClain

outside, half carrying him. They moved several feet toward a beat-up pickup truck. The kind the Somali militia used. Tiger Face helped McClain onto the tailgate.

McClain crawled in next to another guy lying in the bed of the truck.

A skinny.

Shit, a dead skinny, he thought as he pulled himself forward on his hands and knees. Totally naked, too.

The guy's open eyes were glazed over, a trace of bloody froth at the corner of his lips. McClain saw raw welts on the skinny's face and chest. Large welts, zigzag patterns, some ripped open and filled with congealing pools of blood. When McClain brushed against the man's hand it felt like long, wet stubs instead of fingers.

"Let's get you some more room," Tiger Face said. He grabbed the dead skinny's feet and pulled. As the body slid past him, McClain saw the bloody stubs that had been the skinny's fingers. Each one looked twisted at impossible angles. The dude had bloody nubs where his fingernails should have been. McClain's right hand suddenly throbbed with a stinging reminiscence.

"Come on, ladies, let's move it," the craggy guy said in a harsh whisper. "West, take that piece of shit inside. Lee and Doc are rigging the place to blow."

Tiger Face hefted the dead man's body. "Just wanted to thank this skinny one more time for his help." The golden smile flashed again as he patted the corpse's leg. Two other guys pushed a field stretcher with Fisk on it next to McClain.

He heard the craggy man's voice again: "Come on, move it. We got five minutes to get to the LZ."

McClain rolled over on his side and silently started to cry as they clipped the tailgate into place and loaded into the truck, but no tears came out. His eyes only burned.

It was almost over. He was going home.

McClain's memory of his time in the field hospital awaiting medical evac to Germany was vague, clouded by painkillers and other meds. It hurt to breathe. They told him he had some internal injuries and four broken ribs. He kept envisioning Lynn's face smiling at him. He'd wanted to call her to let her know he was all right, but they'd kept him flat on his back, either drugged or away from any phones. An army chaplain came by and asked if he wanted to talk. McClain said he did, but only to his fiancée in the States. His words sounded garbled. He could barely understand them himself. The chaplain smiled and said that would be arranged soon, but there was someone else to see him now.

McClain closed his eyes. When he opened them again he saw a big man sitting in the chair where the chaplain had been. Short, iron-gray hair, craggy face but without tiger stripes this time. McClain was surprised to see the black oak leaf insignias on the man's collar. A light-colonel. Yet he'd been out in the field on an operation.

"I stopped by to see how you were doing," the colonel said. "You're bound for Germany and rehab."

"Fisk?" McClain had trouble forming the word.

The colonel poured some water into a plastic cup. The water tasted like nectar from heaven.

"Your buddy's worse off than you," the colonel said. "Still in a coma. Got some extensive injuries, but he's expected to make it."

McClain closed his eyes and nodded a thanks. Poor Fisk.

"I never had any doubts about you, though," the colonel said. "McClain. That's Irish, right?"

"Scots-Irish," he managed to say.

The colonel grunted an approval. "I need to talk to you about the video."

McClain's mind flashed back to the event he'd been trying so hard to forget. He'd almost been able to convince himself it was a bad dream. Would he face charges? "Sir?"

"It never happened."

McClain felt stupid. His mind moved in slow motion. He had to reach out and grab each word, then write it on a mental chalkboard so he could read it. "What didn't happen?"

"Any of it." The colonel shook his head. "Black ops. It never happened. Got it, troop?"

McClain wondered if they'd watched the camcorder's tape, watched his cowardice. He wondered if his injuries justified it. He tried to speak but was ashamed, the wetness rolling down his cheeks. Then he felt a large hand on his shoulder.

"I know what you're worried about," the colonel said. "But like I told you, it never happened. Got it?"

"Yes, sir. How did you find us?"

The colonel flashed a quick smile. "Let's say we had assistance from some indigenous personnel and leave it at that."

McClain took a moment to think. He remembered the dead skinny in the truck. He'd been worked over pretty good. But it had saved him and Fisk. "Thank you, sir."

He felt the large hand patting his arm. "You'll be going home soon, soldier. Word is we'll all be out of here sooner than expected. You did your duty to God and country."

McClain tried to raise his arm to salute but the colonel held it down.

"You got too many IV lines in you to move," he said. The pressure eased on McClain's arm and the colonel leaned close, his craggy face only inches from McClain's. "I don't know what those bastards did to you and your buddy in that hut, son, but know they paid for it in spades. And like I said, it never happened. Got it?"

McClain stared into the other man's face, clearer now than it had been in the cast of the shadows.

"Black ops," the colonel whispered.

"Black ops," McClain repeated.

It never happened.

But McClain knew better.

CHAPTER 1

Washington, D.C. ~ Present Day

The rotating red and blue lights of the squad car blinked in the darkness. A crowd was gathering at the end of the alley, but luckily the yellow crime scene tape kept curious onlookers back.

Better than cement barriers, thought Detective Kevin McClain. The scene was only a few blocks from the Jefferson Heights Housing Projects. If this was gang-related, the offender was most probably close by, admiring his work. McClain made sure he stared directly into faces, looking for any concealed smirks. He was running late, thanks to a long-winded call from Lynn. Another bitch session. She always had to get the last word in, and then some, even when his alert page went off and he told her he had to go.

"That's more important than our daughter's health?" Lynn's tone was caustic. He wondered how they once had been so much in love.

"Nothing's more important than that," McClain said right before he disconnected. He heard the phone going off with Lynn's ringtone again, all the way to the homicide scene, but let it go to voice mail. She could wait. He was in no mood for Round Two. He had to get his head back in the game. A white van with the ZCCN News logo on the side was across the street. It didn't take those guys long. Glancing at his watch, he wondered by how much of a margin Kelly had beat him here.

He saw an ET getting the black body bag out of his van. A dark alley was sandwiched between rows of abandoned buildings beyond the squad car and the yellow tape. The perfect spot for a homicide. Nobody around to see anything, nobody who cared.

The folded corner of the ET's body bag snared the yellow crime scene tape. Before McClain could call to the ET, the guy felt the snare, reached around, and pulled hard on the tape. It had been stretched too tight and the tension along with the stretch caused the tape to pop loose. The entire line went slack and fell to the ground, its ragged ends fluttering in the cold September wind.

It shouldn't have been that brittle. Must have been old or something. Or stretched way too tight. McClain flipped up his jacket collar. It wasn't supposed to be this cold in the fall. Not in D.C. In Chicago, maybe. Thoughts of home shouldered their way in, like a blast of chilly wind, which in Chi-town was called "The Hawk."

"McClain, Robbery/Homicide," he said to the uniformed MPDC officer guarding the perimeter.

The officer recorded McClain's name and rank on the log, then said, "It's over there, by the dumpster."

"Detective Kelly here yet?"

The uniform ran his finger down the log. "Yeah. About twenty minutes ago."

"The press is on scene." McClain gestured with his thumb over his shoulder. The guy with the camcorder had already set up his stand and was focusing on them. "See if you can reconnect that tape, will you?"

The patrolman looked down at the fluttering tape and said, "Sure thing."

McClain thanked him and glanced over his shoulder. At least they'd strung the red tape at the inner perimeter and it had remained intact. McClain stooped underneath the horizontal line. The sweet smell of rotting garbage mingled with something else. McClain couldn't quite put his finger on what it was: familiar, distinctive, but undetermined. Bright halogen flashlight beams darted around the confines of the alley as the two techs continued going over it, one photographing, the other taking notes.

The camera flash popped in the ambient darkness. The tall, lean figure of Joe Kelly leaned off to one side. Kelly brought a cigarette to his lips and the tip glowed bright red in the dim light. The tight coils of his 'fro were going gray.

"Smoking at a crime scene?" McClain stepped forward and made a *tsk* sound. "And here I thought you were a professional."

"You know how I love stretching them rules." Kelly's voice shifted to an ersatz Irish lilt. "About fucking time you got here, laddie."

McClain chuckled at Kelly's pathetic attempt to fake what he thought was a brogue. "What's with this 'laddie' shit? You trying to convince people you're black-Irish or something?"

"Might have been a white boy in the woodpile somewhere." Kelly's dark face crinkled. "You do know you're the designated primary on this one, don't you?"

McClain smiled. Kelly had been a surrogate father and mentor to him since he'd come to MPDC. "Yeah. I'm sorry. Argument with the ex."

Kelly's thick gray eyebrows lifting as his face twitched. "Where would we coppers be if it weren't for our ex-wives keeping us working all this overtime? What's Miss Scarlett's problem this time?"

"The usual." McClain surveyed the scene. He knew to wait till the techs had finished their preliminaries before going in for a closer look. "Taking me to task about Jen's current teenage angst."

Kelly shook his head. "Good thing you married money way back when. How do you think I feel, knowing my pension's gonna get sliced up like a fucking pie when I retire. I got three exes looking to hang my ass. Least you only got one." He squinted down at McClain. "For the moment, that is. You still kinda young and capable of making more mistakes."

"Don't remind me. What we got?"

"Looks like a dump. Just remember, it's your turn in the barrel."

"How could I forget? You keep reminding me." McClain smelled the booze on his partner's breath. He took out a pack of gum and offered a stick to Kelly in case the brass showed up. The flash popped again, illuminating a bare foot and shin of the supine body between the dumpsters. What he could see of the corpse was odd-looking. It was also nude. "Any sign of clothes around?"

Kelly shrugged as he popped the gum in his mouth. "I haven't been dumpster-diving yet. That'll be your job."

"Is that so?"

"Yeah, you airborne troopers are supposed to be tough, ain't ya?"

"As tough as we want to be," McClain said. "Look like a suicide?"

"Not unless he stripped and set himself on fire and walked here. You ain't gonna be able to close this one that easy, laddie."

"There you go with the 'laddie' shit again. Where you getting it?"

"An old Bing Crosby movie, the one where he sang 'Too-Ra-Loo-Ra-Loo-Ra.' "

"Man, I'm sorry I missed that."

"Don't be dissin' the Bing now," Kelly said with an exaggerated squint. "But I wouldn't be too concerned. It's probably some poor, homeless dude that no one gives a shit about."

McClain stared over at the bare foot sticking out. "I could use a bit of luck. You got any other predictions?"

Kelly took a last drag on his cigarette and ground it out against the brick wall. Then he turned and flipped it far away from the busy techs. "I did get a chance to view the decedent before the ETs got here. Looked beat up pretty bad."

"Beat up? How?"

Kelly shrugged. "You'll see soon enough."

McClain glanced over his shoulder and noticed the yellow crime scene tape was still fluttering in the night wind.

He sighed. So much for nice requests. It looked like the techs were still busy so he walked back to the perimeter. The uniform was busy trying to keep the crowd back—the evening's entertainment in this neighborhood.

With the news cameraman getting it on video.

McClain snagged the fluttering tape, pulled the band tight, and retied the knot.

The gym was hot tonight. Drops of sweat littered the lacquered, wooden floor. It smelled like a hamper full of dirty clothes. Felicia Knight watched as the white girl on the other team tossed the volleyball in the air and smacked an overhand serve over the net.

Felicia thought her name was something like Heidi. Like a model's name. She looked like a model, too. Probably old money from Fairfax County.

The accompanying thump told Felicia that Heidi had put a lot of top spin on the ball. Better to set it up, she thought as she moved forward, using the customary bump pass with inverted forearms to deflect the serve, setting up the tandem play. The ball spun upward, sending it toward her teammate, the setter, who used a brush of her fingertips, allowing Felicia to time her approach and do the spike as the ball descended to the right level above the net.

"I got it!" she yelled.

The multicolored sphere shot down and bounced off the floor on the other side as Felicia's feet touched back on the floor. She was one of the few girls on the team who could spike. The ref's whistle sounded from his elevated platform, and he lowered his hand toward their side, indicating a score, and flipped the score card up to twenty.

Thank God for rally-scoring.

Felicia was also glad he'd called this one right for a change. So many others on the line had gone against her team, she wondered if he needed new glasses.

Down by one. Our serve.

She ran to the back and stepped out of bounds, making sure everyone was set. As she tossed the ball upward, ready to power-serve it back, she heard the all-too-familiar ringtone of her boss, Section Chief Woodrow S. Joiner, on her cell.

The phone was against the wall and off to the side. She could easily ignore it.

However, with her game concentration compromised, her serve went flat, barely making it over the net and flapping the top band, allowing her white girl nemesis on the other side to slip underneath and set up the spike. White Girl went up and executed a perfect blow, sending the ball back over the net like a bullet. It hit the wooden floor and bounced so high, Felicia thought it might hit the rafters.

The ref's whistle sounded again. Match point. Her team had lost two out of three.

After the obligatory fist-bumps with the other team, Felicia walked slowly toward the sidelines and retrieved her phone. She glanced at the screen: missed call, no voice message.

The white girl came over and smiled.

"Great game," she said. "You've got real lift in your verticals."

Felicia smiled back, giving her one of those "lips-only" smiles that she hoped would be gracious and also a warning not to violate her space. Sort of a "stay outta my face" smile. Heidi apparently got the message as the blue eyes blinked twice, followed by a nervous smile. Felicia pressed the button to redial the missed call and listened for the ring. She knew she should have been nicer—shown better sportsmanship—but she wasn't looking for a girlfriend, and of late her intensity about competition in general had increased. It probably had to do with her divorce becoming final. At least her second round of HIV tests had come back negative. That, in itself, was something to be thankful for.

Just like in *Diary of a Mad Black Woman,* she thought. Well, almost. Jerome hadn't left her for a white woman. He'd left her for a white man. Still, it would be nice to have dumped him into a hot tub and watched him squirm. She shook her head. When was she going to wake up from her personal nightmare? About all she had was the joy of volleyball once a week, and now even that wasn't sacrosanct.

Joiner's voice boomed on the phone. "Knight, where you at?"

"I'm at the gym. It's my league night."

"What?" Before she could reply, she heard his frustrated sigh and, once again, his Southern drawl. "Look, we're coming under pressure to have the report on the Guantanamo abuses completed. It looks like the AG's going to be moving on this sooner than we anticipated."

Oh, great, Felicia thought.

Somebody scored on an adjacent court to a cacophony of hoots and cat calls.

"What's going on there?" Joiner asked.

"I'm at the gym. It's my night to play volleyball, remember?"

"Volleyball?" His twanging accent drove her nuts—the way he drew out the Ls, putting an extra syllable into the word. Felicia could almost taste the derision in Joiner's voice.

"Well," he said, "there's been a significant new development."

Everything with Joiner was a "significant new development."

"A new development, sir?"

"Operation Prometheus." He sounded like someone talking to an ignorant child.

"Sir?"

"Our surveillance team lost track of subject three-eighty-three. We've got to incorporate that update into the report before I turn it in tomorrow morning."

Three-eighty-three. With 625 prisoners mentioned in the report, and 123 of those released, three-eighty-three should have had little significance to her. But she had a head for numbers. At least that's what her father always said. He'd told her to become an accountant. She remembered three-eighty-three as Mohammed Amir Fassel, mainly because of the surveillance detail that Joiner had assigned when Fassel snuck back into the U.S. and came to D.C. As far as Operation Prometheus, she'd heard Joiner talking about it at the team briefings, emphasizing the highly sensitive nature of the topic. She was surprised that he'd even mentioned it now. He was probably ultra-upset that they'd lost Fassel.

"How did that happen?" she asked. "Who was on him?"

"Beaumont and Johnson."

Thank God she hadn't been on that detail. If it had been anybody else but his good old boys, they'd probably be packing their bags for Podunk or Bismark.

"So," Joiner continued, "as I told you, I'll need that updated report on my desk first thing in the morning. Are we clear?"

Of all the supervisors in all the world, why did he have to walk into my corner of the world? Or did I walk into his?

Had she known what life in the D.C. branch of the Bureau would be like, she would have never transferred from Omaha.

"Knight? Did you copy?"

"Yes, sir." Who did this cracker think he was talking to?

"Are we clear that I'll have the report tomorrow morning?"

She resisted the temptation to mimic Tom Cruise in *A Few Good Men* and say, "Crystal." Instead, she murmured that he'd have it in the morning. That meant a stop back at the Federal Building on the way home to load up her flash drive so she could finish up the report tonight, once she got home.

Joiner's voice intruded again. "I don't need to remind you that Operation Prometheus is ongoing, do I?"

"No, sir."

"I'll expect that report in the morning then," Joiner said. "Enjoy the rest of your night off."

Didn't this man listen? Was he repeating himself for reassurance? Or maybe he was so dense he didn't understand. This eleventh hour, off-duty request would effectively kill the rest of her night off. Plus, she was walking a tight line downloading top-secret FBI material that was considered too sensitive to put on her laptop, even if it was her government laptop. But she couldn't worry about that now. Joiner didn't want excuses, only results. She'd have to worry about the consequences if she failed. Or if she got caught in some violation. God forbid that jackass Joiner would back her up. She would have to get hold of either Beaumont or Johnson, neither of whose numbers she had on her cell, and get an update. Operation Prometheus—the way Joiner talked about the surveillance of some possible terrorist wannabes planning who knew what, you'd think the world was coming to an end. Still, after nine-eleven, the Bureau couldn't afford to drop the ball on anything.

She felt totally sweaty now and knew if she didn't get a hot shower soon she'd catch cold. She debated the always dreadful consideration: should she wash her hair or pull it back? It was starting to curl up on the sides where she'd been sweating. She opted for the second option.

I've got enough shit to deal with, she thought. She grabbed her bag and headed for the locker room. As she walked by the section of the gym that had the boxing equipment, she glanced to the right.

The speed and heavy bags hung in silent tranquility. No white boy working out tonight. She didn't know his name but secretly enjoyed catching a glimpse of him skipping rope or pounding the bags. Reddish blond hair cut short and pale skin. Nice build. Irish, from the looks of him. Maybe a few years older than she was. He usually looked intense and really into things. Like he wouldn't notice her if she'd walked by stark naked. She wondered if he would. But she had enough problems in her life without stepping into some kind of interracial interlude. She was curious, sure, but if she ever did consider something like that, she had to be sure she wasn't doing it to get back at Jerome. Plus, Joiner would love that if he found out, especially with his southern gentility attitude. Was it any wonder he treated her like shit?

He probably has fantasies of me shuffling up from the slave quarters.

Seated in the semi-darkness of his den, surrounded by the many trophies and spoils of his various wars, Colonel Claymore Jefferson Viceroy thought about the unfairness of life, the intrusion of occasional serendipity, and what might have been. While he waited for his special phone to ring, he fingered the fine paper of his Cuban cigar. Doctor Wallace would not approve, but what the hell, Viceroy liked to live on the edge. He'd been there his whole life. He rolled the unlit cigar between his fingers, then set it in the glass ashtray in front of him where he could still see it. He didn't want to light it right now. Better to wait until the proper time. When he knew the mission, or at least this phase of it, was complete. Postponement of gratification, followed by a small reward.

He drummed his fingers on the teakwood desk he'd had shipped from one of Saddam's palaces. He'd done it by going through Jordan and then to Canada. The black market was a snap when you knew the ropes from working black ops. Ironically, he'd used almost the same route that the enemy was using now. Operation Prometheus, the mythological theft of fire from the gods. Appropriate name on so many levels.

He drummed his fingers again and thought about his last good mission, the last time he'd been in the field during the Iraq invasion—the last time he'd really felt alive. Everything had been going according to their op's plan when he'd felt a twinge in his chest. Like his heart skipped a beat. He ignored it. On with the mission. But, suddenly, he felt a tightening steel band around his chest. His breathing became labored. On with the mission. The band tightened another notch. Then West was at his side, telling him they were going to abort and get him out of there with a dust-off.

Abort? Viceroy wanted to knock West on his ass, but he couldn't raise his arms. He couldn't do shit.

The helicopter arrived, taking him back to base where the doctors told him he'd suffered what they termed "a myocardial infarction."

It hadn't felt mild. As he lay there, flat on his back, looking up at the young doctor's face framed by the bright overhead lights, Viceroy knew it was over. He'd never be leading his squad in the field again. It was an epiphany.

Like a great athlete coming back from a career-threatening injury, he had to modify his stance. He was shifted to M.I.—Military Intelligence—and eventually back to D.C., where he rode a desk. But at least he'd been able to take his team with him. Still in charge, but at a distance. Still be a part of it, but only vicariously. Ironically, he found it both frustrating and stimulating. But one thing hadn't changed. The waiting was still the hardest part, but the sweetest too. Now he savored every tick of the clock.

He remembered the old days and the good missions. Hitting them where it hurt in Iraq and Afghanistan. That had only been a few years ago. Smacking the cartels way south of the border back in the late nineties. And back in ninety-three in Somalia. That was something. Kicked ass and took names and capped some skinnies along the way. Him, along with West, Polmroy, and Lee, of course. He couldn't forget his son. They were all winners. Especially Lee. And you didn't break up a winning team.

He flashed back to the roof of the embassy in Saigon, the human sea trying to work up to the roof to get on that last chopper, and him standing there pushing people back. The woman's face, high cheekbones framing her almond-colored eyes, imploring eyes, asking him to take her baby. The kid looked so small, so vulnerable. Viceroy turned and ripped one of the fat-cat Viet diplomats out of the chopper and threw the man down into the crowd. Then he lifted the woman and her son up onto the metal ledge and gave them freedom. He'd felt like a god.

And now, with a little luck and the grace of the real God, the team was still in place. They would be able to set things in motion for the crowning advancement. He had to get there before his time ran out. But with the present administration sitting on his promotion, under the guise of the secretary moaning about how overstaffed the military was, he knew the clock was ticking double time. He also knew he had to get that star. He deserved it. They couldn't deny him. From there he could rise to General of the Army, and then even higher. He smiled at the thought. There hadn't been a general to accede to the presidency since Eisenhower. Haig might have made it if he hadn't blown it with his "I am in control" gaffe after Reagan was shot.

Avoiding the mistakes of others as I make my own climb, that's the name of the game.

And if he kept to his game plan, he was sure he could get all the way to the mountaintop.

The key was getting his brother-in-law into the White House. As a former vice president, Big Willie had easily won his party's nomination. Now all that was left was to win the big one, a brutal fifteen-round fight, and they were in the middle of it. Getting the nomination had been the first step. Next they'd have to win the election and to do that they needed to disgrace the incumbent—an operation that had to be played as delicately as handling a Stradivarius.

He glanced at his watch again. Twenty-fifteen. Six minutes after the last time he'd checked. Was this what he'd been reduced to—a rear-echelon clock-watcher? He picked up the remote and flipped on the TV.

The close-up of Allison Hayes's beautiful face filled the flat screen as she arched an eyebrow and asked, "Mr. Thomas, this week you announced the indictment against Robert Saxon, an undersecretary of security in the Reed/Bernard administration, for approving the use of torture against suspected terrorists held at Guantanamo . . ." She paused as the camera lingered on her attempt at a thoughtful expression.

This broad knows what she's doing as far as screen presence, thought Viceroy. Big Willie must have given her a few lessons.

"Why did it take this administration almost three years to bring this indictment to fruition?"

The camera shifted to Attorney General Reginald Thomas, or "The Little Prick," as Big Willie liked to call him. Viceroy smirked. Thomas was a gad fly, nothing more. A puppet. His brother-in-law was giving him much more attention than he was due. Once the dust had settled, "The Little Prick" would be nothing more than a distant, unpleasant memory.

"The key word in that is *suspected,* Allison," Thomas said. "We're talking about holding men without the benefit of counsel, without charges, in a harsh prison environment for a protracted period." The camera caught his forward lean, the set of his jaw as he added, "And using inhumane methods to systematically torture them. The civilized world has a policy against such torture."

The camera shifted back to Hayes. "What would you say to those who would argue our national security was at stake?"

"National security," he repeated, letting derision seep into his voice. "We've been hearing those two buzzwords since the seventies."

Hayes smiled before she spoke. Her teeth looked flawless on camera. Viceroy wondered what they looked like up close, in real life. He also wondered if Big Willie had sampled those goods.

"We have indeed," Hayes said, "but you must admit we live in a different world today than we did back then. A post-nine-eleven world."

It was Thomas's turn to raise an eyebrow, try to look thoughtful. "Admittedly, we do. But I would also say the end doesn't always justify the means. If you violate the very principles this nation was based on, who really wins? Isn't that what the terrorists are striving to have us do?"

Back to Hayes. "So you're saying that suspected terrorists, our enemies in our ongoing war on terror, should be given the same rights afforded our citizens? Aren't they considered enemy combatants?"

"I'm saying that the government of the United States must stand ready to obey the Constitution, no matter who our enemies are and how low or high up the food chain they are."

Viceroy knew they were setting the stage and wondered if

they'd rehearsed this beforehand.

Hayes waited for a beat, then said, "Mr. Attorney General, there's a lot of speculation about this indictment and how far it will lead. With former Vice President William Bernard clinching his party's nomination, and the November election only a few weeks away, do you anticipate this trail will go any farther?"

Viceroy had the impression she'd been dying to ask that question.

Thomas swallowed, a sure sign that he was both prepared and anxious. "I have no comment on that at this time. I will say, however, that the investigation is continuing and ongoing."

Continuing and ongoing? A bit redundant. Clearly he'd laid the groundwork through clever innuendo that Big Willie was on the indictment list. This could call for an adjustment to the plan. Still, it was way too early in the game to worry about this shitbird of an AG. There'd be time to deal with him later, and in the proper fashion. It had to be smoke and mirrors at this point. Indicting a former vice president on the eve of an election would take audacity. It would be unprecedented, or almost so. But then again, Spiro Agnew was indicted while he was still in office. Nothing was impossible. Did Harris have the balls?

"So it's safe to say then," Hayes continued, "that there's more to come?"

"It wouldn't be prudent for me to comment further at this time." Thomas looked like a catfish trying to imitate a shark. "I will say that Undersecretary Paul Ross will return shortly from Guantanamo with new information and we'll be conferring later this week."

Viceroy assessed Hayes again. The camera loved her, and she seemed to ask all the right questions. Either she was damn sharp, or she had someone behind her who was. Viceroy made a mental note. She'd bear watching, and listening, down the road.

His cell phone rang. It wasn't the call he'd been waiting for, but he had to take it. He flipped it open and answered with his usual salutation.

"Clay?"

"Who else were you expecting?" Viceroy let a little levity creep into his tone.

Big Willie chuckled too, a nervous laugh. The stress of recent events was taking its toll on him. Viceroy could hear the other man's breathing. It was a long run to the White House. "What is it, Will?"

"That damn interview was on Allison Hayes's show tonight. You know, the one with—"

"I was watching it. I recorded it earlier."

"Well, what do you think?"

Viceroy took a deep breath, purposely letting his brother-in-law dangle. "I think you need to concentrate on our plan and not worry about trivialities."

"Trivialities? But—"

"Have you met with your man Roger about how to respond?"

"No, I wanted to call you first."

Viceroy smiled. It was reminiscent of Shakespeare's plays. *Henry the IV, Parts One* and *Two:* Prince Hal making his ascendance to the crown as Henry the V more stellar by manipulating Falstaff. Viceroy preferred Shakespeare's histories because they dealt with military battles and court intrigue. Perhaps some future playwright would write a play about him someday. He hoped it would be a history and not a tragedy.

"Clay, you there?"

The man's whine set Viceroy's teeth on edge. "Let your campaign manager figure out the right spin. And relax. You're in Virginia, I take it?"

"Yeah, we're practicing for the debate," Big Willie said. "Roger says I'll kick his ass."

The schedule called for two debates between Big Willie and

the current president, Anthony Harris. This first one was to center on foreign policy. Viceroy knew the torture allegations would come up: *The previous administration, under the direction of Vice President William Bernard, had allowed and encouraged torture to be used against the inmates of Guantanamo.* Right now Harris wanted to let Big Willie sweat in anticipation. Rattle the man. Despite the pending indictment of an underling and the purported case in the works against Bernard, Viceroy wasn't worried. They were telegraphing their strategy to shake up Big Willie and scuttle his chances in the presidential debates and then the election. Politics as usual. But if Harris found himself behind in the polls, he might try to use the indictment against a current presidential candidate as a Hail Mary play. If he had the balls.

"The debate's more than a week away," Viceroy said. "What's your next TV appearance?"

"Allison Hayes's cable TV show, *In the News.*"

Viceroy wondered again about Hayes. Word was they didn't call his brother-in-law "Big Willie" for nothing. Roger A. Jetson, the ace campaign manager, or "Roger Ram Jet," as he called himself, would have to prepare Big Willie well for the interview.

"Any news on the other matter?" Big Willie asked, his voice tense.

Viceroy's cell signaled that he had an incoming call. He glanced at the number on his caller ID screen. It was Lee's disposable.

"I'll call you back," Viceroy said, and switched to the incoming call. "Sit-rep."

"I dropped that item off as you instructed," Lee said.

Damn, he was proud of that boy. Viceroy thought again about Saigon so many years ago. Lee and his mother. The flash of terror in the woman's face. The baby boy unaware that his world was coming to an end. The winding, serpentine tail of people slithering out of the emergency door on the roof of the embassy toward the helicopter.

"Outstanding," Viceroy said. "Any problems?"

"No, sir." Lee maintained military courtesy, even though Viceroy had adopted and raised the boy as his own after his mother died. "Are you watching the news?"

"No, I'm not."

Viceroy was confident that no one was listening on this secure line due to the scramblers they'd installed, but he always stressed discretion unless speaking face-to-face. It was the rule of black ops.

"Check out ZCCN," Lee said. "They're covering something I passed by a little while ago."

Viceroy flipped the remote. The twenty-four-hour cable news show materialized on the screen. A reporter stood against the backdrop of a darkened D.C. street corner—Lee's way of covertly telling him the Arab's body had already been discovered. Viceroy watched as the camera focused on the oscillating red and blue lights and the fluttering yellow crime scene tape.

"Looks like crime in our nation's capital never ceases," Viceroy said. "And what about that stuff you were looking for? Find it?"

"Affirmative. Rolley's looking into that as we speak. Looks like we'll be traveling north, as we anticipated."

Rolley was their code name for Master Sergeant Roland West. Next to Lee, West was the man Viceroy trusted the most. Viceroy knew this part of the mission had been a total success and felt a partial wave of supreme satisfaction. The only thing that could have made it better would have been if he'd been there with them. But that wasn't an option anymore. "Excellent work."

"Thank you, sir. Is there anything else you need tonight?"

"Negative," Viceroy said. He contemplated his next couple of moves like a game of chess. You always had to think a few moves ahead. "Thanks for the call. I'll talk with you tomorrow. God-speed."

Viceroy smiled with anticipation as he picked up the cigar and inserted the tip into the circular hole of the cutter. The crew would already be preparing for their trip to Maine for the intercept. Viceroy knew he had to call that asshole Joiner and keep him in the loop on Operation Prometheus. Keep the fish on the line was more like it. More court intrigue. But he needed Joiner. Thanks to the good old *Posse Comitatus Act,* the FBI had jurisdiction inside U.S. borders, not the military, even though this intercept was on the border with Canada. It was all about not leaving a discernible trail.

He'd have to call Big Willie back, too, and give him the news. Allay the man's anxiety a bit. It wouldn't do to have him toss and fret all night and emerge tomorrow with bags under his baby blues. Still, Viceroy decided to let the other man simmer a bit more.

First, he'd enjoy the Havana.

CHAPTER 2

Ted Lane bumped his glasses up on his nose. It was tight quarters in the preparation rooms at Zenith Cable Network News headquarters and Lane smelled Allison's perfume. It mixed with the hint of muskiness in Allison's scent as they watched the image of the fluttering crime scene tape on the monitor.

No wonder she was so popular, he thought. Her sexiness came through in so many different ways. And she was so good at parroting information. Programmable. Those who watched would never dream she was something of an intellectual lightweight. But who wasn't, compared to him?

Their arrangement worked for both of them. She was in line for a network spot, if things went well with this current series of stories. And as her news researcher, he'd be ascending with her. The top echelon knew he was the real brains behind her carefully manufactured image. The screen goddess and the ogre. What the hell, he didn't have to be photogenic. He more than made up for it in intellect. But everything in today's world was visual, about creating image. Too bad the print media was going the way of the dinosaurs. Lane knew he would have made as good a columnist as Woodward or Bernstein. One way or another, he was going to get to the top. Using Allison as a means to this end would benefit both on them, as long as he stayed in control. At the moment, that didn't seem to be a problem.

"What do you think?" she asked, turning to him. "I kind of

like that tape blowing in the wind."

He smiled. "It does add a bit of metaphor to the scene. The fleeting transience of life, so to speak. Just like the old Dylan song."

"Who?" A crease appeared between her brows, like it always did when he lobbed one over her head.

"Never mind."

She turned toward the tech guy editing the footage. "Okay, use that for my voiceover."

Lane held up his hand. "Better cut out that idiot stooping down to tie it up first. He ruins the effect."

"Right," Allison said. "Lose that loser. Must be a cop." She smiled and canted her head. "Are you sure we should use this instead of the update about the AG and the torture investigation? My *In the News* segment is set to run again on Sunday."

"Which reminds me, we need to go over that. But in the meantime, use conventional wisdom," Lane said, admiring the sweep of her neck. "If it bleeds, it leads."

Allison bit her lip and focused on the image again. "I wish I was as sure as you are."

She flashed her perfect smile. The dentist had done a magnificent job on her veneers. Her boob-job was first rate, too. Lane hoped none of it would need a makeover before they reached the network position. He didn't want any delays.

The tech guy was hunched over his keyboard, glancing at the handwritten copy Lane had given him. "What's this word, Allie?"

The prick was asking her, like he didn't know who'd really written it. *Next time I'll have to do it on my laptop and eliminate the middleman. He can copy and paste.*

Allison bent over and squinted at the handwritten notes.

"Smoldering," she said.

The tech guy went back to typing.

Good thing she's so adept at reading my writing, Lane thought.

Allison's hand surreptitiously brushed Lane's crotch; her way of letting him know she'd thank him formally later tonight. In the meantime, he knew better than to get between her and her chance to do the lead-in story. When they were between the sheets he'd let her make it up to him.

"I'll be back. Ted and I need a smoke." Allison leaned over and placed a hand on the tech guy's shoulder, letting her breast brush against him at the same time. She knew how to manipulate men all right. But as long as he stayed in control, he'd be the manipulator.

He and Allison stepped into the hall, all business again, in case someone was watching, but then again, when wasn't someone watching? They were in a cable news television station. Eyes were everywhere. He followed her swaying hips down the corridor and into the break room. It was their regular meeting place, rather than his cramped cubicle or her trailer dressing room. Nobody would be listening in the break room.

Allison closed the door behind them and shot him a piercing look. "You call *this* a hot story? Some homeless guy gets whacked and left in an alley?"

"If it bleeds—"

"Don't give me that shit." She waved dismissively. "I mean, shouldn't we be capitalizing more on my coverage of my interview with the AG?"

Lane shrugged with a quick smile. "It's best to leave the public tantalized. Champing at the bit to find out more."

"And when are we going to give it to them? Should I follow up with the torture theme? Then I can press Bernard before they do the debate."

Oh, Christ, Lane thought. There she goes, trying to think like a real reporter again. He took a deep breath. "Let's skip around it for now. With the economy in the toilet, Harris will have to bring up the torture issue. He wanted it out there, which is why he had his AG lapdog break the news of the Saxon indictment. He wants Bernard to sweat a little. I'm sure Big Willie will be ready with a sound bite response if it's brought up. At this point, all we have to do is keep people interested in the whole torture issue. Once our big story breaks, we'll be leading the pack."

She studied his face. "You keep saying that, but where do we stand on this big story? You keep teasing me. And what if the AG does go ahead with the case against the higher-ups of the old administration for using torture tactics?"

"Trust me, he won't. Harris knows the key is to give Bernard enough rope to hang himself. Let him make the statements of denial and justification right now. Just like handing him more rope."

Lane had to play it close to his vest with Allison—give her too much info and it would be like putting all his research and covert investigation up on a billboard. Allison had presence and grace in front of the camera, but in real life she couldn't hold water. She'd blab to somebody about what "they" were working on, and the rest of the newshounds would descend on his story like a hoard of locusts.

He liked that image, his flair for metaphor. It would have translated well into print had he been born thirty years earlier, when reporters were really reporters. Now it was all about the image and glitz and telegenic personalities. It didn't matter who the real reporters were, as long as the network had someone like Allison reading the news off her teleprompter.

"The AG is helping us by keeping the issue out there," he said. "Trust me on this. It's all about timing."

She compressed her lips, then picked up the glass pot and poured some coffee into a Styrofoam cup. She held it out to him with both hands, smiling like a nineteenth-century painting of one of the king's courtesans. When they stood face-to-face she practically towered over him because she was wearing heels. Short and stubby, overweight, glasses—on his best day he looked like a refugee from a nerd contest. In high school he'd been ridiculed when he asked the girls out, but not anymore. And pretty soon he'd be running this outfit as the top news editor. Then he'd be able to write his own ticket to anywhere he wanted.

She leaned against the counter, sipping from her own cup with a sexy delicacy and stared at him over the white rim. "What are you thinking about? You look a million miles away."

Not a million miles. About twenty years in the past. It had forced him to become cerebral. Use his wits to survive, to endear himself to those in power. It forced him to become mentally shrewd, mentally tough. He was driven to become the best. It got him the scholarships, the minor accolades, and now it got him Allison. She knew he could deliver the goods. The goods that would finally take them both to the top. Her looks riding on his brain. It was an unbeatable combination.

"I was thinking about the future," he said. "Our future."

CHAPTER 3

McClain felt the comfort of his shoulder holster bouncing along under his left arm as he ran through the deserted, but still mean-at-any-hour streets. The constant bouncing bothered him, but it also gave him some kind of lingering reassurance. *Don't leave home without it. At least not in this neighborhood.* Recent days had seen some signs that the gentrification was gradually sweeping his way. Once the rents caught up with the wave of encroaching yuppies, he'd have to get another apartment. He came to a hill and increased his pace, wanting to work his legs some more. He felt the sweat pour down his face and sides despite the cool temperature. He'd have to wipe down the Glock when he was done, even though Glocks were practically rust-proof.

To the east the sun was an orange glow peeping between cracks in the skyline. Predawn, the only time he could feel safe doing his roadwork. Early enough to beat the commuter traffic, and late enough that the bars had closed. The idiots retreated, like a legion of vampires, back under their rocks with the purifying morning sunshine.

Lately, running was the only way he could get rid of stress, but he felt like he was cheating this morning. Going for a run during the crucial first forty-eight after catching a homicide. But this was a different kind of case. The victim was unidentifiable. Burned to a crispy critter. The apparent mutilation, missing fingernails, bothered McClain. It brought back unpleasant memories of a land far away, a time long ago. Still, without an ID on the victim, backtracking through his life was virtually impossible. And Kelly had assured him that it was okay to take off.

"Leave the canvassing to me," Kelly said. "I'll start hitting my street sources. If I find out who it is, I'll call you and wake you out of your beauty sleep."

"You sure?" McClain asked.

Kelly winked. "With the roll I bet on you, you can't afford to skip training."

McClain felt a twinge in his legs. Running every day for the past month had put him in pretty good shape, and he needed to get into the best shape he could. Kelly had entered him in the Police vs. Fire Boxing Tournament.

The thoughts of some hose-hauler cleaning his clock gave McClain the incentive he needed to keep running, even on days when it was all he could do to roll out of bed. Sleep had been as elusive as the leads on this latest case. He'd used the same technique when he'd been in the Gloves back in Chicago. He'd been the only white kid in his weight class, and every black and Puerto Rican opponent did their best to humiliate and punish him in the ring. But he'd walked away with that golden glove on a chain around his neck. It had been one of his proudest moments. And one of the few moments when his father had told him he was proud of him.

More ghosts from the past resurrected themselves as he quickened his pace against an encroaching fatigue. His conversation with Lynn last night drifted back, her shrill tone slashing him like a straight razor: "What do you mean, your insurance won't cover her visits to Dr. Moorefield? This is our daughter we're talking about."

No, we're talking about some quack who charges twice as much for an hour as I make in a month.

"It's what our daughter needs," she said. "Try thinking of her instead of always being focused on yourself."

Focused on himself? With her family the epitome of "old Virginia money," her father could afford to send Jen to anyone Lynn wanted. But the divorce settlement specified he was responsible for his daughter's medical needs until she turned eighteen. Not that he wanted it any other way, but this Moore-field guy was something else. The latest kid-shrink fad in rich, D.C. circles. Why raise your kid the old-fashioned way when Dr. Moorefield could screw their heads on at a new angle?

He forced the conversation from his mind and rounded the last section of streets before entering the park. Once through the park, he'd be back at his apartment. Some gym time would be nice, but that would be more elusive than catching his steamy breath. He'd have to hope his timing hadn't totally deserted him once he stepped between the ropes. Otherwise, he'd get his head handed to him. And Kelly would lose his money.

McClain glanced at his watch as he finished. Forty-five minutes for five miles. Not bad for a homicide-day run. Almost ring-ready. But the toughest tests weren't always in the ring. The stomach-churning autopsy awaited.

Felicia Knight was clamping the flat iron over a thick strand of hair when her cell phone rang. Joiner's ringtone. *Did that man have extrasensory perception or something? He had a natural knack for calling at the most inopportune times.* She debated letting it go to voice mail, but Joiner would keep calling until she answered, and then he'd lecture her about official policy "of keeping the Bureau phone on at all times." Damn, it was only six-forty. Didn't she deserve a modicum of privacy?

She extended her arm, watching the kinks flatten out, then set the iron on her dresser.

"Good morning," she said as she flipped open the phone.

51

"Knight?"

Who else did he think it would be on her official Bureau phone? She mulled over the possibility of making a smart-ass reply, but knew she'd regret it later. As Joiner always reminded everybody at his weekly meetings, "An agent is never off the clock. We're all government employees twenty-four hours a day, seven days a week."

"Knight?"

"Yes?"

"What are you doing?"

"At the moment I'm getting ready for work." She purposely omitted the "sir."

"What about the adjustment to the report? For three-eighty-three. You get it done?"

Felicia took a deep breath. She had to keep her cool or this asshole would get her transferred to some remote location in Podunk, Nowhere. She'd waited too long for her shot at D.C. So she answered with a professional tone, even though the rest of her was screaming to tell him what he could do with his report. "Yes, sir. I finished it last night, as you instructed."

"You went into the office?"

What was his problem? Isn't that what he'd told her to do? No, more like ordered her. "I did, but took the file home and finished it here."

She heard a little squeak over the phone. "You didn't e-mail it, did you?"

Now she understood. Joiner distrusted Internet technology and constantly worried about transmissions being intercepted. Also, it left a time-stamped trail his bosses could follow.

"No, I didn't," she said. "It's on my flash drive. I can send it now if you want."

"No, no." His voice cracked. "Get in and print me out a hard copy."

Felicia smiled, glad she'd been able to press the right buttons to make him jump for a change. "I'll be in as soon as I finish getting ready."

"What's your E.T.A.?"

She glanced at her wall clock. Six-forty-five. If this idiot hadn't interrupted her, she'd have been walking out the door by now. She forced herself to sound calm. "An hour or so."

That seemed to mollify Joiner, at least for the moment. He was silent and Felicia could almost hear the rusty gears grinding in his head.

"Okay," he said. "Make sure you bring me a hard copy as soon as you get in. Highlight the section about three-eighty-three."

"Will do. Anything else?"

"What?" Annoyance. "No, no. Dammit! Hold on."

He'd put her on hold. Must be taking another call. The silence droned on. She cradled the phone between her shoulder and neck and began fitting more strands of her hair between the paddles of the flat iron.

"There's been a new development," Joiner said. "You got your go-bag ready?"

"My what?"

"Your damn *go-bag*. Bring it. I'll brief you when you get in."

Before she could reply, he hung up. Her go-bag? That meant traveling. To where and for how long? Felicia took a deep breath and remembered her mother's advice: *Girl, don't be borrowing worries till you know what's going on. Lord knows, you be getting enough of them anyway.*

She smiled at the memory and figured whatever was waiting for her, she'd deal with it. Still, she wondered exactly what it was, which brought her back to Joiner's phone call.

Three-eighty-three. The man was obsessed with that number and with Mohammed Amir Fassel. They'd lost track of him, but he'd pop up again. They knew three-eighty-three was part of a larger plot. How significant could his disappearance be?

She wondered if Podunk would be so bad if she was away from Joiner. Her hand accidentally brushed over the edge of the hot pads of the flat iron. Recoiling, she stuck her burned fingers in her mouth and raced to the sink to run cold water over them.

Damn that man! Is anything gonna go right for me this morning?

CHAPTER 4

Viceroy fingered the general's stars that he hoped would soon replace the eagles on the epaulets of his dress uniform.

His den was adorned with photos of him at various stages of his military career: his service as a young marine, guarding the embassy in Saigon during the pullout, receiving his college degree, graduating from OCS, going from former enlisted gyrene to army officer.

The phone interrupted his reverie. Glancing at the screen, he frowned. "What is it, Will?"

"You see what they're saying about me this morning?"

Big Willie sounded like a pig about to be castrated. Viceroy took a deep breath and spoke slowly, keeping his voice low and flat. He'd done this countless times during combat and black ops, scaling down the emotional level to quiet a man under stress. "Calm down. Relax. What are you talking about?"

"That damn Allison Hayes interviewing the little prick. The bitch. And I know her, too."

Viceroy smirked, figuring Big Willie had almost slipped and said he'd fucked her. But since he was married to Viceroy's sister, he didn't always mention his escapades. As if Viceroy didn't know. It was unfolding like a Shakespearian play. From the whine in Big Willie's voice, Viceroy thought of it as a comedy. No, more like a history with farcical elements. Like Prince Hal and Falstaff in *Henry IV.* Viceroy decided to move Big Willie like he'd move a chess piece. His brother-in-law was a bishop—a rook at best. He was certainly no queen. The distaff metaphor bothered him. Not a queen. The king, seemingly in control, but protected by all the other pieces.

Viceroy thought wistfully of his past missions, of being close to the action. Now he was relegated to protecting the king from afar. But he was controlling all the pieces on his side of the board, able to order a strike when the opportunity arose.

"Clay?" The other man's voice continued to bleat.

Was he really a rook? This would be a good chance to test how fast Big Willie could think on his feet. "What do you mean, you *knew* her?"

"I gave her a couple of interviews when I was V.P.," he said, already starting to regain his composure.

Not too bad. Push him up against the wall and he regains his cool. Still Viceroy wouldn't want to take this one into real combat. Chances are he'd fold when the shit hit the fan. *Better surround him with some strong advisors once they got to the Oval Office.*

"I see." Viceroy gave Big Willie a couple of beats to let him think. "Don't be too worried. As far as I can tell, she's a lightweight."

Big Willie snorted. "Easy for you to say. You know what they said about me?"

The petulance in the voice, the pathetic whine, had returned. Time for more reassurance. It was good practice manipulating him. Good practice for the ultimate plan that would unfold down the road. "Actually, I did see the segment."

"You did?"

"It was recycled bullshit. Nothing that hasn't been said before."

"It's like I told you." Viceroy could hear the other man's breathing on the phone. "We need something else to knock the torture matter off the headlines."

"We got a lot riding on this master plan of yours, don't we?"

Viceroy felt his anger suddenly well up. Even though he was reasonably certain that no one was listening, he always stressed to his team to act like there was, in nonscrambled conversations. Especially with what was at stake. Especially in Washington, D.C. If they'd been in the field, Viceroy would have knocked the man's mouth all the way down to his ass.

His ops phone rang. It was time.

"I have to go," Viceroy said, forcing his voice to sound calm and flat.

"Huh? What's up?"

"You can discuss your campaign plans with Roger. In the meantime, keep all your concerns to yourself, all right?"

He didn't wait for a reply.

As morgues went, the one on Massachusetts Avenue wasn't bad. It was clean and well scrubbed. Even the usual refrigerated storage room stacked with bodies was neatly organized, but one thing couldn't be erased: the smell. That was what got to McClain the most. The pervasive odor of death that reminded him of Mogadishu. Bodies left to decay in the hot sun. Bloating. Stinking. Kids poking the bodies with sticks. Those kinds of memories stayed with you, beneath the surface of your consciousness, waiting to spring upward like a coiled serpent hiding in dark water.

The waiting room was comfortable: soft chairs, a sofa, and a couple of vending machines, but it was still part of the morgue. Thank God he'd only have to deal with the odor for a short while, unless the ME got long-winded and wanted to demonstrate his findings by holding up the severed organs. McClain leaned back in the chair and hoped this would yield some sort of lead.

A lab attendant in scrubs opened one of the swinging glass doors and waved at him.

Great, that meant they'd already opened John Doe up. Now the stench would be really bad. McClain rose to his feet and shuffled over. It hit him as soon as he went through the flimsy swinging door—a combination of blood and rotting garbage. The body lay on a metal table, its feet sticking up at relaxed forty-five-degree angles, like the guy was asleep, except for the open flaps of skin and ribs that exposed the red meat of his chest cavity. The doctor, a youngish guy with dark rimmed glasses named Norwood, looked up. His face was reed thin under the plastic flap of the protective mask. He labored with something inside the body's lower groin region.

"Ah, Detective. Glad you're here. I may have something." Norwood's gloved fingers continued to probe.

McClain heard a squishing sound and felt a wave of nausea creeping up from his stomach.

"Henry," the doctor said, "I may need your help here."

The lab attendant moved over to the metal table and the doctor spoke in an indistinct tone. He straightened up and came over to McClain, holding his gloved hands outward, the light green latex covered with red smears. "I've found some interesting things with this one."

McClain took out his notebook.

"First of all," Norwood continued, "someone preferred him well done." He snorted a laugh.

A thousand comedians out of work, McClain thought, *and I have to walk into his autopsy room.* The lab assistant picked up an electric saw and leaned over the lower portion of the corpse. The blade made a humming whine as it met the tissue, setting McClain's teeth on edge.

"I took some swabs to formally identify the accelerant on the skin," Norwood said, "but to me it smells like plain old gasoline."

McClain wondered how the man could smell anything, even gasoline, in this place.

"Did I ever tell you about my friend, Dominic?" Norwood asked. "He uses gasoline on his charcoal grill. Makes the meat taste sort of metallic."

The saw made a grinding sound. Bone.

"Moreover,"—Norwood raised his voice to talk over the whine of the saw—"I'd say they took extensive steps in an attempt to obscure identification."

McClain scribbled that in his notebook.

Norwood pointed at the head. Facial skin had been peeled back and what remained was a mixture of white muscle tissue and blackened charred sections. "All the victim's teeth have either been removed or broken off. Some of the roots remain so it was probably done with pliers." McClain caught the doctor's impish grin flashing again under the plastic shield. "So I think we can rule out a bad dentist."

The noise from the saw stopped. McClain felt the tingling along his neck start to fade.

The lab attendant straightened up. "Got the hip-joint out, doctor." He held up a whitish section of blood-covered bone with a metallic flange about the size of a large faucet. The flange was connected to a circular ball joint. Norwood took it and went to the counter. He flipped a switch and a large circular magnifier illuminated. He held the bone under the big lens. "All right, here's your ID number. G, as in George, one-zero-nine-four-four." He paused and looked at McClain. "Appears to be a government serial number. Could this man be a veteran or government employee?"

"Don't know."

Norwood held up the metallic hip socket. "Well, this should help." He shot McClain another sly grin. "Are you hip?"

"Anything else you can tell me, doc?"

"He was subjected to a protracted beating." Norwood told the aide to raise the body. The aide's gloved hands grabbed the corpse by the arm and lifted. Norwood traced his fingers along with the charred flesh of the man's back and side, peeling the separated skin away. It had obviously been cut away before because it separated like a zipper now. "These subcutaneous hematomas—I had to fillet a good portion of his skin here to check, but the secondary tissue damage is obvious. This indicates that he was beaten severely prior to his death." Norwood motioned for the aide to lower the body, then picked up a charred hand. "It also looks like his fingernails had been removed premortem."

A twinge ran up McClain's spine. He remembered the intense pain from losing only two fingernails in Somalia.

"Detective? Are you all right?"

McClain blinked. "Just remembering an unpleasant experience. So what was the cause of death? The beating or the fire?"

"I'm not done yet, but at this point I'd have to say neither."

McClain gritted his teeth. This joker was making him wait for every tidbit. "What's your best guess?"

Norwood pointed to the open chest cavity. It looked like a hollowed-out hunk of raw beef. "There were no signs of soot in the nasal cavities or bronchial tubes. The burning occurred postmortem." He reached inside the corpse's throat and pulled a section of pink tissue, scrutinized it, then jammed a syringe into it. "Want to get a sample for analysis. Should tell us something about this subterfuge."

"Subterfuge?"

"Yes, subterfuge. Something done or performed to obscure one's real intention."

McClain frowned. He knew what it meant. "Obscure what? His identity or the cause of death?"

"Water trapped in his vocal folds," Norwood said absently, pulling back the plunger. The syringe filled with a semi-clear-looking fluid. "He'd aspirated quite a bit of water into his lungs as well, causing asphyxiation." Norwood raised his eyebrows and looked thoughtful. "I'd have to say the cause of death was drowning."

Missing teeth, ripped off fingernails, a gasoline broiling, and a drowning on dry land. Not your ordinary way of killing, McClain thought.

His homeless guy's murder had become a complicated whodunit.

CHAPTER 5

Viceroy fingered another Havana but didn't even consider lighting it. He was saving his cigars for special occasions, like the previous evening. It wouldn't do to get into the bad habit of smoking again. Not with his cardiac condition. The ubiquitous cigarettes had been his downfall before. So an occasional cigar would do little harm as long as he didn't let it become a regular habit. He put the Havana back into the humidor. On to more important things: he had a mission to set up. His phone chimed with a text alert from Lee: *b team gone. we're ready to go. permission to disembark.*

He texted back: *Has other party arrived yet?*

Not yet.

Viceroy frowned. *Negative. Wait till further.* He prided himself on always using proper grammar in his texting. The devil, after all, was in the details.

roger that. standing by, Lee sent back.

Viceroy looked at his watch. Zero-nine-seventeen. Where the hell were those damn feds? What kind of outfit was that jackass Joiner running where he couldn't mobilize a squad to be on time? Still, he was dealing with civilians and that in its own way gave him an innate advantage. He took a deep breath and glanced out the window of his den. It was a lovely late September day. The last vestiges of summer transitioning into autumn. As inevitable as the sunrise, and as unpredictable. Right now it was time to deal with another intangible. But this one was totally manageable. He went to his contact list, scrolled down to Joiner, then hit the call button.

It rang three times. "Special Agent Joiner."

"Woody," Viceroy said as cordially as he could manage. He detested the FBI man—a buffoon, but a necessary evil for the moment. A means to an end. "It's Clay. My men are standing by, ready to go. Are your guys close?"

Viceroy heard the other man swearing under his breath. "Shit! I told them to hurry it up. I knew I shouldn't have sent that damn Knight."

Viceroy chuckled. "Knight? That's an appropriate name for a crusader in law enforcement."

"Affirmative action is more like it," Joiner said. "She's on colored people's time."

So Joiner was a misogynist as well as a racist. Something to file away until it was time to jettison him. When that time came, Joiner would make a good fall guy. Setting things up in the proper fashion required a bit of finesse, but it all came down to managing your battlefield, whether you were on foreign soil, here at home, or on the chessboard. "You got time for a meet at the Mall? I'd prefer to give you an update face-to-face."

"I'll be there in twenty minutes," Joiner said. "Where exactly?"

"By the merry-go-round." An appropriate metaphor for keeping the FBI man in a state of ignorant anticipation.

Felicia was feeling every bump as Beaumont drove. He even managed to go over the corrugated shoulder before straying back into the lane. He and Johnson sat up front, having relegated her to the backseat. At least this way she could hold onto her laptop to keep it from thrashing about.

"Will you slow down a little bit?" she said. "It's not going to make that much difference since we're already late."

She caught a flash of Beaumont's disapproving look in the

rearview mirror. "When the SAIC says to use all possible speed getting there, that's what we do."

"When the SAIC says jump, we say, how high?" Johnson added.

Felicia frowned at their tag-team bullshit and thought about mentioning that if they hadn't lost their assigned surveillance target, they wouldn't be rushing like this. Still, arguing with these two assholes served no purpose. She had to spend the rest of the day and probably well into the night in their company. Clutching the laptop to her breasts, like a school girl, she put her head back and wished she could have gotten one more hour of sleep last night.

"Turn there," Johnson said.

"I know," Beaumont grunted.

Felicia couldn't help but smile. They were turning on each other now.

The car lurched into a turn, approaching Dulles. With any luck they'd be at the military section of the airport in five minutes. She wondered how cold this aircraft would be. If only she'd known she was going for a ride she'd have brought a sweater. She'd have to update her "go-bag."

She reviewed the almost frantic instructions Joiner had spewed out. "I've gotten word about a new development involving target three-eighty-three," Joiner had said. "He's involved in an attempt to smuggle a WMD into the U.S."

If that were the case, she couldn't blame Joiner for being nervous and abrupt. The fact that Military Intelligence had intercepted and developed this information, especially when the Bureau was assigned to follow Fassel, could be embarrassing for everybody concerned.

Screw embarrassment, she thought. *Let's concentrate on stopping these fanatics.* She mentally added, *by any means necessary.* She smiled. If Joiner knew she was quoting Malcolm X, even mentally, it would send him up a wall.

The car made another turn, approaching the military gate. It wouldn't be long now.

Viceroy reviewed the incoming text message: *feebies finally here.*

A few people were jogging around the grassy edges of the Mall. Others were buying ice cream and taking pictures. Workers were taking covers off the plaster horses on the merry-go-round. The midmorning sun silhouetted the Washington Monument, and best of all, he saw Joiner waddling down the sidewalk toward him, the man's head bobbling like one of those flocked dogs on a dashboard. He carried a blue folder.

"Semper fi," Viceroy said, extending his hand. He knew Joiner had been a marine. Once a marine, always a marine.

"Semper fi." Joiner's face looked flushed.

"My squad sent me a text. Your agents arrived."

Joiner let out a heavy breath. "Sorry it took so long for them to get there."

The wetness seeped through the front of Joiner's blue shirt. The man was so out of shape, a brisk walk had made him sweat. Viceroy wondered how this jerk had ever made it through Marine Corps boot. Still, it meant for sure that Joiner wasn't wired. Sweating like that would short-circuit any remote mic. Not that Viceroy was worried about being recorded. He just liked to have every possible contingency covered during an op.

"They'll be underway shortly," Viceroy said.

Joiner fell into step beside Viceroy. "What's the latest intel?"

"As you know, three-eighty-three has been a busy boy since he was released from Gitmo."

"Yeah, and I told those idiots in the Justice Department there was no way he should have been repatriated back to Saudi. But the Commander-in-Chief's so caught up in not offending those fucking towelheads—"

"You're preaching to the choir, Woody."

Joiner compressed his lips. "They're going to have a lot of crow to eat when they find out about this."

"That's the thing. With the AG so bent on following all the rules on *Posse Comitatus,* we have to tread lightly. You know how they'd react if they found out the military was involved in this one."

"They've forgotten we're all on the same team."

Viceroy knew he had to walk a delicate line: tell him enough to keep stringing him along, but maintain overall control of the operation.

"Have we located Fassel yet?" Joiner asked.

Viceroy feigned a grim expression. "He's dropped off the radar. But we did intercept more intel about their intercept tonight."

"The WMD?" Joiner's head popped up like an anxious dog. "Where our teams are going, right?"

Viceroy had to suppress a smile at "our teams." In a way it was true, except Viceroy knew it was more like some division-two football players being brought into the NFL for a few plays. Still, he had to keep the FBI man satisfied but hooked. "Fassel's associate is making the meet tonight."

"Hassan Omar Mohammed, right?"

Viceroy nodded. Let the fool think he knew more than he did. "We call him HOM for short."

"Outstanding. I like that."

"HOM's meeting the group smuggling the WMD in tonight. As I said, the rendezvous point is at that abandoned border crossing in Maine."

"How reliable is the intel about the WDM?"

"First rate," Viceroy said. "I've had people tagging them since they left their point of origin."

"And you're sure they've actually got—" Joiner glanced

around "—Sarin?"

"Ever wonder why we never found any WMDs in Iraq? They've been moving the components around like Chinese checkers. From Iraq to Jordan to Yemen to Canada." He paused for effect. "And now, here."

Joiner frowned. "Dammit. We can't let them get that stuff into the U.S."

"Agreed, but we also want to be able to connect it to the dormant cell. Otherwise they'll go underground and resurface at another location. Besides, it's a binary gas. As long as we keep the two halves from getting together, the gas is inert."

Joiner bit his lip. "I need to start notifying my higher-ups on this one."

"Ah, that might be a mistake at this juncture." Viceroy waited, then said, "All we have in the way of tangible proof are some vague messages. Let's intercept the shipment and you'll come out smelling like a rose. But if we get a bunch of other people and agencies involved right now, it'll only muck things up. Plus, they'll come down on me like a ton of bricks for running this as an MI mission within the continental United States. You know how this current administration feels about *Posse Comitatus.*"

Joiner looked worried. "I hope you're right."

Viceroy placed a hand on the other man's shoulder. "Don't worry, Woody. My team's got it covered. With your guys there, too, what can go wrong?" He watched the man's mouth twitch again. "Come on, there's a small coffee joint on the next corner. Let's grab a cup and you can show me your report. We won't know anything more for a few hours. They'll call me once they arrive and set up."

"Sounds good to me."

Viceroy felt like he was moving another chess piece in place, this one a pawn.

★ ★ ★ ★ ★

Felicia was still clutching the laptop as one of the crew showed her how to buckle herself in. This was the first time she'd been in a helicopter this large. Two rotors, front and rear, and an interior as big as a train car. Canvas seat against a metallic wall, no frills, and certainly no flight attendants. Just three pilots. And when those big rotor engines started up, it was noisy as hell.

Everyone sat in silence as the crew went through some sort of checklist before takeoff. Beaumont and Johnson were to her right. A group of hard-looking men in uniforms sat across from her. Eleven of them. Army on one side, civilians on the other. She assumed they were army. None of them had any rank insignias and their uniforms were darkened BDUs. One thing for sure. They were armed to the teeth. Each had a rifle or an MP-5 machine gun dangling between his legs. Very phallic, she thought. These guys probably sweated pure testosterone. They all had sidearms, too. Except the guy directly across from her. He was in civilian clothes, but she had him pegged for a soldier. The others called him "Top." His nickname? He was black with a shaved head and looked to be in his forties. She'd noticed him as they boarded. Not real tall, but his shoulders and arms were massive. The man next to him was Asian, with dark eyes that stared at her. She pressed her legs together and crossed her ankles. The bald guy grinned.

"First time flying in a CH forty-seven, miss?" he asked.

"Yes." She didn't smile back. He wasn't bad-looking, but reminded her too much of Jerome. She didn't need another man in her life at the moment.

He glanced at the cockpit area and yelled, "How long?"

"About five mikes," one of the pilots answered.

The bald guy unbuckled his safety harness and moved forward. Felicia thought he moved very smoothly for such a big

68

man. Like a running back. He returned with a blanket and plastic bucket and handed them to her.

"It's going to get cold real fast once we get up there," he said.

She looking questioningly at the bucket.

"You might need that, too," he said. "These Chinooks can be a bit choppy, if you're not used to them, especially your first time."

"Chinook? That what this helicopter is called?"

"A lot of our birds are named after Native American tribes."

Felicia set the bucket on top of the laptop.

The black guy turned to Beaumont and Johnson. "You guys want puke buckets too?"

Beaumont smirked. They both shook their heads.

The bald guy shrugged. "Suit yourselves." As he buckled himself in again, he exchanged a wink with the Asian guy, whose embroidered name tag over his pocket said *LEE*. The two of them seemed to be sharing some inside joke. They'd obviously worked together before. Like they could read each other's thoughts. It was a degree of comfort she'd never share with Beaumont or Johnson. Joiner either, for that matter.

The engines revved up and the helicopter jerked back and forth. Felicia heard a loud whining sound before she felt the craft lifting off. She assumed it would be called a liftoff, rather than a takeoff, like a plane. Immediately, she felt the chill and pulled the blanket over her legs. She still held the plastic bucket on her lap. The noise was offsetting. It increased as the helicopter gained speed. She felt like asking how fast this thing would go, but knew they wouldn't be able to hear her.

A zigzagging motion started. The front end jerked as the back end came forward, then it reversed. Almost like they were taking steps in the air instead of flying straight. It caused a constant shimmy and she knew why the man had given her the plastic bucket. She clutched it tighter in her hands, praying she'd be able to keep her breakfast down. Coffee, juice, and an egg sandwich. She wished she'd skipped it altogether. Her stomach twitched with the constant back-and-forth motion, so she concentrated on the report that Joiner had been so insistent on getting "first thing this morning." She'd barely walked in the door when he asked her for it, Beaumont and Johnson right behind him like two oversized lap dogs.

"You bring your go-bag?" Joiner had asked. "Get ready, you're going on a field assignment."

Now she let out a breath and her stomach started to relax. Her breakfast was going to stay put for the moment.

Someone grabbed her plastic bucket.

Beaumont. His face was flushed and contorted. He held the bucket under his chin and puked, the stench of the vomit assailing her nostrils. He kept right on puking while Johnson fought him for a space around the edge. Johnson tore at the bucket and it twisted from Beaumont's hands, spilling the vile contents over both their laps. Thank God she had that blanket or it would have gotten all over her, too. Felicia recoiled, looked away, and saw the black guy. He had a wide grin on his face.

CHAPTER 6

Back at the office McClain replayed the autopsy in his head. The man's mutilated body bothered him the most. Maybe it was the fingernail thing. A long forgotten, unpleasant memory. He rubbed his fingertips together as he recalled the pain of the Somali torture. And he'd broken. Cried like a baby.

No, like a pussy. Airborne ranger, my ass.

Time to get back to reality. The past is the past. Now is now. Get it together. But McClain couldn't help wondering why this victim had been tortured. Maybe when he figured out who the victim was, he'd be on the track to finding out why, and then who. Step by step.

The ME had given him the sanitized hip replacement joint in a plastic evidence bag. The serial number indicated it was GI— Government Issue. Had the vic been a member of the military, a veteran, or a civilian employee? Trying to find which branch of the government to check was a problem in itself, not to mention where the surgery had been done. McClain had the needle. All he had to do now was find the haystack.

The manufacturer, Otis-Veal Medical Supplies, an outfit out of Cincinnati, proved less than helpful. After dealing with a computerized switchboard, he finally got a human voice. McClain said he was working on a homicide investigation.

"Just a minute," the bored-sounding receptionist said.

After several minutes of dead air, another person came on the line with a quick, "How may I help you?"

McClain said, "I'm working a homicide case and trying to identify the victim. It's extremely important." He gave the serial number and heard keys clicking on a computer.

"That particular batch was sold to the government back in 2006, sir."

"Is there any way you can tell me exactly where it went? Which branch of the government? Which hospital it might have gone to?"

"No, sir. The only thing I can tell you was that it was part of a larger order that year. It shipped on April eighth."

At least he had a general time frame. McClain tried to figure out his next move. His new lead was turning into an old-fashioned crap shoot. Without knowing which governmental branch to check, he was still up the creek without a paddle. He began checking them all, getting the runaround until he was finally referred to a branch called GMIS—Governmental Medical Inventory Services. After speaking with at least five different people, he finally got someone who asked for the serial number. McClain read it off to him. He heard the promising sound of keyboard clicking again, but tried not to get his expectations up too high.

"All right," the voice on the other end of the phone said. "I've traced that particular one to the Miami Veteran's Hospital in Florida. You want their number?"

"Please," McClain said.

"A word of warning, though," the guy said. "They probably aren't going to give you any patient information without a subpoena."

"Yeah, thanks."

Kelly was supposed to be walking a general, nonspecific homicide-inquiry subpoena through court this morning, but he wasn't back yet. McClain could fax it down to the hospital in Florida if they hesitated in giving up the patient info, even though a person's expectation of privacy ended with death. He dialed the number for Miami VA, and was put in touch with the head of the purchasing section.

"What's the serial number?" the guy asked.

McClain could almost recite it by heart now.

"Okay," the guy said, "that one was sent to the U.S. Naval Hospital, Guantanamo Bay, on June 7, 2007."

"You have any patient information?"

"I don't have any specifics, but I can probably get you a name. Hold on."

McClain felt a sudden elation. It was about time he caught a break in this case.

"All I'm coming up with is a nondescript. Patient X-three-eight-three," the man said.

"What's that mean?"

"Shit if I know. They do that sometimes, for whatever reason. You got to call down there for more info. Sorry."

McClain checked the computer listing for the medical hospital for the marine base in Gitmo. The vic could be Navy, Marine, or civilian. Or an enemy combatant. He dialed the number and asked for the medical records section. The person who answered was initially helpful until the brick wall popped up.

"Uh, I'm sorry, sir," the hospital clerk said. "I can't release any patient information."

"Come on," McClain said. "The guy's dead. I'm trying to identify him."

"I'd need a subpoena, sir."

"There's no more expectation of privacy, damn it!"

As McClain's frustration was building to the breaking point, Kelly came in with a big grin on his face. McClain told the guy to hold for a minute.

Kelly held up a folder.

"What's your fax number?" McClain asked. "I'll send it right down."

The crew wouldn't give Beaumont and Johnson new clothes until they'd cleaned up the mess they'd made. Trying to hide her glee, Felicia stood by while they sprayed and scrubbed. Beaumont looked up at her, his lips twisting into a snarl. "Least you could do is help us."

"You're doing fine without me," she said. "Besides, I didn't contribute. Tell me you'd be helping me if I'd been the one up-chucking."

"Don't tell the SAIC, okay?" Johnson said.

Felicia didn't reply. Little chance she'd be running back to Joiner to dime them out. The asshole would probably see it as disloyalty and hold it against her. But if she'd been the one puking, it would have been a source of jokes around the water cooler for weeks. The Asian guy named Lee motioned for her to step over and handed her a nylon flight jacket.

"You said you were cold," he said.

She thanked him, slipped the jacket on, and caught him watching her breasts as she moved. There was something cold and scary about his eyes.

"We're going to have to shove off now, ma'am," he said.

"Can't you wait for us?"

Lee glanced toward the Chinook then shook his head.

"Not enough time. We've got to locate our target area and set up." He peeled back a black Velcro strip uncovering his wristwatch. "Ten hours and counting and we have to recon."

Felicia was ready to go, but Bert and Ernie still scrubbed their vomit patches. "I don't think my partners are quite done yet." She smiled, but he showed no emotion. All business, this guy. As emotional as a feral tiger.

"I've arranged for your group to accompany our surveillance

vehicle," he said. "B team's standing by to bring you. Once they finish with their cleanup."

This was starting to sound less and less like a Bureau case and more like one they were on the sidelines observing. What would Joiner have to say about that when he read her report?

"Okay," she said. "Are we going to be brought up to speed anytime soon?"

"Later. Right now, all we're worried about is making sure we get our hands on that Sarin."

"What time's the meet with the suspects set for?"

"Twenty-two-forty. Late enough for it to be dark, but early enough for there to be vehicles on the roads."

The helicopter had made better time than she'd figured, but the rendezvous point was still a good two or three hours away by car. "Who will I be with?"

"Sergeant Baker, ma'am," Lee said. "He's good."

Felicia hoped he was. She hoped they all were. This was one mission they couldn't afford to screw up.

Kelly set the document down on the desktop in front of McClain and said, "Let's go hunting."

McClain glanced at it. An arrest warrant for Rewaldo M. Snopes for attempted murder and armed robbery. He looked up at Kelly.

"I'm about to finally find out who my vic is."

"Thanks to me," Kelly said, "for walking that subpoena through the court system this morning for you. Let's not forget that."

"Yeah, partner. It's called division of labor when we're working a homicide, right?"

"Ain't gonna make no difference on a bullshit murder like that. I bet they end up reclassifying it as a misdemeanor."

"I'm the primary, remember? I can't afford to take time away from this one."

"Yeah, and I'm the one got you that subpoena, remember? Now let's go serve us a warrant and get credit for an easy arrest and clearing a case."

"One of your cases."

"Right. Make my stats look good. Besides, who's gonna be that concerned about some poor, dumb, homeless dude who got fried in an alley?"

"Hey, I think the guy might have been a veteran."

"We got a long history of forgetting vets in this country."

McClain rubbed his forehead. Some time out of the office would be a welcome break. He was still spinning his wheels and this case was probably one step away from being turned over to the cold case squad. He stood up and stretched.

"All right, where we going?"

Kelly read him the address and McClain flinched. "Are you kidding me? The housing projects?"

"Not to worry. Got some tac guys to go with us."

McClain was grabbing his coat when his cell rang. Glancing at the caller ID screen, he grimaced. Just when he thought things couldn't get any worse. "Give me a minute, will you?"

"Don't tell me Missy Lynn picked this time to reach out."

McClain pressed the button and answered the call with, "This is a real bad time."

"Is there ever a good time with you?"

"I'm on my way to serve a warrant."

"I thought you were going to get this insurance matter straightened out."

McClain grabbed the bridge of his nose and squeezed. It felt like his head was going to explode.

"Kevin? Are you ignoring me?"

"Now how could I possibly do that?"

★ ★ ★ ★ ★

Viceroy waited for his special phone to ring. He amused himself by playing chess against his computer and watching Big Willie being prepped by his campaign manager, Raymond A. Jetson, Junior, or "Ram Jet." Viceroy figured the man could call himself anything he wanted if he could lead Big Willie to the White House. This afternoon that was proving to be an arduous task.

"What about the rumor that's he's a closet homosexual?" Big Willie asked.

Ram Jet shook his head. "Just that—a rumor. Plus, we can't risk alienating the gay vote. The polls have us—"

"Don't talk to me about the fucking polls."

Ram Jet threw up his hands. "Do you want to win this or not?"

"Ah, hell, I'm a scrapper. That's all I'm saying. He wants a street fight, I'll damn well give it to him."

Ram Jet massaged his temples. "We have to keep this civil for now, remember? The public doesn't like negative campaigning. Plus, we have our own baggage in that department. You haven't always been Mr. Clean yourself."

Viceroy figured he must be referring to some intern turned personal assistant named Regina, one of Big Willie's "dollies." Big Willie didn't know that Viceroy knew, and he wanted to keep it that way for the moment.

"What if he brings up the torture issue during the debate?"

Big Willie sipped from a glass of bourbon, his second glass since he'd arrived. Viceroy knew his brother-in-law could usually hold his liquor, but today Big Willie's facial muscles were beginning to sag and the usually well-coiffed pompadour looked a bit ragged and oily. "And what about that asshole, Paul Ross? Who knows what kind of shit he'll throw at us."

"Don't worry." Ram Jet placed a reassuring hand on Big Willie's knee. "It's all a smoke screen."

The move made Viceroy wonder if Ram Jet was secretly gay. Since the overturn of Don't Ask, Don't Tell, he'd reexamined his view of homosexuality and while he still felt they had no place in the military, he had assumed a position of benign tolerance. If Ram Jet could reshape Big Willie's image into that of the next president, Viceroy didn't care who the man slept with. But it was interesting information to have on file, in case he needed it later on down the line. That was how things worked when you were a king-builder. Ram Jet gave the knee a final, affectionate squeeze.

"It's a bluff," he said. "Something to get you off your game. Remember, he's running on his record this time, and that gives us the advantage."

Big Willie took another sip of the amber liquid. Despite all the booze, he was an impressive figure of a man. It had led him to the vice presidency in the previous administration, and Viceroy knew that Big Willie had been instrumental in running the whole show. But he and the blithering idiot who had previously occupied the executive office had run things into the ground: poor war management, lack of follow-through, inability to get enough funding through the Congress, mishandling the economy. They'd let the country down and ensured the election of Harris. Viceroy didn't think the country, much less the military, could survive another four years of a Harris presidency.

Not if we want to remain the preeminent super power. Something must be done. The time is now.

The computer moved its black bishop to black queen's four. Viceroy brought his full attention back to the screen. The machine had boxed him into a corner. He would be checkmated in three moves. He'd been too damn distracted.

Big Willie laughed his horse's laugh—a side effect of the booze that sounded more like a forced guffaw than a sincere expression of merriment.

"You got to work on your laugh, Will," Ram Jet said. "Make it sound more sophisticated."

"What wrong my fucking laugh?" The words were slurred now. Viceroy glanced at his watch as he exited the game and watched the computer reset the pieces. He didn't like the way it always made him white, forcing him to make the first move. Black was better. Thirteen-fifteen. West should have called.

"Will," Ram Jet said, "go easy on the booze, okay?"

Big Willie slammed his glass down on the coffee table.

"Hey," Viceroy said, "that came all the way from Morocco."

"Morocco?" Ram Jet said. "That's a Muslim place, isn't it?"

"Oh, loosen up." Big Willie got to his feet. "Clay, you got any more scotch?"

"You've had enough," Viceroy said.

"He's right, Will," Ram Jet said. "We've got work to do. Basic strategy to discuss here."

But Big Willie looked in no condition to discuss anything. The corners of his mouth drooped and he sat back on the sofa with a plop. "Aww, shit, I know you guys are right. I need to win this debate."

Ram Jet clapped his hands together. "Great. Now we're cooking."

"With this damn shit storm that's coming, it could derail everything." Big Willie's gaze swiveled toward Viceroy. "Any word from your man yet?"

The fucking idiot couldn't hold a secret to save his life. Viceroy stared back at him.

Still, if I want that general's star, the one that's been denied me, and all that will follow, Big Willie in the White House is a necessary evil. At least until I assume command.

Ram Jet looked perplexed. "What man is that, Clay?"

Viceroy realized it was a mistake letting his brother-in-law in on so much, but it was the only way to keep the son-of-a-bitch lucid and quiet. Otherwise he'd be digging his own grave, trying to justify all of those allegations of encouraging torture when he was VP. But perhaps it was time to let Ram Jet become more aware of what was to come, if they wanted to get maximum usage out of it.

"We're working an operation," Viceroy said. "Domestic terrorism. When we take this cell down, it'll make everyone, the press included, forget this torture bullshit."

"Tell me more."

"I wish I could," Viceroy said. "It's classified."

"Classified? Clay, come on. I'm the guy who's trying to get your brother-in-law in the White House, remember? If you can't trust me, who can you trust?"

Who did he trust? Lee, West, and the rest of his men. They'd been there together, their backs against the wall, and he trusted them with his life.

Part of the op was assessing the weak links. Would they hold? And if they made it all the way to 1600 Pennsylvania Avenue, Ram Jet could then be erased. Another expendable pawn.

With me wearing a general's star, and soon a couple more stars when I'm in charge of the Joint Chiefs of Staff, I'll be able to call the shots. I'll play him like my old six-string guitar until it's time for me to take my place in the Oval Office.

Viceroy's cell phone rang. He flipped it open. "Sit-rep."

"About to begin set-up now. Feds in the van, about ten clicks back."

"Roger that," Viceroy said. "Proceed as planned. And be advised, use proper protocol. Report to me upon completion."

Viceroy terminated the call, totally confident that they were on a secure line but still miffed at Lee for the breach of protocol—mentioning the "feds." Take a tiger out of the jungle for too long and that's what happens. He gets lax, cocky, loses his feral edge.

"Who was that?" Ram Jet asked, while Big Willie shuffled back to the sofa, his glass sloshing amber liquid over the edge. He'd taken the respite of the phone call to raid the liquor cabinet again. "Was that Lee?"

"Was that him?" Big Willie asked.

Viceroy studied the frozen potential hidden behind the silver pompadour, the chiseled, patrician features, the steady ooze of political charisma. Could he really ride this horse all the way to the throne room so he could lead the king's armies and conquer the world?

He'd already broken the first rule of espionage: Never trust anyone outside of your op's team and your immediate chain of command. But he needed to keep his brother-in-law in the loop for damage control. Big Willie was involved up to his neck. Now it was time to bring in Ram Jet as well, so the silent spin doctor could keep things on track.

Heavy lies the head that wears a crown, Viceroy thought. *Henry IV, Part Two.* His favorite of the histories. His brother-in-law was Falstaff to his Prince Hal. But could the fat fool ever become king?

Ram Jet said, "Did I miss something here?"

"Maybe it is time to bring you up to speed on the operation." Viceroy reached over and took the glass of booze from the table. "You need to sober up," he told Big Willie. "About six months ago we received intel that a former prisoner from Gitmo, who had been repatriated by the Harris administration, had made his way back into the United States via Canada."

Ram Jet's eyes widened. "This is dynamite."

Viceroy held up his palm. "It gets better."

CHAPTER 7

McClain spent the next five minutes listening to Lynn's rant about Dr. Moorefield. Not only was this guy not covered by McClain's insurance plan, but Jen hated the man. When he mentioned this to Lynn she tore into him worse than ever: "That's typical of you. Always spoiling her, letting her have her own way instead of what's best. That's why *I've* got custody."

He didn't like taking it and not answering back, but didn't want to get into an argument. Not with half the squad room listening in. Plus, he couldn't afford to give his ex any more ammunition about him shirking his paternal responsibilities. Not if he wanted to remain a part of Jen's life. Finally, Lynn said, "After all, you *are* her father. Take some responsibility, for Christ sake."

Taking the Lord's name in vain, he thought to himself, silently chuckling by thinking that her straight-laced, Bible-thumping, congressman father would castigate her for that transgression. If he were listening. But he was probably greasing up a pork barrel somewhere. His father-in-law had never approved of him. But so what? Congressman Robert E. Vernon was an idiot. He was, after all, the prime mover behind getting former Vice President William Jefferson Bernard, aka "Big Willie," his party's nomination for president.

"Are you listening to me?" Lynn asked.

"That's all I've been doing, isn't it?"

"You'll get this insurance problem straightened out then?"

82

"I will. Soon. This is my weekend coming up, right?"

"Yes, but . . ."

Okay, here it comes, McClain thought. The real reason she'd called to bitch him out. She wanted something. He waited.

"I need you to reason with her about something." Her voice sounded sweet as peach pie now.

He said nothing. It was like a boxing match. Sometimes you were better off as a counter puncher.

She cleared her throat. "Rex and I are planning a trip."

"Where to?"

"That's none of your, that's not important. Make her understand I need some time to myself."

"How long are you going to be gone?"

"A week."

"The whole week?"

"Of course, the whole week." The sarcastic lilt was back. "She doesn't want to stay here with my parents at the house. She's insisting she wants to stay with you. She's actually threatened to run away, which is why I've got her scheduled for another session with Dr. Moorefield."

Marvelous, McClain thought.

Lynn's voice hardened slightly. "It would help if you'd speak to her about her behavior. She's been talking back to Juliana a lot lately. Dr. Moorefield says it might be due to a chemical imbalance. She might have to go on bipolar medication."

Juliana was the Vernons' live-in nanny. She'd been with the family forever and had raised Lynn as well. That's what you get when you marry into old Virginia money, he thought. Nannies raising your kids and a forced enema in divorce court. But if Jen was rebelling against the Old South gentility, she must have more of his Chicago Irish blood in him than he thought.

"Bipolar medication," McClain said. "No way."

"What?"

He repeated his comment.

"Whatever," she said. "We can discuss that later. In the meantime, can you spare a few moments to talk to her this weekend?"

At least the sarcasm was gone for the moment. But she still needed something, didn't she?

"All right," he said. He wondered where Lynn and good old Rex were going. Probably someplace where they could both get tanked at ten in the morning. McClain had met the guy and didn't like him much. The less time Rexie spent around Jen, the better. "I really have to go now."

"You'll look into getting that insurance problem corrected?"

"Yes."

He felt a wave of relief wash over him when she terminated the call and strode over to Kelly who was engaged in telling a joke to the other detectives.

Maybe it'll do me good to get out of here, McClain thought. After dealing with her, going after a bad guy will be a welcome relief.

Felicia had managed to secure herself a seat in the dark-colored van while Johnson and Beaumont were relegated to one of the rented tail cars. Maybe the surveillance team was afraid they'd have a relapse and upchuck again. She smiled at the memory of the big helicopter. This assignment wasn't half bad. The scenery rushing by had a strange look to it. Like rural Minnesota or Wisconsin. She'd never been to Maine before. It was so pretty. Then the reality of the situation bounced back and hit her: They were stalking some terrorists who were smuggling a WMD into this beautiful place. Into her country. They had to be stopped. Were they up to it?

She eyed Baker, the guy who was driving. He looked young. Maybe in his early twenties. Younger than she was, at any rate, yet he seemed like a pro. The military had a way of doing that—drawing the best out of people. Certain people. The military could break you just as easily, she'd noticed. But so could life.

"Where's the rest of your unit now?" she asked.

Baker pointed to a small GPS screen on top of the dashboard. "Looks like about twenty clicks ahead of us, ma'am. That's kilometers, not miles." His voice had a southern twang to it.

She smiled again. These young guys were certainly polite. Too polite. Making her feel like a lady of a certain age. She decided to try to break the ice a bit.

"So how long have you been in the service, sergeant? It is sergeant, isn't it?"

"Yes, ma'am. I'm an E-six, though. That's a staff-sergeant, noncommissioned officer's rank."

"I know. My brother's in the service."

"Oh yeah? What branch?"

"Navy."

Baker grinned and shrugged. "Same side, different team. He enlisted or officer?"

"He's a lieutenant. He's aboard the U.S.S. *Enterprise.*"

"That's a carrier, right? Never been on one myself, but Captain Lee has. Him and Sergeant West worked with Force Recon and the SEALs a lot in their black ops."

Black ops, thought Felicia. "Captain Lee said you'd brief me on the operation. I kind of need to be brought up to speed from the beginning."

Baker took a deep breath, like he felt uneasy telling her. "We received intel that a shipment possibly containing a WMD, a quantity of Sarin gas, was circulating in Damascus. By way of Yemen originally."

Felicia knew he was intentionally trying to be vague.

"So," Baker continued, "we received further intel that Al Queda was in communication with a terrorist cell operating here in the U.S. and that they were making arrangements to ship the WMD here, via Canada."

"Any idea where this WMD originated from?"

He grinned. "Well, actually, we heard it might have come from the Iranians."

"I thought they'd be too busy trying to collect enough uranium to make a nuke."

Baker grinned again. He was obviously feeling more comfortable discussing this now. "Shucks, they got a lot of shit they're cooking up over there. Anyway, MI—that's Military Intelligence—has been working with the boys from Langley on this. They found out that an enemy combatant who'd been released from Gitmo and repatriated had been coordinating the operation."

Mohammed Amir Fassel, Felicia thought. Number three-eighty-three.

"Turns out you guys had been monitoring him as well, and that's about it," Baker said. "Our mission is to set up at the rendezvous point tonight and intercept the shipment as they cross the border."

She suddenly knew why they needed the Bureau along for the ride. Neither the military nor the CIA was authorized to carry out this type of operation inside the U.S. Not without specific executive authorization. "We're the sanctioning agency," Joiner had told them. "Do nothing except to accompany the squad up to Maine and monitor the exchange." It was time to catch up on the big picture.

"And that's where exactly?"

"It's an old, abandoned border crossing called Willis Point. The A-team, led by Captain Lee, is setting up there now, reconnoitering."

Felicia considered this. "Are they certain the shipment's coming through tonight? I mean, we were tracking the guy from

Gitmo, too, but our team lost him."

"Colonel Viceroy's sure, ma'am," Baker said. "And if the Colonel's sure about something, you can take it to the bank."

I hope so, Felicia thought. God, I hope so.

Ted Lane leaned back in his car seat, sipped his coffee, and glanced at his watch. It was quarter after three. He had a few more minutes to wait in the parking garage across from Capitol Hill. His view through his windshield was speckled with dead bugs and lines of street grime. Time to hit the car wash. But the view held nothing interesting anyway: row after row of parked cars, cement pillars, and illumination provided by overhead vapor lights. Almost all the stalls were full, on this floor. It was better that way. His was a tree in the forest, to strike a metaphor. Did journalists even use metaphors now? The good ones did, he thought, glancing at his watch again, then looking around.

Nobody.

But with all the surveillance cameras nowadays, you had to assume that everything was being recorded somewhere. Even five levels up.

He swallowed some more coffee and his stomach quivered. He wondered if Woodward and Bernstein had felt this much anxiety when they were going to meet Deep Throat. That had been Woodward alone, though, hadn't it? Bernstein was more on the periphery, like Allison. That made him grin. As if Allison had the journalistic savvy to even fathom how big this story was. Her thinking was limited, but she was ideal for his purposes. Use her looks and poise as the vehicle to get to the network, and from there the sky was the limit.

He looked at his watch again. Closing in on three-nineteen. After this was over he'd stop on the way back and order a slice of hot apple pie with ice cream on top. He might as well give himself an early treat. His cell phone rang. The tones jarred him.

"Where are you?" Allison asked.

"Meeting a source. I told you—"

"Yes, yes, I know." Her voice sounded drawn. "But I've been running into some problems here. Bernard's office called, wants to preview and approve my questions for the pre-debate interview."

Lane snorted. Bernard—what a controlling, duplicitous bastard. "I hope you told them to go pound sand."

"How could I do that? He offered me an exclusive." Her tones were now clipped. "How far am I going to get with him next time if I don't agree?"

Lane exhaled slowly, assessing what would be the best way to handle her. All he wanted was for everything to stay on an even keel until he'd nailed down enough information on Bernard to hang him out to dry. And he needed Allison for that.

"Okay," he said. "Call them back and say we'll be glad to accommodate them." He always referred to the former vice president in the plural because the man was so shallow he needed an army to prop him up, cover for him, and feed him his lines. All Bernard had going for him was his charisma. He looked so damn presidential, and could read a speech off the teleprompter with the best of them. Yet there was a sinister side to the man. Lane knew Bernard had been the orchestrator of the use of torture in Guantanamo. He waited for Allison to respond, but heard nothing. Had they lost the connection? "You hear me?"

More silence. Then, "Ted, I don't want this interview to come off looking like a watered-down sound bite."

"Look, don't worry about it." If she could keep her cool long enough, he'd be handing her the biggest story of the year. Perhaps of the decade. "Keep stringing them along. Keep them happy. I'm working on something. Something big."

Lane's cell phone vibrated. A text.

Shit, it had to be the signal. He had to get rid of Allison fast.

"Something big." Her voice had gone from anxious to sarcastic. "And when are you going to share it with me?"

Share it. He might as well try discussing the theory of relativity with a fifth grader. "Soon. Look, I gotta go."

He heard her quick sigh. "Are you coming back to the office?"

"After my meeting. We'll talk about it then."

He terminated the call and glanced at the phone.

New Message.

He hit the options button and went to his inbox.

i'm here pulling in now.

ok, he texted back. *on my way.*

Lane glanced around again. No one. Not that anyone would recognize him. Few people knew him outside of the news business, and he used his mask of anonymity to his full advantage. The invisible man, capable of fading into the background and listening to the most intimate of secrets. He heard an approaching vehicle. His gaze shot to the rearview mirror. The tan Honda passed by and pulled into an open stall two cars down from him. He heard a car door open and slam, then the skitter of footfalls. If he'd lived in another era, he'd have made a good spy.

He waited what he felt was the appropriate amount of time, then got out of his car and walked toward the stairwell. He detected the delicious trail of her perfume. Chloe. Allison wore that brand, too. Pleasant-smelling, like a spray of lilacs, leading him through the catacombs toward his reward.

CHAPTER 8

McClain slouched in the passenger seat and glanced at the imposing brick building down the block. The Jefferson Park Garden Homes, also known as JPGH, was not so affectionately called the briar-patch by MPDC. The briar-patch, a euphemism for "pure ghetto," was a dangerous place, especially for cops, and he knew he should get his mind on the game instead of mulling over Lynn's latest harangue. She had never understood the nature of the job. Or him, for that matter. He wondered how they'd ever fallen in love. It seemed a lifetime ago. If not for Jen, he wouldn't think of his ex at all. His thoughts turned to Dr. Moorefield and good old Rex. "Sexy Rexie," he overheard Lynn saying once. He allowed his mind to slip into a quick fantasy of persuading Rex to step into the ring with him and tattooing the guy's face with a flurry of blows before crowning him with an overhand right. McClain wondered where the hell Rex and Lynn were going that they couldn't take Jen.

He heard Kelly emit a low whistle and looked across the seat. His partner held his radio in one hand, his cell phone in the other.

"No need to slouch and hide your white face, laddie," Kelly said. "They already know we're the police. Who else drives a ride like this." He patted the steering wheel with his radio hand.

They were in one of the standard black Ford Crown Vics, equipped with the side spotlight. They might as well have had a sign on the roof, too.

"I'm wishing I was someplace else."

Kelly smiled. "You will be soon enough." He held the radio to his mouth. "You guys in position yet?"

"Stand by."

The reply was static-laden. Typical for a sideband channel in this area. McClain hoped it wasn't a sign of things to come.

"What apartment is he in again?"

"Three C. His mama's place." Kelly grinned and shook his head. "I love public housing. Easy to find all about somebody."

"You sure Rewaldo is gonna be there?"

"As sure as I can be," Kelly said. "These boys always go home to Mama. Plus, it's getting close to four. Our boy should be waking up pretty soon."

McClain flipped the visor down and looked at the color mug shot photo of Rewaldo Snopes. Mohawk hairstyle, dark-skinned, thick neck, cold-blooded brown eyes. Photo looked like the portrait of a young killer. Big guy, too. Six-three, two-twenty, probably with a jail-house body. McClain flipped the visor back up. "He still got the Mohawk?"

"Far as I know." Kelly smirked. "He thinks he's an Indian."

"I'd hate to go breaking down Mama's door and get shot only to find out he ain't home."

"Me too, which is why I'm wearing this." Kelly patted the front of his Kevlar vest. "And this." He used two fingers to pull open the front of his sport coat to show McClain the shiny wooden grips that adorned the pistol grip of his chrome-plated, six-inch Colt Python. "I got the snake with me."

"You're going to get in trouble carrying that thing," McClain said. "Not departmentally sanctioned. Plus, it's only a six-shooter."

"It's my back-up." Kelly pulled out the opposite lapel and showed McClain two dangling leather cases on the other side of the shoulder holster. "And I got two fully loaded speed-loaders and an extra handcuff key in these."

"The key's the only thing authorized."

Kelly grinned and patted his side. "Shit, don't worry. I got my MPDC-issued Glock, too. But that ain't all."

McClain raised his eyebrows.

"I got a foolproof plan." He set the radio on the dash and flipped open his cell, punched in a number, then said, "Laureen? Kelly. You ready to do that little job for me, baby?" He paused and then added, "Okay, do it now. I'll stay on the cell."

McClain shot a sideways glance at his partner.

Kelly placed his palm over the cell speaker and said, "I'm having one of my ladies call his house, asking for him. She let me know if he's there."

One of his ladies. That probably meant a hooker or an informant who needed a favor. McClain suddenly felt more uncomfortable. The pit of his stomach felt tight. "She know him?"

Kelly shook his head. "She'll ask to speak to Rewaldo. His mama is probably gonna answer anyway."

"And if Mama lies?"

Kelly snorted. "Think she's gonna miss a chance to get him out of her hair by having him go to some ho's crib?" He winked at McClain. "And don't you never go messing with a black woman's hair."

"I've heard that," McClain said. "What if Mama has caller ID?"

"Laureen's using a near-antiquated method of communication. Your friendly neighborhood pay phone."

McClain grinned. "A pay phone? They still have those?" He sat up, anticipating the pending action as Kelly shifted the car into drive.

"They're almost extinct. Hey, girl, what's the story?" He

listened, glanced at McClain, and pulled out of the parking spot. He flipped the cell phone shut and stuck it into his jacket pocket. "It's a go," he said into the radio. "We're moving on the front now."

"Negative," the radio voice crackled. "We're not in position yet."

"What?" Kelly said, the irritation obvious in his voice.

"We had to move. We got made."

"Shit," McClain said. "What the fuck have they been doing?"

"We gotta move now," Kelly yelled into the radio. "Back us up. We going in. Meet me in front and send the second unit around to the back door." He accelerated the half block then jammed on the brakes, stopping the car in front of the building. "Go cover the back, bro. I'll tag up with one of the tac guys and rattle the front door."

McClain ran down the decrepit sidewalk, a cracked ribbon of cement with bare patches of dirt on both sides that led through a narrow gangway between two buildings. The temperature cooled noticeably when he got into the shaded area where the fading sunshine was blocked out. He stopped running as he came to the end of the walkway. Voices, laughter, the sweet scent of weed. McClain stopped and glanced around the corner. A group of four black teenagers sat on the rear steps and passed a blunt around. One of them looked up in surprise and grinned.

"Who we got here?" he said. "A honky in the woodpile."

The others looked around.

Before anyone else could say anything, McClain reached inside his windbreaker and withdrew his Glock. "Police. Get outta here."

"Hey, man, fuck that," one of the teens said. "We live here."

"Beat it, if you don't want to get busted or shot." He brought his radio to his mouth and said, "Send me some units to the back. I got some suspects back here."

He heard a faint click of the mike, Kelly acknowledging his transmission. They both knew there were no additional units, but McClain hoped the group of young assholes wouldn't know that. They bought into the ruse, quickly tossing the joint away as they ambled out toward the alley.

The porch went up for four stories, with mid-sized enclosures at each landing and a winding staircase. McClain scanned the yard, which was surrounded on three sides with a tall but decrepit wooden fence. The quartet of punks opened the rear gate and left, one of them pausing to stare at McClain and spit.

McClain heard a rapid thumping coming down the back stairs that sounded like a herd of scared antelope. It had to be Rewaldo. Kelly's girlfriend calling and hanging up, coupled with the tac unit squad car getting made, must have sent the word through the building. McClain held his gun close to his chest and stepped back around the corner. The porch itself offered little cover, but if he could catch Rewaldo coming down and swing out at the right time, he could grab him. The heavy footsteps continued. McClain grabbed one of the more solid-looking slats from the wooden fence. It was stuck firmly in place, though, and he needed to holster his weapon and use both hands to pull it loose. It remained firmly in place and McClain got several slivers in his palms for his efforts.

More footsteps. Getting closer. He twisted and pushed the slat with more vigor. The footsteps hesitated, as if rounding the last corner before the bottom.

The slat came loose and McClain decided he'd keep his weapon holstered and his hands free. If he could maintain the element of surprise, he'd have Rewaldo cuffed in a heartbeat.

He waited, listened as the sounds grew louder, and then spied a figure darting from the stairway toward the opening that led to the back porch steps. McClain shoved the long slat forward, placing it in between the running man's feet. The guy tripped and spilled forward onto the cement.

McClain was on him, yelling, "Police! Don't move. You're under arrest." And twisting the dude's arm back in a hammer lock. He held the guy's wrist, twisting upward to exert more pressure, and held it with his right hand, reaching back for his cuffs with his left.

"Man, I didn't do nothing," the guy screamed.

"Shut up, Rewaldo," McClain said. But something was already registering that looked wrong. This guy was slender— probably only a buck and a half at best. And his hair was clipped short. No Mohawk.

"I ain't him," the guy yelled. "I'm Jay-Jay."

McClain pulled the guy's head back to look at his face.

Shit! It wasn't Rewaldo. He held the guy in place and took out his radio instead of his cuffs. As he keyed the mic to call Kelly, another transmission blocked his with a sharp squelching sound. McClain took his finger off the button and waited. Two units transmitting at once, walking on each other.

"Kev, he's headed your way," Kelly's voice said.

McClain held the radio to his mouth. "That's a negative. This guy's not him."

"Negative." Kelly's voice had the urgency of authenticity. "I repeat, he's headed your way. Down the back."

McClain glanced up at the stairway and saw a quick shadow vaulting over the second-floor balcony railing.

A shadow with a Mohawk.

McClain extricated himself from the tangled figure on the ground. Jay-Jay was probably wanted for something. Around here everybody was conditioned to run from the police. The shadow hit the ground next to the building and sprang upward, running toward the back gate. McClain ran on an intercept path.

The man's head swiveled in McClain's direction, the big

Mohawk bobbling in the wind, then he cut left and jumped high, grabbing the top of the fence and pulling himself up and over with the ease of a thoroughbred jumping a steeplechase barrier.

The guy had probably been scaling fences since he was two, McClain thought. He grabbed the top of the fence, but his weight suddenly shifted and he felt the strain shoot through his shoulders. His feet skidded over the surface of the fence, seeking purchase. Regaining his strength, he pulled upward with his arms, like a chin-up, kicking his feet at the same time, and got his gut over the top of the fence. He saw Rewaldo already scrambling over the fence on the far side of the next yard.

McClain powered himself over and landed on his feet, feeling the shooting pain come up through his feet as he hit the uneven ground. He ran across the yard and scaled the fence Rewaldo had gone over. The asshole turned and grinned at him.

McClain pressed the key on his radio as he ran. "Rewaldo's running east through the backyards," he yelled into the mic, hoping someone heard him. He jammed the radio into his pocket and hit the second fence running. This time he was able to get up and over with almost as much precision as the guy he was chasing.

But Rewaldo was already scaling the next yard's fence, another of those big, solid wooden fences. It shook visibly.

Shit. I'll never catch him now! McClain reached for his radio.

It wasn't there.

Had he dropped it going over the last fence? He felt like he'd been hit with a gut punch. His legs slowed and he knew it was over. Then he heard a snarling, barking, snapping, screaming sound coming from the next yard ahead. The scream was human.

Rewaldo.

He must have come down on the wrong side of the neighborhood dog.

McClain felt a surge of renewed energy and hit the fence hard as his hands shot toward the top. Suddenly, the section fence collapsed forward, McClain holding on and riding it down. He saw Rewaldo punching at a pit bull tied to a long chain, the dog's jaws locked on Rewaldo's pant leg. As McClain got to his feet, Rewaldo pulled loose from the dog, ran toward McClain, and assumed a boxer's stance.

McClain raised his hands and moved forward.

Rewaldo threw a looping roundhouse right. A Superman punch. McClain blocked it with his left and shot a straight punch into Rewaldo's nose. The bigger man recoiled, then swarmed forward, his arms flailing like a windmill, getting in too close for McClain to use any long punches, so he did a shoeshine set of body uppercuts. Rewaldo continued to push forward. McClain felt the man's smelly, ragged breath. The big arms circled McClain and they both went down in a heap, each struggling to be on top.

McClain's right hand instinctively sought the grip on his weapon to make sure it was still in its holster. His back hit hard on the framework of the fence. He was cognizant of the loud barking and snarling, the dog pulling at the end of its chain, wanting to join in. Rewaldo was on top, his head butting into McClain's forehead and left cheekbone like a dribbling basketball. Rolling away from the dog, they rained blows on each other. Rewaldo outweighed McClain by a good forty pounds and was strong as hell. McClain prayed the others would find him quickly.

They had to be looking, right?

More blows stung his side. McClain kicked and managed to partially knee Rewaldo's groin. The big man grunted. McClain twisted his body back and then pulled loose from Rewaldo's grip. He crouched and sent a left-right pair of hooks to Rewaldo's head. Rewaldo looked stunned and McClain repeated the punches. His breathing sounded ragged, like he'd run the hundred-yard dash.

Rewaldo shot a punch at McClain's balls and grabbed him around the knees, twisting him downward again.

They rolled over the fence. McClain reached again for his weapon. He felt Rewaldo's hands groping for it, too.

McClain was conscious of his breathing again. Rapid breaths, in and out.

Off to their left, the dog made a diving jump at them, but was pulled back with a jerk by the confining chain and collar.

Rolling again, McClain felt himself coming out on top. He pulled his right hand back, holding Rewaldo off with his left, and smashed three punches downward, as hard as he could. Extricating himself and again managing to get into a semi-crouch, he saw Rewaldo struggling to his knees. *Marquis of Queensbury be damned,* McClain thought, and smashed a left hook to Rewaldo's temple.

The big man sagged but straightened up.

McClain began pummeling Rewaldo with more punches to the head and body, anywhere he saw an opening.

He heard the barking again. Then something else. A different sound. Voices.

"There they are." Kelly's voice sounded like a trumpet from heaven.

With renewed energy, McClain sent two more punches into Rewaldo's gut and face, watching him crumble downward. McClain followed him down, collapsing to his knees, struggling to crawl forward on top of the fallen man and reaching for his handcuffs.

He felt someone's hands on him and he pulled back, ready to punch.

"Easy, brother. We're here."

Kelly.

His partner held the big chrome Python in his right hand. He pressed the barrel onto the side of the prone Rewaldo's temple. "You move, fucker, and you're dead." He leaned closer. "And you know I'll cap your black ass, too, don't you?"

McClain watched as Rewaldo's left eye twittered and then closed. It was over. A stream of blood ran down from a gash on the asshole's eyebrow. McClain suddenly wondered if his own face had been cut. Just what he needed, more stitches.

Other coppers arrived, helping McClain up and twisting Rewaldo's arms behind him, ratcheting on the handcuffs. McClain felt relief surge through him, like the end of a ten-round fight. He wiped at his mouth and looked over at the snarling pit bull, saw the foam collecting at the sides of the dog's jaws.

"Glad that chain held," he managed to say.

"Shit, that dog deserves a medal," Kelly said. "Or at least a bone. Him barking was how we found you. Why didn't you call for help?"

McClain patted his side, checking again for his weapon. Still in the holster.

"I lost my radio when I was jumping fences."

"We'll find it," one of the tac guys said. Two uniformed officers were on the scene now, lifting Rewaldo up and pulling him through the gap in the fence.

"Let me check you out," Kelly said, his fingers gently tilting McClain's head back. He studied McClain's face. "Don't see nothing but a few scratches and some red marks."

"Tell that to the rest of me." The adrenaline was wearing off and he felt a bunch of aches in various places.

"No problem. The other guy looks a lot worse."

★ ★ ★ ★ ★

Felicia looked at the array of screens in front of her. They were covering both walls of the van. No windows, but with all this technology you didn't need them. Only one of the monitors was lit up at the moment. She knew it was dark outside, but on the monitor screen things looked as bright as day, in a green-image sort of way. The decoy van sat in perfect emerald tranquility— broken once again by her radio.

"Knight, any updates?" asked Beaumont.

Felicia adjusted the headphone set that allowed her to scan the various radio frequencies. "Negative." She wanted to keep it brief.

"Repeat that. I didn't copy."

"Nothing at this time," she said in clipped tones.

"Don't forget to give us updates," Johnson chimed in. "Remember, we're the senior agents here."

"Ten-four," she said, swallowing her exasperation. She wondered which of the two was the most irritating. Senior pukers, too. If they hadn't lost their respective cookies back in the Chinook, they would have had the chance to be with the advance team, not relegated to the rear guard. She glanced at her watch. Nine-thirty. Hopefully, they wouldn't have to wait much longer.

Baker, the young soldier next to her, licked his lips and his mouth pulled into a taut line. He pulled one of the earphones away from his head and said, "Ah, ma'am, I got to ask you something." His voice had a Southern twang to it.

"Yes?"

"You guys got a scrambler on those radios?" The twin creases between his eyebrows seemed to punctuate his anxiety.

Now it was Felicia's turn to be anxious. She wasn't sure. She assumed so, but didn't want to say they did only to find out later she was wrong. "I don't know."

Baker clucked. "Probably be better to maintain radio silence then. We have to assume that the towelheads have a scanning system for all the regular frequencies, even if the chances are they don't. It's part of being prepared for as many eventualities as you can."

Felicia felt like an amateur along for the ride. So far the operational precision of these army guys was putting the Bureau to shame. They were so organized, so well trained, so disciplined. The kind of professionals she wanted to be. And she was stuck with Beaumont and Johnson—Bert and Ernie, all grown up and wearing three-piece suits. Or in their case, mismatched neckties and out-of-style sports jackets.

Baker seemed to sense her concern and showed her a lopsided grin. He looked so young, his blond hair cut close to his scalp. A spray of freckles dotted his pale cheeks.

"Like I said, it probably won't matter none," he said. "But it's gonna be a while yet. Our intel said the meet's set for twenty-two hundred. It's all about the waiting now."

Twenty-two hundred—ten o'clock. A good time. Late enough to assure darkness to conceal their movements, and early enough so as not to look too conspicuous driving on the roadways. That's what Captain Lee had told her. She glanced at her watch again. Seven-oh-nine. Yeah, it was going to be a while, and Baker was right—it was all about the waiting.

CHAPTER 9

"Jesus, Kev. What the hell happened to you?" one of the dicks said as McClain and Kelly walked into the detective squad room. McClain didn't answer. His whole body hurt and he knew he stank of sweat, mud, and who knew what else. Still, he felt good for having gotten Rewaldo. *Things could be worse. I could have landed in a pile of that pit bull's shit.*

"Gentlemen," Kelly said, gesturing toward McClain. "May I present to you the middleweight champion of the D.C. ghetto."

"Middleweight?" McClain said over his shoulder. "Light heavy, please."

"Whatever. You the bomb, my man."

"Yeah, well, he's somebody else's bomb, too," one of the other dicks said. "The El-Tee's waiting in his office for you, McClain. And I'd hustle if I were you, pal. He's usually at home with the Mrs. El-Tee by now."

The Lieutenant? McClain glanced at his watch. Seven-ten. What the hell was Beasley still doing here? "What's he want?"

"To talk to the champ, I guess." The dick laughed. "At least till he gets a whiff of you."

McClain wished he'd stopped in the washroom to clean up. But he'd been so anxious to fill out his time sheet and get out of there, he hadn't taken the time. He looked at Kelly, who lifted his eyebrows and made an "I got no idea, either" shrug.

"Hey, maybe he wants to compliment you on a job well done," Kelly said.

"Look at me. I'm a fucking mess. I stink."

"That's right. You do." Kelly grinned. "But it's all man-sweat."

"Next time you can go chasing the guy."

Kelly grinned as they walked. "I been thinking about that. What we need is one of them Versitrack 1500 robots. Saw one of them on the History Channel the other night. Save us walking up a lot of stairs. Send that robot thing up there and watch it all on your MDB."

Through Beasley's pebbled glass, McClain could see him talking on the phone. Beasley was a big, beefy man and the shadow of his form hanging up the phone and rising from behind the desk seemed to fill the door. He pulled it open and regarded them with a querulous look.

"Where you guys been?" He waved a hand in front of his face. "Jesus, McClain, you stink."

"Out picking up a robbery suspect, Lieu," Kelly said. "You know that robbery and shooting we had on—"

"Robbery suspect," Beasley said. His face scrunched up, the lines looking like a fish net pulled taut. "What the *fuck*. You're supposed to be working a homicide, McClain."

McClain took a deep breath. This was turning into one hell of a messed-up day. "Yes, sir, I've been working on it. Reached a sort of plateau and was waiting for some more info to come in."

The lines deepened in the Lieutenant's face. "More info to come in." The sarcastic lilt told McClain that something must have come in all right. And it wasn't good. He swallowed.

Beasley motioned them in. "Jesus, I'm gonna have to get this office defumigated. Shut the damn door."

Kelly eased the door shut behind him.

Beasley sorted through some papers on his desk and said, "Don't even think about sitting down." He grabbed a piece of paper and held it out toward McClain. "The ID on your homicide vic came in. Trouble is, it set off some bells and whistles on the THL"

"The Terrorist Hit List?" Now, the Guantanamo surgery and all the stalling red tape made sense. The guy had been a prisoner there. "I'll get right on this, Lieu."

"Huh-un." Beasley shook his head. "You go home and get cleaned up, and bright and early tomorrow touch bases with the feds. They want to talk to us on this. And then report back to me. I'll have to decide how we're going to proceed."

McClain took the paper from Beasley's hand. Lately his life seemed to consist of stumbling from one shit storm to another. But at least he had his victim identified: Mohammed Amir Fassel.

As soon as Ted Lane got back to ZCCN, Allison spied him and grabbed his arm.

"Let's go outside," she said, giving him a squeeze. "I need a smoke."

Actually, neither of them smoked cigarettes. They used the excuse to vacate the building so they could talk in what they felt was semi-privacy. Lane smiled and walked with her. Outside, the sounds of nighttime traffic filtered through the cool darkness. Lane glanced around at the lights of the cityscape, purposely making her wait for the update.

"Well," she said. "What happened?"

"Big Willie's worried," he said.

She rolled her eyes. "No shit, Sherlock. I could have told you that. You should have seen the outtakes of our interview. He broke into a sweat when I mentioned Thomas or Ross. And now Ross is supposedly on his way back, right?"

"Due in later tonight."

"Do you think it would be worth sending a crew to the airport to tape him when he touches down?"

"Thomas isn't going to want to let someone else share the spotlight, especially his lackey. Besides, Ross is probably flying in to the military section. He's coming back from Guantanamo."

"Yeah, you're right. So what else did our source say?"

He considered how much to tell her. Could she be trusted or would she inadvertently spill the beans and tip their hand? Plus, she'd said "our source" like she was really a part of this. For the moment he was content to let that lie. He shot her a crooked smile. "Big Willie is concerned over something big on the horizon. But our source doesn't know what."

"Something big?" Her forehead furrowed. "He has his party's nomination and is running for president. I'd say that's pretty big, wouldn't you?"

Lane canted his head. *She still didn't get the big picture. Couldn't see the forest for the trees.* "Yeah, that's big all right, but remember, he doesn't want to just run. He wants to win. And there's something in the wind that might keep him from doing that."

"Like the attorney general threatening to indict him for ordering torture? Like I didn't already know that?"

He couldn't believe she was trying to get more info out of him. Amusing that she persisted in deluding herself, believing she was more a partner than a vehicle for him. Still, a pretty nice vehicle. Lane felt some stirring in his groin. "I think there's something more in the works. An ace Big Willie's tucked up his sleeve. Something to offset the torture issue."

"And that's what we have to concentrate on finding out, right?"

Maybe there was hope for her, after all. But he'd rather keep her as a vehicle than a full-fledged partner. That way he could ride her to the top. He looked at her breasts pressing against her blouse, her nipples showing through her bra. "Speaking of riding."

"Riding? What are you talking about?"

Lane loved it when she looked inquisitive. That little double crease forming between her eyebrows. "Just thinking out loud. Come on. Let's get back and close up shop for tonight."

"But the story—"

"Will wait. Besides, we can't move till Paul Ross gets back." He was thinking of getting her into the bedroom. It had been a long-ass day and he deserved some recreation. And the story, the really big one, would unfold at its own pace.

Viceroy had always enjoyed the fine architecture and sense of history that a walk through the Hill provided. Unfortunately, his brother-in-law's nearby campaign headquarters provided none of that. The place was staffed by at least fifty workers, busily making phone calls and typing on their computers, even at this early evening hour. Big Willie's personal assistant, Regina Griggas, noticed Viceroy and tapped Roger Ram Jet, who'd been busy in a conversation. Ram Jet turned, waved to Viceroy, and motioned for him to come over by the back room, which he did. He extended his hand.

"How's my favorite soon-to-be-general?"

Viceroy shook his hand but didn't respond to the bait. Instead, he simply said, "Will sent word he needed to talk to me."

"Of course, of course." Ram Jet lightly slapped Viceroy's back and ushered him forward toward an office door. "He's right in here."

William Bernard, who was on the phone, looked up when Viceroy entered and showed him a weak-looking smile. Or was it a grim one? He ended the phone conversation and stood, holding out his hand for Viceroy to shake.

"Thanks for dropping by, Clay," Big Willie said "Roger, give us a few minutes, will you?"

Ram Jet's eyes shifted between the two men. Then he left, closing the door behind him.

When Big Willie spoke, his voice was a harsh whisper. "I've heard some scuttlebutt that prick Ross is bringing back some irrefutable evidence linking me to this god-damn torture issue." He wiped his hand over his face. "The question is, what do we do now?"

Viceroy smiled. "It's a moot question."

"Moot? I'm telling you he's on his way back now. He's due to land with his findings at ten o'clock, D.C. time."

Viceroy wondered again if the man had the *cojones* to make it through this damn campaign. Still, when he was on his game there was nobody better at performing before an audience, so long as some of the peripheral distractions were cleaned up.

"Relax, Will. I told you I have it covered."

"Covered?" Big Willie's jaw tightened, making his quizzical expression look like a great photo op for a *Time* magazine cover: *William Bernard Questions His Advisers.* The man was photogenic, Viceroy thought. The perfect foil.

"Yes, covered. He's taking a military flight out of Gitmo, and it's been delayed due to a storm approaching. He won't be touching down until well after midnight."

"You're sure about that?"

"Got the word a little while ago." Viceroy smiled. "In fact, I orchestrated it."

"What?"

"I told God to summon one up." Viceroy watched for his reaction, then laughed. "Haven't I told you, I'm the ultimate multi-tasker."

Big Willie licked his lips then smiled too. "Well, put in a good word for me next time you talk to Him." The chiseled features took on another photogenic pose. It would have made a great campaign poster.

Good, he was starting to relax a bit. But Viceroy figured his brother-in-law would still need a little more reassurance. And Big Willie didn't disappoint.

"And you've got the Ross thing taken care of?"

"I've already got B team on it. Right now I'm more concerned with this other matter."

"The other matter. You mean the—"

Viceroy's special cell phone rang, keeping the idiot from mentioning the Sarin by name, and it was a good thing. At that moment the door opened and Regina walked in. She put her hand to her pretty lips and mumbled some sort of inadequate apology about sorry to have interrupted. Big Willie dismissed the intrusion with a grin and a wave. He slipped his glasses on as she handed him some papers to look at.

It was one of the man's major faults: his propensity to open his mouth and mention sensitive things at inopportune times. That was how this whole damn torture thing got leaked in the first place. Viceroy glanced at the LCD screen and pressed the button to answer the call as he appreciated the rounded curve of the secretary's ass. Big Willie was checking it out, too, indicating his second major fault: his inability to keep his pecker in his pants.

He's probably fucking her, Viceroy thought. He told the caller to stand by and waited until Bernard had finished signing the papers and the girl had once again left the room. It was a mistake meeting him here. Too many prying ears. He told the caller to proceed.

"Sir," the voice on the phone said. "There was a THL activation on a subject earlier today."

"What was it?"

"MPDC Police, sir. A hit on an identification request on Mohammed Amir Fassel."

Viceroy was stunned. He hadn't anticipated that they'd be

able to ID Fassel so quickly. Not with the precautions they'd taken. If news got out of his demise prior to the plan being fully executed, it could be disastrous. "Do we know who put in the request?"

"Detective Kevin McClain."

McClain . . . The name struck a distant chord with Viceroy, but he couldn't recall why. "See what you can find out about him. Were protective measures taken regarding the inquiry?"

"Yes, sir, although identification was confirmed."

I'll have to contact Joiner on this, Viceroy thought. He glanced over and saw Big Willie staring at him intently. To reassure his brother-in-law he smiled as benignly as he could, as if he'd been conversing with an old friend about the weather. He issued a few more precautionary instructions designed to slow the whole identification and response process down and terminated the call. As soon as he did, Big Willie asked him what was up.

"Nothing," he said. "Only a minor inconvenience. A small change in plans."

"Change?" Big Willie's face took on an ashen look. "It's not anything to do with Ross and this torture thing, is it?"

Viceroy repeated his casual smile, exuding confidence that everything was totally under control. And it was. After all, a good commander planned for every contingency and was used to working in a changing environment. It was also the part of the game that he loved the best. When things didn't go totally as planned and he had to improvise.

"I told you I've got that covered."

Big Willie's face still looked ashen.

"Everything's fine, Will," Viceroy said. "Not to worry."

"Well, what was it?"

Viceroy considered not telling him, but decided it was probably better to let him know now than to have him find out tomorrow and get one of his panic calls.

109

"The police identified Fassel."

"What? I thought you said we wouldn't have to worry about that? Didn't you take precautionary measures, for Christ's sake?"

Pulling out all his teeth and setting his body on fire after searing his fingerprints. I would think that constitutes precautionary measures, Viceroy thought. He suppressed his irritation with the other man and said, "Don't worry, I'm dealing with it."

"What does that mean?"

"It means what I said. Haven't I had a good handle on this whole thing from the beginning?" Viceroy stood so he towered over the other man. Spatial intimidation. "Rest assured, we've planned for every contingency."

Big Willie's face relaxed, his mouth gaping a bit like he was between rounds of a tough preliminary fight. That brought an idea to Viceroy. "Say, Lee's going to be fighting on an MMA card in Alexandria next week. Want to go?"

"I don't know. Let me think about it." Big Willie took a couple of quick breaths. "You're sure it's nothing to worry about?"

"Absolutely," Viceroy went around the desk and opened a drawer—the one where he knew Big Willie kept the bourbon. Taking out two shot glasses, he set them side-by-side on the desk. He smiled again as he poured.

This should calm him down, he thought. But his mind still focused on the name. Kevin McClain. Where the hell had he heard that one before?

A light rain had begun to fall. Felicia looked at her watch again. Ten-twenty-five. They were running late. They'd give it a while longer, but if the assholes didn't show they'd have to figure out their next move. She wondered if anyone had the target under surveillance on the Canadian side. Ten-twenty-six. Soon, she thought. And it couldn't come too soon either.

Her radio crackled. "Knight, you got any updates?"

She heard Baker's disapproving grunt. "Them guys sure ain't used to this stuff, are they?"

She shook her head, then said into her radio, "Negative. I repeat, maintain RS, please."

RS—radio silence. She was going to bring all this up to Joiner when she got back, but then had an afterthought: A fat lot of good that'll do. She saw Baker silently chuckling. "Those two guys . . ." She left the rest of the sentence unfinished and shook her head, smiling.

Baker smiled back. "I can tell you never served in the military, right?"

She shook her head.

"We never say 'repeat' over the radio," he said. "It's a code word for sending in another bombardment. We always use, 'say again'."

Felicia smiled, trying to make light of her embarrassment. "Well, I'd like to bombard my two partners."

That got a laugh from him.

"That's wonderful resolution," she said, trying to change the topic. "Even with the rain."

"Yes, ma'am. This here is an LRS Thermo Sight. Three-forty-by-two-fifty ATI—that stands for advanced thermal imager. It's got interface optics that'll see through fog, smoke, and dust, which came in real handy when we were doing ops in the sandbox, as well as being able to see in extreme darkness like we got here. Maintains boresight and reticular calibration up to five hundred yards." He moved over and started typing on the keyboard of another laptop. She saw a bright yellow billow moving over a map. "Looks like this storm's gonna get worse. Moving up the coast from the D.C. area now."

"Wow, that's pretty impressive," Felicia said, trying to sound genuine.

Baker's smile looked a bit self-conscious. "Sorry, ma'am, I guess I get kind of technical sometimes. That's my end of things. The gadgets. I'm sort of a back-up portion of the team, but they treat me like one of them."

"Well, you are, aren't you?"

"Thanks for saying that, but, Lord knows, I'd much rather be out there on the line with them taking care of business."

Baker's radio crackled. Lee's voice said, "Alpha-one to team. We got movement up by the bridge."

Felicia's pulse quickened. "Is that them?" She realized her voice had been a whisper and she felt silly. They were at least a hundred yards away from the target point.

"Could be," Baker said. "Captain Lee wouldn't break radio silence unless he thought it was something real important."

She wondered if he was making a dig at the Bureau and the constant inquiries the pesky Beaumont and Johnson had been making over the last few hours. Still, he had a point. They're making us look unprofessional, she thought. Maybe he's fishing for a compliment.

"Your team's very disciplined."

"That's why they're the best," Baker replied. "Especially Captain Lee and Sergeant West. They got so many black ops operations between them, you'd need a year to count 'em all." He checked his radar screen and said into the mic, "Looks like bogies moving in. Truck-sized vehicle and two stragglers about one hundred clicks behind."

"Confirmation," Lee's voice said. It sounded matter-of-fact. Devoid of any excitement or nervousness. "We'll commence broadcasting."

Baker tapped the screen above the one showing the decoy van. A green background featuring an old stretch of decrepit roadway overgrown with weeds and surrounded by a wooded area. The image of an approaching truck, moving slowly and without lights, appeared on the road. Lee and his team must have been set up on the side of the road in the trees.

"Knight?" Beaumont again.

"Tell them to maintain radio silence, please," Baker said. His voice had an edge to it now.

Felicia was angry, too. "Stand by till further. Maintain radio silence. It's going down." She hoped that would shut those two idiots up.

She watched as a second screen came to life with more crisp green images of another truck, this one a big U-haul type, approaching. The resolution was so good she could read the lettering on the side of it. It was some kind of Canadian rental company from Nova Scotia. She jotted it down.

"Is this being recorded?" she whispered to Baker.

"Yep. And no need to whisper. We got no hot mics in here." He pointed to his headset. "We can hear them, but only transmit if I press this button."

Felicia felt silly for getting so caught up in the moment. But most of her job was in an office going over reports. She longed for the times when she could get out on an actual assignment.

The image on the new screen tracked the approaching truck.

"That's got to be from Captain Lee's spotter," Baker said. "He's on the point with the react team."

Felicia knew the drill. Sergeant West was by himself in the decoy van. He was to meet with this group, pretending to be a member of the terrorist cell, and hopefully acquire the Sarin. She couldn't help but admire his bravery and silently prayed that everything would come out all right. The second screen showed West getting out of his van as the truck approached. The bigger vehicle slowed and three men got out. A third screen suddenly illuminated, but this one only showed some vague shapes accompanied by sharp movements.

"What's wrong with that one?" Felicia asked.

"Nothing. That's Sergeant West's hidden body camera. It was set up in sleep mode—only active when it detects movement. He's turning it on to full record now."

Felicia looked at that screen again and saw the blurry image sharpen into three figures approaching from what must have been West's point of view.

The first man in the group looked swarthy in the green light, his hair long and combed back from his face, which was covered by a thick beard. The other two men looked like carbon copies of the first: dark and beardy. They all wore what appeared to be black clothes.

"Where's his camera at?" she asked.

Baker grinned. "It's a super-micro. The lens is only point three-seventy-five millimeters. Designed to look like the button on the front of his shirt. We see what he sees, except about a foot lower." He chuckled. "Built-in microphone transmitter, too."

Felicia watched the little drama unfold.

"*As-salam Alaykum,* my brother," West said. The audio was as crisp and clear as a television program.

"*Wa-alaikum assalam,*" the other man said. Felicia detected a bit of trepidation in his voice. Oh-oh, she thought. Does he suspect something?

West moved forward and Felicia saw his arms stretching outward, as if to perform an embrace, but the other man stepped back, reached into his jacket, and pulled out a gun.

"Stop," the man said in heavily accented English. "I do not know you. Where is Amir?"

Baker had told her that Amir was the code name for Mohammed Fassel.

"He couldn't come," West said. "Too dangerous. They're following him. He sent me in his place."

"And who are you?"

"I am Hassan Omar Mohammed," West said.

"I have not heard of you." The bearded man's head cocked slightly to the side. "Amir did not say this in the texts."

Felicia knew that West and these guys had been texting earlier. This wasn't going well at all.

The image jerked. West must have shrugged. "There was no time. And we didn't want to take the chance of missing you. Allah's will must be done." He began speaking in Arabic again. It was a long discourse and sounded authentic. Felicia could have sworn West was a native.

"Sergeant West's trying to reassure him that the other dude, Amir, couldn't make it due to the infidels following him," Baker said.

"You speak Arabic too?" Felicia asked.

"Yeah. We all speak it pretty good." His voice was tight—no more than a whisper.

"He sounds fluent. Very authentic." She realized she was whispering too.

"Shucks, ma'am, Sergeant West speaks Arabic like a regular towelhead," the young soldier said. "He knows the Koran, too."

"Where did you learn to speak it so well?"

"They sent us to all kinds of language schools that teach them real good, plus being deployed so many times. I can understand it all right, but don't speak it too good. They say I couldn't shake my accent." He shook his head and grinned. "Go figure, huh? Augusta, Georgia, my whole life until I enlisted."

Felicia smiled. She couldn't help but like the young man's lack of guile.

"Shucks, ma'am," he continued. "Sergeant West even had them take the gold cap off his front tooth so he'd look less like

115

an American."

They looked back at the monitor. The conversation between the two men had been continuing in the foreign tongue. Suddenly, they both were silent.

The swarthy man stood still. His eyes looked dark and foreboding in the greenish tint. He licked his lips then brought his gun up, holding it outstretched toward West's face. Even on the monitor screen the bore looked deadly.

Oh my God, Felicia thought.

"Call Amir," the swarthy man said over his shoulder. One of the others took out a cell phone and began dialing.

West said something in Arabic. Felicia looked to Baker. "What did he say?"

"He's telling him there are no cell phone towers close enough to use the phone," Baker said, his voice barely audible.

West continued speaking to him in the foreign language that Felicia couldn't understand, but his tone was cajoling. The bearded man spat back, the cadences and rhythms of their respective dialogue almost identical. Both of them stopped talking.

The one near the truck held the cell phone up and shook his head.

The image of the bearded man's face twisted into a contemplative sneer. "Amir would have called me to tell me this before. And why didn't he?" He kept the pistol outstretched. "I think you are a spy. Or a traitor."

Felicia recoiled, almost forgetting that she was only watching this from a remote monitor.

Baker's mouth twisted a bit. "Shit, this ain't looking good." He pressed a button on the monitor. "Alpha-one, are you copying this?"

"Roger that," came the reply. "Moving in."

"Do you have the gas?" West asked in English.

The swarthy man extended the gun so it was only a few inches from West's face. "Get in the truck. We are going to go back across the border until we hear from Amir. If you have lied to me, you will beg for death a thousand times before it comes to you."

"I have not lied," West said. His voice sounded exceptionally calm. "And I have a question to ask you."

The swarthy man's face contorted. "What?"

"Do you really think there'll be seventy-two virgins waiting for you in hell?"

The swarthy man blinked, then his face contorted again. West's hand lashed out, smacking the outstretched pistol away from his face. The camera image blurred. Movement punctuated by grunts. Felicia knew they must be struggling. She looked at Baker. His face was drawn, intense.

"What's happening?"

"A-team's moving in." He reached over and pointed to the second monitor. It showed the overview of the scene from the decoy van. In front two men struggled. Beyond that other shadows moved toward the truck.

Two loud cracks burst from the speaker, then more subdued cracking sounds. Gunshots?

Felicia gasped. Her eyes went from monitor to monitor.

The view from West's camera came into focus. She saw his outstretched hand holding a gun, then a flash of green light exploded momentarily on the screen accompanied by a piercing discharge. The image returned showing the man with the cell phone clutching his chest. Another flash, another shot. The man's head snapped back and he fell forward.

West was moving forward now. When he came abreast of the truck the camera view panned on the third man by the truck. He was on the ground. West stepped on the man's hand, which held a pistol, and stooped to recover the weapon. When he stood the image of a soldier with a darkened face came into view.

"Vehicle secure, top," the soldier said.

"Roger that, target secured," West said. "Any other bad guys on lookout?"

Lee's voice came over the radio: "We've got those two about a hundred yards back. Lex, you got 'em?"

Felicia heard two more remote-sounding pops, followed by, "Targets neutralized."

"What happened?" she asked, although she was pretty sure already.

"Our snipers iced two more towelheads." Baker's grin was wide now. "Like clockwork."

"Move in to confirm," Lee's voice said. "Baker, sweep the rest of the area for any other hostiles."

"Yes, sir," Baker said into his mic. His face seemed to swell with pride as he scanned the monitor with the rotating radar grid again. "All clear, sir." He turned to Felicia and held out his palm for a high-five. "Now all that's left is we have our haz-mat team move in now and secure the gas."

Felicia felt a wave of relief sweep over her. The whole thing had taken less than a minute. Five terrorists killed and the truck with the gas secured.

These guys are good. Really good.

CHAPTER 10

It was close to midnight and Undersecretary Paul Ross felt his stomach lurch as the Lear jet touched down on the runway. Smooth landing, thought Ross. At least that was one benefit of being flown by a military jock. They knew how to set these planes down. He exhaled and leaned back, still buckled in his seat. Coming through that damn storm had been dicey. One of the crew came back and told him that the ride was going to be bumpy, but there was nothing to worry about.

Nothing to worry about, Ross thought. If there was nothing to worry about why had they delayed taking off so long, and then flown through the storm anyway? Ross sighed. Hell, at least he'd gotten back safely, even if it was late.

He'd flown through storms before, but this one made him feel extra queasy. Maybe it was due to the load of dynamite he was carrying. He had enough info on his laptop to make Big Willie crap his drawers. Ross smiled. When his boss heard the stuff he had—names, statements, times, dates, details of waterboarding—even some closed-circuit videos of a few of the procedures on his hard drive. Ah, the power of those federal subpoenas. Makes even the most macho most compliant. And best of all, the footprints lead right back to the office of Vice President William Bernard, the previous administration's point man in the war on terror. The only question remaining was when to use it. Yeah, after this his boss, Attorney General Thomas, was going to be saying, "Paul, you can call me Reggie."

The pilot's voice came over the intercom. "We're approaching the gate, sir. Should be able to deplane in about ten. You want me to call for a ride for you?"

"No," Ross said. "That's already been taken care of." He held up his cell phone and admired the screen saver—a photo of him and his family. If it wasn't so late, he would have called them too. Another nice thing about being a diplomat on a military ride. No need to abide by those ridiculous in-flight restrictions. He'd called the service when he'd been about forty-five minutes out. The driver should be standing by. Outside the night looked cold and rainy, the bright lights reflecting off the dark tarmac.

Big Willie, we've got your balls in a vise, you son-of-a-bitch.

Time was dragging on and Felicia was feeling impatient. "Can I go over there now?"

Baker, his mouth half twisted, shook his head. "Not advisable, ma'am. If it is Sarin, it's highly unstable. Usually it's transported as a binary gas in two separate containers, and only lethal when it's mixed. Our haz-mat team's still in the containment and evaluation phase."

"How much longer will it take?" she asked, thinking that Joiner wouldn't be pleased if she didn't do a hands-on verification.

"Hard to say, ma'am," Baker said.

"Well, can I at least get in on part of the debrief? Is Captain Lee available?"

Baker bit his lip. There was something he wasn't telling her.

"What's wrong?" she asked.

"Captain Lee departed already. A while ago."

"What?"

"After the initial phase of the mission was finished he left and went back to the base. They had a special flight waiting for him."

"Why?" she asked. "This is a pretty big mission, isn't it?"

"Yes, ma'am, but he was called back to D.C. by mission control ASAP. He turned things over to Sergeant West."

She didn't remember seeing him leave, but then again, she hadn't seen him get there either. These guys were like ghosts. "Well, perhaps I could talk to him then?"

"I'll see if I can get him on the radio."

Felicia looked at the monitor watching the haz-mat crew busily working on the two trucks. Hopefully those guys knew what they were doing, but they dealt with this kind of thing all the time, didn't they?

She heard a knocking on the van's door and it opened. Johnson stared at her and said, "Hey, Knight."

Felicia turned. The man's expression told her all she needed to know. He was about to ask her something and didn't want Baker to hear it. His face looked like he was anticipating a root canal. He cocked his head and said, "Step out here a second, will you?"

Felicia said she'd be right back and got out of the van. It felt good to stretch, even if it was into the damn rain. She tucked her hair under her FBI baseball cap as best she could. When she stepped down she was surprised at how soggy the soft ground felt, the mud rushing up over the side of her shoe like a cold, dirty wave. She grimaced and set the other foot down gingerly. Why the hell had she worn pumps instead of gym shoes?

Out of the corner of her eye she caught Johnson's smirk at her dilemma. The asshole.

"What?" she said.

He scratched a nostril. "You got any idea how much longer this is gonna take?"

"Not really. We can't go down until the scene is secure."

He blew out a slow breath. God, it stank. A stale combination of halitosis and cigarettes. She was glad she hadn't been cooped up in the same car with him and Beaumont.

"Me and Beau been thinking," he said. "There's no sense all of us staying up here now that the operation's mostly complete."

"Complete? Are you serious?" Obviously, they wanted to bail out and leave her holding the bag.

"What I mean is, if you were to stay here, we could head back to D.C. and give an oral briefing to the boss. That way we'd be ready to jump on new developments should they come up."

"And how are you figuring on getting back? Are they going to give you a special helicopter ride?"

"We'll drive, use one of the cars we rented," he said.

"Why drive? We can catch a ride back with those guys. There's got to be plenty of room."

"Who knows if they'll be flying in this weather. We're ready to go now. Besides, who knows how long this decon is gonna take. We could be up here waiting all night."

"That's got to be better than driving back," she said. "You'll be *driving* all night."

"We'll take turns driving." He grinned. "You've got your laptop, right? You can work on the report as it unfolds here and e-mail us so we can give it to the boss. Then come back with your little army buddies."

Fear of flying or fear of puking? You and Beaumont don't want to be riding in that chopper. That's what this is all about. Felicia canted her head. "Leaving me to do all the work, huh?"

Johnson glanced around, looking everywhere but into her eyes. His upper lip bulged as he ran his tongue over his teeth. "We estimate, with both of us switching off, we can be back in D.C. in about twelve hours," he said. "That beats waiting around here, don't it? It's mostly all freeway."

"Twelve hours," she repeated, looking him in the eyes. It was time to show this cracker that she was his equal, if not his superior. "That's if you don't get pulled over by some state trooper!"

"Hey, we're on official government business."

All things considered, it seemed like a good plan, but not for any of the reasons Johnson had given her. If they left now, she'd be rid of them for twelve hours and might still beat them back if things went smoothly. "Sounds okay to me, but you're on your own as far as your reports."

Johnson exhaled loudly. "Come on, can't you be a team player for once?"

"A team player?"

"Yeah, like I said, it doesn't make sense all of us being trapped up here."

Felicia considered telling this asshole to go fuck himself, but she decided to handle it the smart way: cool and professional. "You and Beau go ahead in the car. I'll stay here and work on *our* report."

"And you'll e-mail it to us when you're done?"

She smiled, unable to resist one last score against the opposition. "I hope you don't get carsick."

Johnson's face reddened. As he walked away, he muttered, "See you in D.C. Whenever you get there."

You mean whenever you get there, asshole, she thought.

Paul Ross came through the jetway and headed for the terminal, his suitcase in tow and his computer case slung over his shoulder. His blood was boiling over having to sit on the fucking tarmac for an additional forty-five minutes while they waited for another gate to clear. Forty-five minutes. What the hell could they have been doing this time of night? He listened to the voice on his cell phone as he walked. "The driver texted us," the limo service said. "He's on scene and waiting, sir."

Ross grunted an acknowledgment. One-fifteen. They'd taken their sweet-ass time hooking up the damn jetway, too. Like the assholes were intentionally moving in slow motion.

The airport was deserted, even on this military side. Just a few guards standing by. They looked bored. As he passed through the security checkpoint, he saw a black man in a chauffeur's uniform. He held a white sign with MR. PAUL ROSS printed on it. A twenty-minute ride into Virginia and he'd be home. He resisted the temptation to call AG Thomas. No sense waking him and his wife up at this hour. No, it would be better to call in the morning. Have the presentation organized.

All Ross cared about now was getting home and taking a long hot shower before getting into bed. He smiled. Well, a nightcap might be in order. Too bad the limo didn't have a bar.

"I'm Ross," he said.

The limo driver asked if he had any other baggage.

Ross pushed past him. "No. Let's get out of here. I'm in a hurry."

"Yes, sir," the driver said. "Right this way, sir."

The driver went through the doors ahead of Ross, then pointed to a limo parked by the curbside with an Official U.S. Government Business plaque slapped on the front windshield. Ross strode up to the right, rear passenger-side door and waited. The driver opened the door. As Ross started to get inside, he saw another figure. A man.

Ross jerked to a stop and said, "Who're you?"

"Get in," the man said, grabbing Ross's left arm. The man's face had Asiatic features. He was dressed in all black, like some kind of military outfit. Ross felt the driver's body behind him, like a hulking shadow.

"What the hell's going on here?" Ross said.

The driver gave him a nudge and he flopped into the rear

seat, his computer case falling to the floor. Then the asshole driver shoved the carry-on case in there, too.

"Put that in the damn trunk," Ross yelled. "Or better yet, get me another car. I'll have your fucking job for this."

"The trunk's already occupied," the Asian man said.

His hands looked glossy. Some kind of tight rubber gloves were stretched over them. Ross felt them clasp around the base of his skull.

"Let me out of here!"

The fucking door handle was locked, the damn carry-on between him and the door. Ross felt strong fingers grip his head and smash it against the separation screen with such force that the plastic cracked. God, the pain! He wiped his face and watched his hands come away red.

Then felt the thrust of the car as it shot away from the curb.

Viceroy had been sitting in his darkened den and fingering the cigar again. He'd purposely been waiting until he heard from Lee. Phase one had come off perfectly. They had taken out the intermediary delivery boys and commandeered the cargo, under the watchful eye of the FBI. You couldn't ask for a more reliable alibi than that. He regretted having to summon Lee back before all the details were done, but West was more than competent to secure the gas. Lee had to take care of Ross.

Viceroy wouldn't light his cigar until he heard from Lee.

A good commander doesn't rest, or celebrate, until all phases of an ongoing operation are complete, he thought. *Relaxing too soon—one of the seven deadly sins for a military man.*

At least he didn't have his idiot brother-in-law sitting here stressing and fretting about everything. He'd finally convinced Big Willie to go home and get some sleep. His movements were creating a paper trail, with the damn Secret Service contingent following him. And that was one thing Viceroy couldn't have.

Meetings had to fall under the guise of friendly family get-togethers. Nothing too out of the ordinary.

His cell phone vibrated. *One new message*—from Lee: *phase 2 complete en route with package.*

Viceroy acknowledged the text, fingered the Havana again, trimmed off the end with his cutter, but still didn't light it.

The rolled paper felt coarse and brittle between his fingers and he longed to experience the taste. He'd earned it. Tonight's ops had gone off without a hitch. But first he picked up the remote and flipped on the TV. The big flat screen came to life with a reporter recounting the day's top stories. Along the bottom, the headline scroll listed breaking news: *Car explosion near Maine/Canada border. More details shortly.*

Viceroy smiled. He'd already received his text from West about that package being secured by the haz-mat team. Everything was fitting into place. Big Willie could relax with Paul Ross out of the way, and the findings of his ill-fated trip to Gitmo, in the clutches of "a watery grave"—something that would no doubt be gracing the breaking news scrolls in a few more hours. And best of all, he had that extra-special ace slipped up his sleeve for his Hail Mary play. He thought about that part of it for a few moments.

The tree of liberty must occasionally be watered with the blood of patriots and tyrants. Jefferson's words. Unfortunate, but true.

The watering would wake this country up, and put him on the fast track to 1600 Pennsylvania Avenue. A circuitous track, but as long as he stuck to his game plan and kept the minor glitches from turning into major ones, it would work. Viceroy smelled the cigar. Minor glitches . . . Like the unexpected identification of Fassel and Detective Kevin McClain. He still hadn't figured that one out yet. But he would.

Sun Tzu said it best: *He who is victorious needs two things—*

Viceroy took out his lighter and flicked it, the flame looking bright and gem-like in the dark room—*the strongest army and the best spies.*

And I've got both, Viceroy thought.

CHAPTER 11

McClain couldn't believe how sore his body felt as he rolled out of bed. The clock's hands were set at a right angle, like a division symbol. Six-fifteen. His head felt like somebody'd cut it in half and slapped it back together. He shouldn't have been this bad, but he was. Shit, I'm supposed to be in shape, he thought.

At least that's what he told himself. Dancing with an asshole like Rewaldo should have been a piece of cake. After all, he was up to going four rounds in the gym. Sometimes five or six. But he knew all the gym work in the world wasn't like being in a real fight, be it in the ring or in the backyard of some tenement house. Plus in this one, there hadn't been any rules.

The pain came jolting back to him as he began shuffling toward the bathroom.

It hadn't helped either that he and Kelly had gone out to tip a few after getting the ass chewing by the El-Tee. Beasley was a prick who didn't react well to pressure, but in this case, the pressure should be off. The victim was a former inmate at Gitmo. What better victim could you have than a potential terrorist. So what if somebody iced him? Who was gonna give two shits? Still, murder is murder, and when you torture somebody, kill them, set them on fire, and dump them, it's a given that somebody should look into it. Just not too hard.

McClain concentrated on placing one foot in front of the other, shuffling along like an eighty-year-old man. He had to shower, eat, and then make his way over to the Federal Building to touch base with the feds at nine o'clock. Beasley wouldn't like it if he was late, and knowing what tight assholes the feds had they'd dime him out if he was. He stumbled toward the bathroom thinking he had a bottle of aspirin somewhere and hoping he'd feel better after a hot shower.

Shit, I'm gonna need more than aspirin, he thought a moment later when he saw his reflection in the mirror. Makeup maybe. But it was only the feds. Those pricks would probably want to take everything over like they always do. Of course that would only be if they were ninety percent sure of a conviction.

His rather hideous reflection continued to stare back at him.

He'd known about the long scratch on the right side of his neck, and his left eye was swollen and turning a nice shade of purple underneath—all courtesy of Rewaldo. He didn't think the fucker had connected enough to do that much damage. Have to work on head movement. But Rewaldo's face had begun to balloon up too when they'd dropped him off at lockup. McClain felt he'd given better than he'd got, which meant he'd won.

He took out his shaving cream and razor, then studied the bruises some more.

"You know," he said in his best punch-drunk Marlon Brando imitation, "I coulda been a *contenda*."

Felicia felt awful as she headed out the door, but that's what a night without sleep would do to you. Make you feel like shit. By the time they'd finished their haz-mat duties and secured the gas, it was close to one in the morning. They drove back to the base in the surveillance van, with her fingers doing double duty on the keyboard. She jumped at the chance to ride back in the Chinook again, this time not even needing the puke bucket because she had nothing to offer up in her stomach. Baker offered to get her a sandwich before takeoff. Most of the other team members ate, but she declined. No sense putting something in there that would maybe come up if they hit some rough spots.

Getting home really didn't take that long either, but it was still way after four-thirty by the time she got back to her place. Knowing Joiner would be expecting her to report in to him on the case first thing, she munched on some cheese and crackers as she sat down in her office and finished the rest of her report. It was mostly done, except for the few details she wasn't privy to, like where exactly they'd taken the gas for destruction and the current location of the dead terrorists' bodies. Pretty soon it was quarter after six—the time she usually got up anyway, so she fixed herself a good breakfast of bacon, eggs, and toast and then headed for the bathroom. Even an hour's nap sounded good. As she got undressed, peeling off all those sweaty clothes that she'd been wearing constantly for almost twenty-four hours straight, her cell rang. It was Joiner's ringtone. She dropped the clothes in the hamper and answered it.

"Knight, you're back?" No cordial "Good morning" from him.

She murmured that she was, and added, "But I haven't been to bed yet."

"Do you have a preliminary report completed?"

No pats on the back from this guy. A kick in the bootie was his standard acknowledgment. "I just finished."

"Good. I'll need to see it ASAP. Are Beaumont and Johnson with you?"

Did he think she was going to take those two idiots home with her? "Of course not. I told you, I'm at home."

"I didn't mean . . ." Joiner grunted. "Did everything go all right? They haven't been answering their phones."

She smiled at the thought. Probably because they'd forgotten their car chargers. Or maybe they'd puked on them. "We didn't come back together."

"What? Why not?" His abrupt change of the subject spared her from having to go into a long explanation of stupid Bert and Ernie's fear of flying. "I'm in the office. I need you to get in here right away."

"Now? I was about to take a nap. I told you I've been up all night."

"Negative. I need you here, with the report, ASAP."

"Can't I e-mail it to you?"

"Negative." His voice was a bark. "No e-mails. Too sensitive. Too dangerous. Bring it in. How soon can you get here?"

Felicia sighed as she thought about making the trek downtown. He saw a Chinese hacker behind every keyboard. "I was about to shower."

"Make it a quick one. I'll be waiting."

It was all smoke and mirrors, Viceroy thought as he seated himself across from Joiner's desk. But then again, all warfare is deception, as Sun Tzu said. Viceroy disliked being in the weak position in front of the other man, but Joiner seemed to know little about spacial intimidation, otherwise Viceroy would have remained standing. But being in the subordinate position, psychologically speaking, in this instance might be an actual advantage. After all, he was here not to praise Joiner, but to play him. Viceroy smiled at the thought of Mark Anthony's clever speech to rouse the masses after Caesar's assassination. At least he wouldn't have to do a soliloquy.

"So give it to me straight, Clay," Joiner said. "You said you had a mixed bag."

Viceroy waited a few seconds before speaking. "I assume you want the good news first?"

"Sure, why not? The mission was a success, wasn't it?"

"I'll let your personnel brief you on the specifics, but suffice to say, the intercept went down flawlessly." It was Viceroy's turn to grin. "If you watched ZCCN News early this morning they had a scroll about a truck on fire up by the Canadian border in Maine."

"I did see that. Terrible thing, terrible thing," Joiner said with exaggerated irony. "And the Sarin?"

"That's where the problem arose." Viceroy frowned. "We didn't know this at the time, or even before your agents were routed back, but the shipment we intercepted wasn't all of the Sarin."

Joiner's jaw jutted out like a befuddled pelican. "Huh? But I thought our intel was good."

"Our intel was good," Viceroy said, thinking he wasn't really telling a lie as much as what you might call a convenient misstatement.

Joiner clasped his hand over his forehead and massaged his temples. "Give it to me straight."

"When transported, Sarin can be very unstable," Viceroy said. "It's often broken down into a binary state, which is not deadly until they're combined. So we were able to neutralize it."

Joiner's mouth tugged back into a tight line. "Which means we've prevented an attack, correct?"

"Yes, but among the recovered items from the five hostiles we had to tactically neutralize, we recovered a cache of information."

"Computers?"

Viceroy shook his head. "Cell phones."

Joiner grunted, as if he was right alongside Viceroy following the trail. The man was pathetic. As easily led as a hungry dog. Viceroy took a deep breath, held it, then exhaled—his way of assuming control over his autonomic nervous system. "Unfortunately, there's another shipment I just found out about."

The space between Joiner's eyebrows compressed with double

creases. "Huh?"

"They had another group meeting at a second location. One that we didn't know about."

Joiner's face suddenly looked ashen. "You mean to say . . ."

Viceroy locked eyes with Joiner. It was the final set-up for his one-two punch. "We have reason to believe that one got through. And at this time, we have no idea where it is, other than our intel strongly indicates it was brought into the continental United States."

Hurry up and wait, McClain thought as he glanced at his watch in the outer office of the Federal Building. They'd treated him like an unwelcome visitor, even though they knew he was coming. That's the feds for you, he thought. Uptight assholes. He bounced the file on his lap and waited. Nobody seemed to notice him and he felt like getting up and walking away, but he knew Beasley would be waiting to hear how his visit with the feds went. No, he was stuck for the time being.

An attractive black girl with a laptop carrying case rushed by him wearing a gray FBI sweatshirt and tight blue jeans, which he immediately noticed. She glanced at him in passing and then it hit him. He'd seen her before, but where?

He remembered seeing a pretty black chick at the gym on more than one occasion, but was this her? He'd seen her at a distance and wasn't sure. Then he noticed how her hair was tied up with a scarf. It was the same girl. He was sure. Once she'd smiled and given him a thumbs-up when she'd passed as he was standing there all breathless and sweaty after a particularly hard session on the heavy bag.

She was one of the regulars playing volleyball. Great height on her spikes. He'd spent many a break between "rounds" on the bags pretending to be exhausted but actually watching her run and jump and thinking how nice she moved, how graceful and attractive she was. He'd even noticed her glancing back a few times, but not with the acknowledging and alluring smile he'd silently hoped for, but with a stern, "what you looking at, white boy?" kind of look. It was enough to keep him at a distance. So much for the thumbs-up.

Momentarily, they stared at each other. Then she moved past him, said something to the secretary at the desk, and got buzzed in to the interior offices. McClain wondered if she was an agent and figured she was since she'd been buzzed in without any wait. She obviously had more clout than he did around here.

He sat back and pictured her in her gym shorts. She probably doesn't even remember me, he thought, and went back to bouncing the file on his leg. He rubbed his finger over his swollen eye. Plus, with this face she probably thinks I'm a kissing cousin to a raccoon.

It was him in the waiting room area. Felicia was sure of it as she walked through the inner office section. The white guy from the gym. Always working out on the boxing stuff. What was he doing here? And what happened to his face? It looked like he'd been in a fight or something. He had a black eye and his face was swollen. Maybe it was from a boxing match.

She'd always figured him connected to law enforcement or the military due to his short hair. He was holding some kind of a folder. She glanced over toward Joiner's office. It was strategically located so he had a bird's-eye view of the entire office and could see everyone's comings and goings. His privacy blinds were open too, and Felicia noticed he was in his office along with somebody else. Joiner's head shot up and he motioned her over. From the look on his face he wasn't happy.

She gave a slight knock on the door before she entered. Professional and courteous, even if it was dubious that Joiner merited that measure of respect. Glancing to her right she saw a big man in an army uniform sitting in the chair in front of Joiner's desk. The guy had steel gray hair, cropped short, broad shoulders, and a craggy face that looked like it had seen a lot of hot places and action. But his expression was placid, like this was merely another day in the game. Joiner's face, on the other hand, looked as tight as a wind-up clock running backward.

"Come in, Knight," Joiner said. "You got the report?"

Felicia held up her flash drive and was a little bit shocked when Joiner told her to hold on to it for the time being. After badgering her into rushing into the office after she'd been up for more than twenty-four hours straight, they suddenly had all the time in the world.

She was wondering if the frustration was showing on her face when the big man seated in the chair stood up and extended his hand.

"I'm Colonel Clayton Viceroy," he said. "Military Intelligence."

"Special Agent Felicia Knight." She accepted his hand. His grip was strong, like a vise. Not that he squeezed hers, but the hint of power was there, without his having to demonstrate.

"Knight? I got some very favorable reports on you from my team," Viceroy said. "Excellent job last night. Woody, you've got a top agent here."

Woody? A nickname for Woodrow? So this guy and Joiner were on a first-name basis? Her amazement continued. *Woody?* It brought a smile to Felicia's lips. Yeah, he was a *Woody*, all right. And this guy Viceroy was actually giving her a pat on the back—a total rarity in Joiner's office. She glanced over at her boss who was sitting there, arms crossed, with a scowl on his face.

"I was telling Woody here," Viceroy said, "that there's been a complication."

"Oh?" Felicia said. *What did that mean?*

Joiner practically jumped to his feet. "Knight, what you're

about to hear has to stay in the strictest confidence. It does not leave this room. Understood?"

His brusque tone told her this must be something really important. "Yes, sir."

Joiner's frown deepened. He looked at Viceroy, then said, "Clay, I got to tell you, I'm still having reservations about this. About keeping everything under wraps for now. I mean, something this big, I should be briefing the higher-ups. If it ever comes out I've been sitting on this . . ." He ran his hand through his greased black hair and looked down at his desktop.

"We've already been over this, haven't we?" Viceroy's voice was calm. "None of this was substantiated until last night. You had a report, an unsubstantiated report, and you acted appropriately, investigating and not wanting to cause undue alarm, correct?"

Joiner's lips bunched up.

"Plus, there's some significant new intel," Viceroy said.

Felicia couldn't believe it. This colonel dude was playing Joiner like a secondhand saxophone. And the music coming out wasn't so sweet.

Viceroy cleared his throat and looked back at her. "As I said, you all did an excellent job intercepting that shipment last night. However—"

"Clay, just a minute," Joiner interrupted. He was really showing the cracks today. Totally off his game. "I still have two other agents en route. Where are Beaumont and Johnson?"

Felicia resisted the temptation to dime Bert and Ernie out. She shook her head slightly. "I'm not sure. As I mentioned, we didn't come back together."

Joiner looked like he was totally disgusted. "Perhaps it would be best to wait to give them the briefing when they get here. That way I won't have to repeat myself. I'm sure they'll be along any time."

Don't count on it, Felicia thought. But what the hell was going on? Was there some kind of a problem disposing of the gas? Had one of the haz-mat team been injured?

"And need I remind you," Joiner continued, "we have the additional problem waiting for us in the outer office." He pointed in the direction of the waiting room.

Viceroy gave a slight nod.

Joiner turned to her. "There's an MPDC detective in the waiting room."

Ah, so he is in law enforcement, Felicia thought.

"His name's McClain," Joiner said. "Yesterday he requested an identification of an unidentified homicide victim through federal medical channels. What led him to this, I don't know."

He paused, as if searching for what to say next. How much to tell her. Felicia knew Joiner had a way of transforming even the simplest things into difficult convolutions, spending countless hours caught in an endless spire of indecision. The typical bureaucrat. And as Special Agent In Charge, he epitomized the old Peter principle—promoted to his specific level of incompetence.

"This said un-sub was identified," Joiner said, then paused again.

She waited for him to continue, crossing her arms and pinching the flash drive that had kept her up the whole night between her thumb and index finger. Was he ever going to ask for it? She felt like throwing it into Joiner's face.

"Do you know who the aforementioned un-sub turned out to be?" Joiner asked.

Felicia shook her head. *Did he have any idea how stupid he sounded?*

Joiner frowned, like he was experiencing some physical discomfort. "It was number three-eighty-three. Mohammed Amir Fassel."

This hit her like a sucker punch. *Fassel dead? Murdered? By whom? And what kind of ramifications was this going to have on their ongoing investigation into this latest threat?* "Is this going to turn into a Bureau case?"

"Not our jurisdiction, although it did set off all kinds of bells, whistles, and alarms with the OHSCT Bureau and the Joint Terrorism Task Force. Besides, we already have our hands full with Operation Prometheus." He shook his head slowly. "Number three-eighty-three's involvement in this has to remain in-house for now. Classified. Talk to this McClain character. Find out what he wants. And what he knows. We're going to have to take measures to put the brakes on him meddling in our present operation."

"You want *me* to talk to him?" she asked.

"Why, of course. You are the case agent on three-eighty-three. And a member of the team that let him drop off the radar."

Felicia was outraged. Sure, she was in charge of coordinating the overall surveillance operation, but she hadn't been the one out in the field who'd lost Fassel. She was way too tired and way too mad to stand there and take the blame for this. "Sir, with all due respect, I think your last statement was a bit of a misinterpretation of the actual facts."

Joiner sat back in his chair as if she'd slapped him.

Felicia caught the hint of a smirk on Colonel Viceroy's lips.

Joiner held up his hands and wobbled his head. The man looked like he was on the brink of a nervous breakdown. "I'm not saying you're to blame. What I am saying is that *we* let three-eighty-three slip through our fingers. *We* were supposed to be watching him, keeping him under surveillance, and he slipped us and turned up dead. We're all part of a team here, and *I'm* the SAIC." He bit his lower lip. "This could be a career breaker."

And they'd probably start with the lower-ranking agents, she thought. Like me.

"Woody," Viceroy said, "if I may . . ."

Joiner looked perplexed.

Viceroy turned to her and smiled. "We know that we have strong indications that Fassel was a member of this terrorist cell operating in the D.C. area. His death, as well as him dropping out of sight, could very well be related to this. If that is the case, we're between the perpetual rock and a hard place. In all probability, Fassel was earmarked as a traitor and killed by the other members of the cell."

Felicia's brow wrinkled. "I don't understand."

"We turned Fassel when he was in Gitmo," Viceroy said. "He was the one who was feeding us the info about the cell and their plans."

Fassel was their snitch? Why hadn't Joiner let her know instead of making them tail Fassel without tying him to this other case? But then again, the military had been calling the shots on this whole thing, hadn't they? So Fassel was how MI had been able to stay on top of this thing, one move ahead of the Bureau. So much for sharing information, but she could hardly blame them for not wanting one of their CIs to be burned. Especially an Arab on the inside.

"If any of this gets out to MPDC, it'll be all over," Joiner said. "Like that Wikileak thing a few years ago."

"MPDC is hardly Wikileak," Felicia said.

Joiner snorted. "We need you to meet with this McClain joker and stall him."

"Stall? Exactly how am I going to do that?"

"Tell him the information he wants is classified," Joiner was getting flustered now. "A matter of national security."

"What information does he want?"

Joiner shrugged.

Felicia strained to keep her voice even. "He already has Fassel's name, right?"

"But not his involvement with Operation Prometheus," Joiner said. "We absolutely have to keep a lid on this thing until the new crisis is contained."

"New crisis?" Felicia said. "Is that the one you don't want to tell me about until Beaumont and Johnson get back?"

Joiner's face reddened, a cherrybomb about ready to explode.

"Aww, hell, Woody," Viceroy said. "Why not tell her now. From everything I've heard she's an exceptional agent. Certainly a standout from your other two."

Joiner's mouth worked, like he was about to speak but couldn't find the words.

Viceroy put a hand up and calmly said, "Let me do it for you." Then, to Felicia, "The Sarin gas you helped intercept last night was a decoy shipment. More gas is still out there, and we're afraid it already made it across the border. We're working this from the other end, with the terrorist cell we got from Fassel. Until we can intercept it, we have to assume that this is still an ongoing threat of the worst magnitude."

"Which is why," Joiner said, pointing his finger at her for emphasis as he spoke, "we're not going to give this MPDC joker anything more than the time of day. Understood?"

Felicia barely listened to the pompous asshole. Instead, she thought about the Sarin.

Oh, my God, she thought. *Oh, my God.*

Viceroy thought about excusing himself before they ushered the cop in, but he wanted to stay and size this guy up. He was still waiting for that damn intel report on McClain.

"Woody, I need to shove off soon," he said as they stood in the office waiting for Knight to usher McClain in.

"Don't worry," Joiner said in a hushed tone. "I'll take care of this little hiccup."

"Detective McClain," Knight said as they walked through the door, "this is my supervisor, Special Agent In Charge, Woodrow Joiner."

Viceroy watched as McClain reached over and shook Joiner's hand. The guy looked to be in his mid-thirties. Good-sized, but not big. Fit-looking, too. Viceroy smiled to himself. *He has that lean, hungry look, but it also looks like somebody tattooed his face with a bunch of punches.* The face looked vaguely familiar. McClain turned, his hand outstretched.

"Kevin McClain, sir," he said.

It was then that Viceroy got it.

McClain.

Suddenly, it all came back. He did know him. Somalia. That hush-hush POW black ops rescue.

Viceroy smiled and squeezed McClain's hand. "Colonel Clayton Viceroy, United States Army." His eyes scanned the other man's face for any indication that the recognition was mutual, but saw none. But then again, McClain had seen him only twice. Once during the rescue operation, and then afterward when the young soldier was recuperating in the field hospital. In the first, Viceroy's face had been camouflaged with black tiger stripes, and the second had probably been through a drug haze.

"Army, eh?" McClain's face twitched. "Have we met before?"

Well, what do you know? Viceroy thought. There was a flicker of recognition after all. Maybe there was more to this kid than he figured.

"I don't know," he said. "Have you served?"

"Yeah, I was with the One-Sixtieth SOAR."

Viceroy raised his eyebrows. "Good outfit. Airborne?"

"All the way, sir."

Viceroy grunted an approval and said, "Next time I'll expect a salute then." He grinned and turned toward Joiner. "Woody,

141

I'll let you brief your people. I should be getting back to the Pentagon to review my own reports." He shook hands with Joiner then turned and offered his hand to Knight again. "Agent, it was a pleasure meeting you. Keep up the good work." He shook hands with McClain next and moved to the door.

The GI from Mogadishu, he thought as he walked out. Never would have figured on that in a million years.

CHAPTER 12

Ted Lane stood on the side of the road next to the line of news vans that were filming the grim scene. From the way the cops and the paramedics were standing around, it was obvious that the limo had been under water long enough to negate the possibility of any survivors. Now it was all about roping the scene off and waiting for the medical examiner's office. Lane really wasn't sure why he'd stopped. He'd been on his way in to the newsroom when the call came over his scanner. Was a traffic accident, even a fatal one, anything to delay his pursuit of his main story? Still, any time there's a limousine with two dead bodies inside it was worth a few minutes. Especially one with government plates.

Always the newshound, he thought.

The cops were keeping everybody way back, but the camera crew had managed to zero in on the two prone figures laid out side-by-side on the plastic tarp. Lane stepped inside the ZCCN News van.

"What's it looking like?" He asked the tech.

"The divers pulled two out of the limo. They winched it out of the water a few minutes ago."

Lane studied the monitor, which gave him a pretty clear view of the two dead men. Both victims looked to be male, one appeared to be wearing some kind of black uniform. The chauffeur?

The other guy appeared to be white and wearing a business

suit, although the corpse was so waterlogged it was hard to tell.

"Any indication as to how long they were under?" Lane asked.

The tech pressed the direct-talk button on his cell. "Hey Tony, they give you any updates as to the time of the accident?"

"No, but they're thinking it happened sometime in the wee hours. People on the way in to work noticed the broken fence and began calling it in about six a.m. It was an hour before they got a squad out here and they followed the tracks into the water." One of the cops seemed to notice the prying eyes of the press cameras and pointed, saying something. The ambulance crew moved forward with the black body bags. As they did, they slipped on their latex gloves.

Another untoward development. Usually the cops didn't give two shits if the press zeroed in on a couple of drowning victims, aware that the footage would probably be considered too graphic.

"Ask if they've got IDs on the bodies yet," Lane said.

The distant voice said, "Nothing yet, but they moved us back some more and started stonewalling. Plus, there's a lot of what looks like federal assistance."

The feds? For a traffic accident? Lane studied the monitor with the overall scene and saw a few black, unmarked cars parked behind the marked units. A couple of uniformed troopers walked toward the group of reporters. It looked like they were trying to widen their perimeter. Lane told the tech to have his camera guy try and zero in on the face of the suit before they zipped him up.

His cell phone rang. Allison's ringtone. "What? I'm busy now," he said.

"They announced a White House press conference at one," she said. "They're sending Carmen, unless you want me to go."

God, no, he thought. *I want to avoid a train wreck if I can.* But Carmen wasn't much better. Not quite as photogenic as Allison, but people tended to focus on her because she was a Latina. "Let me think about it."

Lane continued to study the monitor as the ambulance crew manipulated the body into the black bag.

"Think fast," Allison said. "They're getting a crew ready now."

The petulance in her voice was palpable. Better smooth out her feathers.

"Yeah, Carmen's good," he said. "Probably some routine bullshit."

A cop by the crash was on a bullhorn now, advising the press that they would have to move back and leave the side of the road so as not to create a traffic hazard.

"Who's that?" Allison asked. "Where are you?"

"I stopped on the freeway for a traffic crash."

"What?"

"It's involving someone in G."

"Who?"

"Don't know yet," he said, then caught a glimpse of the face of the corpse in the suit. The head lolled back, the body suspended, as the two men tried to work the black vinyl over the dead man's lower torso. The face looked familiar, but who? The body shifted some more and the dead man's head rotated to the other side, giving the camera an almost full facial. Lane studied the image for a solid six seconds. Then, suddenly, he knew.

"What was the original plan for today?" he asked. "Wasn't Paul Ross supposed to be coming back from Guantanamo last night?"

"Yeah," Allison said. "With his findings on the torture investigation. Thomas mentioned it in my interview, remember?"

"Yeah, well, regarding our boy Ross, I don't think he's gonna make it."

McClain plucked the tan parking ticket from under the windshield wiper of his Ford Fiesta and slammed the door as he got in. The vehicle rattled and at first he was afraid he'd broken something. After a cursory check of the door everything seemed intact and he sighed in relief. Stupid move, taking his anger and frustration out on his vehicle. The car was ten years old, and badly in need of a tune-up, a touch-up paint job, and new tires. He'd bought it used after Lynn had gotten their Escalade in the divorce settlement—the fruits of having a good lawyer. Not that it mattered to him. With the child support and alimony payments he'd been roped into paying, he couldn't afford the Caddie. Anyway, he'd always felt self-conscious driving it. Pretentious—a cop driving a Cadillac—but Lynn's father had insisted that it would be bad for any daughter of his to be seen driving one of those foreign cars.

As he jammed the shift lever into first and eased out of the parking space, he gave the finger to the expired meter and the absent meter maid who'd obviously ignored his Fraternal Order of Police sticker on the windshield. He'd been in such a rush not to be late for the damn appointment with the feds that he'd elected to take his own damn car instead of going by the station to pick up an unmarked. And the meeting had turned out to be an exercise in frustration. Now the icing on the cake was the damn ticket.

No, not icing. A rotten cherry on top of a shit sandwich.

The way the feds had stonewalled him brought his simmering anger to the surface. He caught a glimpse of his purple eye in the rearview mirror. No small wonder Joiner didn't take him seriously.

The asshole barely gave me the time of day. He probably thought I was some punch-drunk idiot.

McClain hit fourth gear and replayed Joiner's stonewalling. "I'm afraid this matter is highly classified." McClain had done his best to be reasonable, but in the end Joiner hadn't given him jack-shit to work with. "You'll have to coordinate your investigation through the OHSCT."

Putting in his request to the Office of Homeland Security and Counter Terrorism Bureau would be another delay on an already ice-cold case. No way of backtracking the victim, no known associates to interview, nothing.

He came to a red light and thought that the only bright spot of the entire thing was finding out the name of the black girl from the gym. Special Agent Knight. Nice name for someone in law enforcement. Nice-looking lady, too. She didn't say much, just went along with her boss. She probably idolized Joiner. Or maybe she didn't suffer fools easily.

Of course then she might not go for me, either.

He let his mind move away from her idiot boss and imagined asking Ms. Knight out to dinner. He hadn't seen a ring on her left hand. He hadn't seen her with anybody at the gym. Then he remembered how his face looked and was glad he hadn't asked.

His cell phone snapped him out of his reverie. He glanced at the screen. Lynn.

Just what I fucking need. Another ass-chewing.

"Kevin," his ex-wife said, the panic obvious in her voice. "It's Jennifer. She's missing."

The meetings with Big Willie had become more and more problematic of late, and Viceroy was glad they'd agreed to come watch Lee train for the upcoming fight. He'd have to steal a few minutes alone with the man, though. There was the ubiquitous Secret Service detail that had been assigned ever since he'd won the party's nomination. And Ram Jet, who seemed to have ears the shape of keyholes. Did people even listen through keyholes anymore? Still, as a campaign manager, Ram Jet was exceedingly competent, and that was what Big Willie needed—someone to keep him focused and on track. Viceroy needed it too, if his overall plan was to succeed. Maybe he'd even use Roger Ram Jet myself, once he reached the White House.

The doorbell rang and Viceroy opened his front door. "Willie, Roger, glad you could make it."

"I've got the camera crew following in a second car," Ram Jet said. "I'm hoping we get some good photo ops this afternoon."

"We will, I'm sure," Viceroy said, and stepped back to allow them entry.

After a brief conversation, the two Secret Service agents said they'd wait in the car.

"Roger, would you mind running down to Starbucks and picking us up some coffee?" Viceroy said in an effort to get rid of Ram Jet. "I'm all out and I've been up most of the night and could really use a shot of espresso." He smiled his most benevolent smile. "Here, take my car." He held out the keys.

Viceroy could see the man wasn't pleased, but what could he say? He said he'd take his own car and shuffled out the door.

Big Willie's eyebrows rose like twin arches. "The gas?"

"Secured," Viceroy said. "For the moment."

"And what about those student radicals?"

"Still on the hook. West is meeting them as we speak at *Asr.*"

"Ass what?"

"*Asr.* Afternoon prayers. You really should become more knowledgeable about our enemies, Will."

Big Willie snorted. "Speaking of enemies, what about the Ross matter."

"All taken care of."

Big Willie's eyebrows rose again. "Exactly what happened?"

"I heard there was a bad accident last night."

"Do tell." Big Willie's face stretched into a wide grin. "Terrible thing. Just terrible."

Viceroy picked up the remote and turned the flat screen on. "Should be making the news shortly." He motioned him to the chair in front of the desk and was about to give him a quick briefing, wondering at the same time how much he should tell, when his cell phone rang. He glanced at the screen, saw it was Baker, and said, "I've got to take this."

"I found the file you were looking for, sir," Baker's voice said. "Kevin McClain—"

"Let me guess. He served with the One-Sixtieth SOAR in Somalia."

He listened to the silence. He loved showing his men that he was still top dog.

"That's right, sir," Baker said. He continued with a list of details about McClain's life up to the present.

Viceroy was stunned when he heard the last part. "Interesting." He terminated the call and looked at his brother-in-law, sitting across from him and leaning forward like an expectant pooch.

"Are you going to give it to me or make me wait?" Big Willie asked. He sounded irritated, but knew enough not to be downright petulant.

"Is everything still on track for that fundraising dinner tonight at the country club?"

"I think so. Why?"

Viceroy wanted to get a read on Big Willie's face when he heard the latest news. "That was Baker. I asked him to do a behind-the-scenes check on the MPDC detective assigned to Fassel's case. His name is Kevin McClain. Fourteen years, the last five in investigations."

"Can he be managed?"

"I'm sure of it. But there are a couple of interesting wrinkles."

"What?" The expectant pooch look was back.

"I was planning on wearing my dress uniform to the fundraiser tonight. You are going, aren't you?"

"Of course. What about this detective who is so interesting?"

"Congressman Robert E. Vernon be there too?"

"Probably. Why? Is he significant?"

"I'd like you to introduce me," Viceroy said. "Detective McClain is his ex-son-in-law."

Big Willie's gaping mouth tightened, forming an O shape. "This is going to complicate things. I don't like it."

"Relax. Everything's under control."

"With this Vernon connection he could get way too close."

"I met McClain this morning. Seems like a nice guy. Unassuming. Drives an old Fiesta."

Big Willie looked at his watch and cleared his throat. "Roger should be getting back any time now. You mentioned a *couple* of interesting wrinkles. What's the other one?"

"It turns out McClain and I have met before. During a black ops mission in Somalia."

"He knows you? Shit, that could be bad."

"Which is why I've already set my contingency plan into motion." Viceroy resisted the urge to open his humidor and take out one of his remaining Havanas. That would be bordering on excess. Plus, it was too premature. Postponement of gratification was in order. He'd look forward to a Havana once the mission was completed. "I don't think he recognized me."

"Okay, so what's our contingency plan?"

Viceroy tapped the top of the humidor. "There might be another traffic accident on the horizon tonight. Lot of those lately."

Big Willie smiled, but it was a nervous smile.

★　★　★　★　★

It took McClain a good ten minutes to get Lynn to tell him the whole story. Jen was supposed to have gone to school for a pre-orientation session, but never showed up. That had been two hours ago.

"Didn't you drop her off?"

"Of course I did," Lynn spat back. "You think I'm an idiot?"

He knew better than to answer that. He was a block away from the station house now and needed to get things rolling.

"Okay, listen—"

"You listen. Our daughter's missing!"

He took a breath. "Lynn, please, I know you're worried and upset. So am I. I'm pulling into work now. What I need you to do is try her cell again. And her friends. I'll see if I can pull some strings and get a location on her cell phone."

"You'd better find her, Kevin. You'd better find her."

McClain took the first space on the street he could find and slipped the parking ticket back under the windshield wiper as he rushed up the steps contemplating his next moves: Call the cell phone company to see if they could triangulate the signal; call the Fairfax County Police and tell them to go to Lynn's father's place to take the report; call in an Amber alert if—

From the other side of the glass he saw a young girl sitting there looking out. The girl waved. She had brown hair, the same as Jen's. McClain raced up the last few steps and went through the doors and felt a rush of relief.

"Hi, Daddy." His daughter's brow furrowed. "What happened to your face?"

He didn't speak, just ran forward and embraced her, squeezing her tight.

"Daddy, please," she said.

He realized his sudden show of emotion was embarrassing her. He released her and held her at arms' length. "Where have you been? Your mother and I have been so worried about you."

"Oh shit, she called you?"

Shit? Where did that come from?

He dropped his hands from her shoulders. The station officer in the circular desk was watching them with a smirk. He flashed his badge and pulled Jen toward the elevators. "Come on. Let's go upstairs."

As they waited by the elevators he studied her. She was fourteen—almost fifteen now—and she had Lynn's looks. She was going to be a knockout, although he still saw her as the little girl he'd bounced on his knee through her terrible twos.

The doors opened and he pressed the button for the second floor. As the doors closed he asked, "You have your cell phone with you?"

"Yeah."

"Why didn't you answer it? Mom said she's been calling you."

"I had it turned off."

"Great. When we get upstairs you can turn it back on and use it to call your mother."

"Me call Lynn? No way I'm calling that bitch."

McClain felt like stopping the elevator and taking her over his knee. But she was too old for that. He'd never been able to raise his hand against her, even when she'd misbehaved. Failure to discipline their child was one of the reasons Lynn had cited for being the custodial parent. But she was crying for discipline now. At least that's what he thought. He raised his index finger and lowered his voice.

"First of all," he said, "it's *Mom*, not *Lynn*. And second, I won't have you using that kind of language, especially about your mother."

She made a *tsk* sound and rolled her eyes. "Whatever."

"There's no whatever about it." He kept his voice firm. The

doors opened revealing the squad room beyond the narrow hall. McClain pointed to the left. They walked to the break room, which had a trio of vending machines.

He reached into his pocket and took out a couple bills. "You want pop?"

"Soda, Daddy. Soda. Saying pop is so uncool."

McClain smiled as he slipped the bills into the machine and pressed the button. "I'm from Chicago. Some habits die hard." The can fell into the slot.

As McClain plucked it out, a dark hand knocked on the wall and Kelly's smiling face appeared.

"Heard you were here." He settled on Jen and the smile broadened. "Well, Miss McClain. How's my best little girl doing?"

Jen smiled back. She liked Kelly. He'd been spoiling her with candies and compliments since she was small.

"She's doing real good," McClain said. "Ditching school and worrying her mom half to death."

Jen's head whirled toward him. "She doesn't worry about me. All she thinks about is that asshole, Rex."

Asshole? Well, at least they agreed on something.

"What did I say about your language?" McClain looked toward Kelly. "I'm going to have to take off for a while, okay? Cover for me with the boss."

"Okay," Kelly said, and disappeared.

After staring at his daughter for what he hoped would be an uncomfortable amount of time, McClain said, "What's the problem between you and Mom?"

"She doesn't care about me. All she does is moon about that ass—that jerk, Rex." Jen's face reddened. "She wants to ditch me so they can go to some nude beach at some Club Med place next month."

McClain was taken aback. He searched for something to say,

but all he could do was hand her the soda. She stared at it, then glanced away quickly, looking on the verge of tears. "I don't want to stay with her and Grandma and Grandpa anymore. I want to come live with you."

McClain felt like he'd been hit with a gut punch. *Could this have come at a worse time?* He'd been wrong. The feds' dismissal and the parking ticket hadn't been the cherry after all. This was. A solitary tear wound its way down his daughter's cheek, then another, followed by a steady stream. He took a deep breath.

"Honey, I think you know that's not an option right now," he said. "But we're going to talk about it. After we call Mom and tell her you're all right."

She looked up at him, her cheeks still wet with tears, as he opened his cell phone.

West laid his prayer rug down and knelt, facing to the East. The micro camera transmitter was once again on his shirt, disguised as a button, and he wondered about the image resolution as he bowed, placed his forehead on the floor, and murmured his devotion. It was *Asr*—afternoon prayers.

It's surprising these assholes find the time to be terrorists, he thought, *doing their prayers five times a day.* He kept his expression devout as he listened to the voices droning in Arabic.

After prayers were over, West folded his rug. Hassan Ibriham, the leader of the student radicals, stood next to him. The man looked like a typical towelhead: bearded and devout. The liberal politicians were so worried about profiling, but who needed it? These fuckers wore blinking signs around their necks identifying themselves as radicals. And he'd killed enough of them in Iraq and Afghanistan to know where to look.

West murmured a greeting in Arabic. Those government language classes had done a good job. Even erased the vestiges of his Ebonics. He mentally chuckled at the thought, knowing he could still "rap black" with the best of them. But the students thought he was Somali. Ibriham said something in Arabic too, then motioned for West to follow him. They walked into a small, private conference room. Once inside, Ibriham closed the door and turned to West.

"*As-Salam Alaykum,* my brother," he said.

"*Wa-alaikum assalam,*" West said, returning the greeting. His voice became a husky whisper. "We had a minor complication."

Ibriham's face grew taut. "Complication? What?"

West placed a hand on the other man's shoulder. "We had to take care of a traitor."

"A traitor?"

West kept his voice calm as he answered. "The man had been turned by the infidels. When he was imprisoned in Guantanamo."

Ibriham's eyes widened. "Not Mohammed Amir? I can't believe it."

West said nothing, keeping his expression totally neutral, thinking, *I should have been an actor instead of a soldier.*

Ibriham's voice raised a few octaves. "Please, tell me it is not true."

"The great Satan is a powerful enemy." West squeezed Ibriham's shoulder. "He works his corrupting ways into many men. But remember, we have the strength of Allah with us."

Ibriham looked down. "The plan . . . is it?"

"Do not worry, my brother. As I said, Allah is with us."

"But Mohammed Amir—"

"He is gone. He is dust," West said. "He is nothing, floating for all eternity in the sea of purgatory."

Ibriham's eyes were still downcast.

"We must not speak of the traitor again." West remembered the man's death squirm under the unceasing flow of the water. *No seventy-two virgins for that son-of-a-bitch.*

155

"Do we still have the weapon?"

"We do."

"Tell me what we must do next."

West made a show of glancing around the small room, even though they were alone. "Tomorrow is Friday. Meet me here for *Jumu'ah*. Bring the others. I will tell you then. Allah's will be done."

"Allah's will be done," Ibriham repeated.

Just like clockwork, West thought. *Everything was coming together according to plan.*

"Regina, it's me," Lane said into his cell phone. "How's tricks?" It was their code for asking if she could talk. She said tricks were fine. "Good," he said. "We need to meet."

"You lucked out today. He's gone for the entire afternoon."

This piqued Lane's interest. "Where?"

She giggled. "Watching some MMA fights or something. With his brother-in-law, the would-be general."

Lane knew Regina hated her boss's brother-in-law, Colonel Clay Viceroy, with a passion. She blamed the colonel for Bernard's failure to divorce his wife and marry her, back when she'd been a young, impressionable intern serving under him. Hell hath no fury, he thought. "The usual in, say, fifteen minutes?"

"Sounds good. Hey, guess what?" She flirted with the silence until he asked. "I've got something neat for you. About that homeless guy who burned up."

"Oh?" Lane searched his memory, trying to figure why she would have info on that.

"Yeah. Tell you later. See ya."

Lane had a hundred questions he wanted answered, but right now, despite her promise of "something," most of his concerns centered on the death of Paul Ross. He had to see if she knew anything about the accident—an off-hand comment by Bernard, fragments of an overheard conversation, anything that would tie the former vice president to wanting the would-be whistle-blower out of the picture. It would be pure dynamite. Or maybe more like nitroglycerin. Regardless, it was too convenient that Ross had an "accident" the same night as his arrival back from Guantanamo with the report on his investigations into the torture policies of the previous administration. This whole series of events was way too pat.

Like a big, fat *piñata* waiting for him to bust it open.

Viceroy watched Lee circling his opponent, toying with him. Even with all the extra duties he'd pulled these past few days, he still looked as deadly as a stalking tiger. That was Lee's ring name: Stalking Tiger. He wore the gold and red colors of his defeated homeland on his trunks—the flag of the Republic of South Vietnam.

Below, two men circled each other in the center of the cage. The opponent threw a double jab, but Lee's head bobbled out of the way each time. The opponent threw an overhand right, which Lee blocked and countered with a left to the man's gut. The opponent backed up, obviously hurt. Lee followed and threw a hard jab. It snapped the opponent's head back. Viceroy knew Lee had knockout power in either hand and the flexibility of a Chinese martial arts movie star. As if he'd read Viceroy's thoughts, Lee pivoted and threw one of his high roundhouse kicks that caught the opponent on the side of the head. The man dropped like he'd been pole-axed. Lee didn't bother to do a follow-up blow. Instead, he walked to the door of the cage and paused to give Viceroy a thumbs-up. The ref and the seconds were attending to the fallen opponent, who was out cold.

Lee flipped out his mouthpiece. "Get me another one in here. I ain't got all day."

Viceroy grinned. There was no quit in his boy. None. He turned to Big Willie. "Did you ever see anybody like him?"

"He's like a movie superhero. Unbelievable."

Ram Jet tugged on Big Willie's sleeve. "Maybe we could get a few of those shots while he's waiting for his next one."

Big Willie took a deep breath and leaned toward Viceroy. "You mind? They want to get a few shots of me punching the bag. Figure it'll be good press for my two-fisted image."

Viceroy nodded. It would look good. A two-fisted fighter. After Operation Prometheus was complete, it would all come together, like the feathers on a duck's ass. But timing was everything. He had to get this op done at just the right moment. He waited until Big Willie, Ram Jet, and the photographers had gone before he took out his cell.

Baker answered.

"Sit-rep?" Viceroy asked.

"Still on surveillance, sir. Subject one was traced to a parking garage near Capitol Hill at fifteen-oh-three. We were unable to follow him inside. We then pulled back and picked him up leaving the facility at fifteen-forty hours, at which time he went back to the newsroom."

Lane must have been meeting his source, Viceroy thought. "See about locating surveillance videos in the area. I'd like to know who he was meeting."

"Yes, sir."

"What about Number Three?"

"He spent the majority of his time this morning at his office. At eleven-thirty he left the building with a female and went to lunch. After two-and-a-half hours they departed and left in his vehicle, heading south on the freeway. We're following in tandem, heading into Fairfax at the moment."

"He still have the female with him?"

"Affirmative. A teenager. Looks to be around fifteen or sixteen."

That would probably be McClain's daughter, Jennifer. And from the sound of it, he was planning to drop the girl off at his in-laws' house. Congressman Vernon's southern mansion. "All right. Maintain discreet surveillance on both and wait for further instructions."

"Roger that, sir."

Viceroy terminated the call. Finding out Lane's source was his first priority. He had to plug that leak, or least control it. How troublesome this McClain character was going to be remained to be seen. He had to keep a lid on this Fassel thing until the op was completed. He looked over and saw Big Willie without his jacket, his sleeves rolled up while one of the trainers fitted some bag gloves onto his outstretched hands.

Good photo op, Viceroy thought, before turning back to the cage to watch Lee going after a fresh opponent.

CHAPTER 13

When McClain got back to work after dropping his daughter off, Kelly greeted him in the hallway and told him it was quitting time.

"For you, maybe. I've got to make up for taking care of my personal business."

"Not to worry. Your trusted partner did his customarily outstanding job of covering for you." Kelly grinned. "I told Beasley you were meeting with the feds."

"Great. Now he'll expect some results. The feds wouldn't give me the time of day. Told me to coordinate everything through the OHSCT."

"Nobody'll be the wiser. We're still riding high from our Rewaldo arrest, and your face looks like it got run over by a truck. Why don't you take the rest of the day off?"

"I wish I could. Got to at least touch base with the task force, first. We've lost so much momentum on this case already."

Kelly put a hand on McClain's shoulder and leaned close. "Take it from me, laddie," he said in his best Bing Crosby/Father O'Malley imitation. "This one's heading for the cold case boys."

Cold Case was the euphemism the department used for closing a case that was dubbed unsolvable. Technically, an open homicide case would always remain active, but if all existing leads were investigated and exhausted without success, the file was placed in an inactive status.

"I can't even do that," McClain said. "I have to show I did some investigating."

Kelly wished him luck and pressed the button for the elevator. "I've got to take a young lady out for a drink."

"If it's the same one who ratted out Rewaldo, tell her I said thanks."

"That's one case we can proudly mark closed," Kelly said as he stepped into the elevator.

McClain looked up the OHSCT Bureau phone number in his Rolodex. He still maintained the numbers on this file instead of relying, like everyone else did, on the computer. He punched in the numbers and found the guy he was looking for: Steve Dylan, a copper who'd worked a few cases with him and Kelly in dicks before going to the task force. McClain gave him the lowdown on what he needed.

"Mohammed Amir Fassel, huh?" Dylan said. "I'll see what I can find out and call you back."

McClain busied himself with paperwork. He still hadn't completed the use of force report on his arrest of Rewaldo. After laboring for close to twenty minutes, and not hearing anything back from Dylan, he rubbed his hand over his face and immediately regretted it. The stinging pain made him more irritable as he picked up the phone and punched in Dylan's number.

"Nothing for you, buddy," Dylan said. "All I got is what we already knew. He was in Gitmo five years. Released back to Saudi Arabia two years ago by the Harris administration, and apparently entered this country on a fake passport. Nobody even knew he was here until he turned up dead."

"There's got to be more to it than that," McClain said. "Why the hell are they stonewalling us if that's all there is?"

"You know how the feds are. They won't say shit, even if

161

they've got a mouthful. Especially when it comes to *classified stuff.*"

"That's bullshit! I thought we were all supposed to be working together?"

"Yeah, but it's more like a one-way street. I'm working in the unit and they don't tell me shit. We give them everything and they trickle back info on a need-to-know basis. It's how the feds operate. I'll keep digging though."

"Thanks, Steve, and keep me posted if you get anything else. I need to make a token effort at investigating this thing."

Dylan told McClain he'd e-mail Fassel's file.

McClain began to wonder what the real story was. He needed an entry into the federal structure and thought about Felicia Knight. She looked like a professional and might be more forthcoming than her asshole boss, in an off-the-record sort of way. Perhaps he could ask her out for a cup of coffee. Maybe even lunch. McClain yawned, suddenly feeling fatigued, and glanced at his watch. It was almost seven-fifty and he was super-tired. With a little creative adjustment to his time sheet, he could probably leave inside of an hour and no one would be any the wiser. He started to formulate exactly what he was going to say to Special Agent Knight when he called.

At all costs, he thought, *I have to avoid sounding like an idiot.*

The insistent vibration of her cell phone woke Felicia up. It stopped as she reached for it. The only light came from the flickering of the television screen. She glanced at her clock. Damn, it was early evening. Seven-fifty-one. And she was still in the same clothes and on her sofa. The TV continued to flicker in eerie silence from across the room. She'd been so tired when she got home after meeting with Joiner and the others that she'd sat down to relax and turned on the TV. She remembered hitting the mute button to make a quick call to her sister and stretching out to talk. She'd put the phone on a TV tray next to her and reached for the remote and closed her eyes for a second. And that was the last thing she remembered. Unbelievably, she'd slept for almost eight hours. To top it off, she still felt groggy.

Her thoughts drifted back to the morning's meeting. Joiner— what an idiot. So condescending, so duplicitous. Worse, she'd gone along with him, keeping that poor MPDC detective in the dark.

She decided to check her messages. With reluctance she dialed her voice mail number.

"Knight, it's SAIC Joiner. I assume you're sleeping, but I want you to be aware that we have to tread very carefully on the matter at hand. The subject we discussed this morning is classified and a Bureau matter. Under no circumstances are you to divulge any of the pertinent information about the case. Is that clear?"

Felicia smiled. Always using his Special Agent In Charge title, even to a machine. The jerk was actually giving orders to her voice mail.

She listened to the next message, again from Joiner, approximately two hours after the first. "Knight, this is SAIC Joiner. I'm assuming you've had time to review your messages regarding my instructions. Make sure you call me and confirm that you've been so instructed."

The man had all the personality of a toad. No, that was too unkind to toads. Joiner was more of a human version of a viral wart—always causing an itch you couldn't scratch.

She listened to the next message sent two hours after the second.

"Knight, this is SAIC Joiner. I'm assuming you've had a chance to get some rest. The two other members of your team have arrived back safely and they've been briefed. Call me ASAP and confirm your receipt of instructions."

Yeah, right away, sir. No mention that the two idiots, Bert and Ernie, had been tardy. She expected as much. On to the next one, sent at six-forty.

"Knight, this is SAIC Joiner." This time his voice had an animated urgency to it. "I'm assuming you've been holding off contacting me due to this mess-up. I don't know who's responsible for this leak, but I assure you the matter *will* be investigated thoroughly. Call me ASAP. That's an order."

Leak? What the hell was he talking about? A leak to whom? The news? Felicia picked up the remote and switched to ZCCN News.

She kept the mute on and listened to the last message, sent a few minutes ago. It must have been the call that woke her up. Joiner again, but this time he'd left his long-windedness behind.

"Knight, call me as soon as you get this." His voice sounded strained. She was about to dial him when the scene showed a backdrop of the FBI seal. She turned up the volume. The seal was replaced by a picture of Mohammed Fassel. An old picture, probably from his internment at Guantanamo.

"The identity of a recent murder victim has been tentatively identified as Mohammed Amir Fassel," the news anchor said. "Fassel's body was found two nights ago in an alley. He received media attention two years ago when he was one of twenty prisoners President Harris ordered released from custody in Guantanamo. Fassel was repatriated to his native Saudi Arabia, and not thought to be in that country. Although police sources have not officially commented, our ZCCN News crew was able to confirm Fassel's identity through confidential sources within the government."

Shit! No wonder Joiner's pissed off. She dialed his number and he answered on the third ring with an angry, "Knight, where the hell have you been? I've been trying to reach you."

Felicia took a deep breath. "I've been asleep."

"Asleep?"

"Yes, sir. I was up for over twenty-four hours straight and totally exhausted."

She heard Joiner snort. "There's been a development. Somebody leaked Fassel's name to the news."

"I know. I just caught it on ZCCN."

"This is turning into an unmitigated disaster."

She was amused by his choice of words, but figured the best tactic was to say nothing.

"And to top it off, Attorney General Thomas wants the Bureau to look into the Paul Ross accident."

"Ross? The Undersecretary? What happened?"

"He was killed last night," Joiner said. "I've got Beau and Jay talking to the Virginia troopers and trying to get a hold of his laptop."

"Oh, my God!"

"Knight, are you saying you don't know anything about these things?"

"No, sir. I told you, I've been asleep all afternoon."

Silence. She could hear his breathing. Finally, he said, "Well, regarding this Fassel thing, we've got a leak somewhere. It must have been that damn MPDC cop. But why would he go to the press?"

"We didn't exactly roll out the red carpet for him this morning."

"You think he did it out of spite? We've got a situation involving national security here, and he's being spiteful? What kind of law enforcement officer is he? Going to the damn press, and ZCCN News to top it off. How the hell did they get that information?"

"I don't know, sir."

"Find out, dammit! It had to be that asshole cop, McClain.

Find him tomorrow and see if he leaked it. Find out how much he knows. Christ, if this operation gets blown because of some oversight on our part—"

"We don't know for certain he did, sir."

"No, but we're going to find out. Knight, this is what I want you to do." Joiner now sounded like he'd chugged too many Red Bulls. "Give him some tidbits, and find out what he knows. We're on damage control now. We've got to keep a lid on this thing until we recover that missing gas and take down these student radicals. Is that clear?"

Felicia felt weariness creeping over her. Blamed for every mistake, whether it was her fault or not, and given no credit.

"Is that clear, Knight?"

"I'll do my best, sir," Felicia said and hung up. Apparently, she was going to see Mr. McClain sooner rather than later.

The waiters were clearing the tables and the band had been playing a series of soft waltzes. Big Willie led his wife, Marsha, back from the dance floor as the circle of onlookers applauded. Viceroy used a folded cloth napkin to brush a sprinkle of dust off the sleeve of his dress uniform. He automatically checked to make sure his medals, starting with the blue and silver combat infantry badge, the silver jump-master wings, and the five subsequent rows of fruit salad, were securely in place.

Big Willie and Marsha looked like a presidential couple. Like her husband, his sister Marsha had a propensity toward drinking too much, but as far as he could tell, Ram Jet had assigned someone to monitor their booze intake and probably waterdown the drinks. He'd let him worry about keeping Big Willie and the future First Lady on track. Right now, it was time to do some reconnoitering on the situation and make a decision. He saw Congressman Vernon heading toward the wet bar they'd set up in the far corner. He stepped over to Big Willie and his sister and mentioned how wonderful they'd looked dancing together.

Viceroy leaned close to Big Willie. "Introduce me to Congressman Vernon."

"Sure, I can do that. Gimme a minute."

His words were slurred and Viceroy realized his brother-in-law was a bit tanked. He clasped Big Willie by the arm, just above the elbow, and exerted enough pressure to make him follow as he moved toward the wet bar. "Introduce me now!"

"Shit, Clay," Big Willie whispered. "I gotta take a piss bad. Why do you think I quit dancing?"

"Introduce me first, then excuse yourself."

Big Willie managed to intercept Vernon, who was walking back toward the tables with a drink in each hand.

"Will, if I'd known you were going to quit the dance floor, I'd have bought a drink for the next president of the United States," Vernon said.

Big Willie grinned, but there was enough jerking at the corner of his mouth to let Viceroy know the man was probably on the verge of pissing his pants.

"Thanks, Bob," Big Willie said. "Say, let me introduce you to my brother-in-law, Colonel, soon to be General, Clayton Viceroy." Willie put a hand on each of their shoulders. "I'll leave you two to get acquainted while I go get rid of some of that after-dinner wine."

Vernon said, "Colonel, it will be my distinct pleasure to shake your hand as soon as I deliver two drinks to the ladies at my table."

They arrived at Vernon's table, where he introduced Viceroy to his wife, a pretty, middle-aged woman who looked like she'd had cosmetic work done.

Vernon's daughter, Lynn Ann McClain, was pretty too, a thirty-something blonde. She stood next to a blow-dried gigolo-type whom Vernon introduced as Rex, his daughter's fiancé.

But it was the daughter's last name that interested Viceroy. "Mrs. McClain," he said, shaking her hand.

"She's divorced," the congressman said, "so I've been trying to get her to change her name back to Vernon."

Lynn McClain shushed her father with an, "Oh, daddy," and Viceroy saw a crimson blush tincture her bare neck and shoulders. She was showing enough cleavage to pique the interest of the males in the room.

A sudden flash stung Viceroy's eyes. One of Ram Jet's ubiquitous photographers was snapping pictures.

"Let me see how that picture came out," Lynn McClain said.

"Sure. I'll e-mail it to you," the photographer said. "Can I get another one of the three of you over here with Vice President Bernard?"

"In a minute," Vernon said, his voice low and well lubricated with alcohol. "We were on our way to the bar."

Good, Viceroy thought. It would be easier getting information from a drunk, and he probably wouldn't even remember the conversation in the morning.

"Your daughter's very lovely," Viceroy said as they walked toward the bar. "You said McClain's her married name?"

"Yeah. Used to be married to a cop."

"A cop?"

"Yeah. He's still on the force. They met back in college in Chicago. Got married, had my granddaughter, then split up."

"What kind of man was he?"

"Decent sort. I liked him, was sorry when they split up. As much as it pains me to say it, I think it was mostly my daughter's fault. She wasn't ready for the responsibility."

"Oh?"

"I know how that sounds, bad-mouthing my own little girl, but my ex-son-in-law was a good guy. Had something rare these days. Integrity. And a stick-to-itiveness that made him a first-rate investigator. The tenacity of a bulldog."

Viceroy had the twenty-dollar bill ready and slapped it down on the bar. "Give the Congressman whatever he's drinking."

The bartender started mixing a whiskey sour. "And for you, sir?"

Viceroy contemplated the situation. "I'll have the same," he said, then added, "but let me step out first."

Congressman Vernon winked.

As Viceroy moved through the crowd, he fished his cell phone out of his pocket. *Integrity . . . A first-rate investigator . . . The tenacity of a bulldog. That was quite an assessment from an ex-father-in-law. Perhaps some preventative measures were warranted sooner rather than later. A good leader is always prepared for every contingency, no matter how seemingly insignificant—Sun Tzu.* As he approached the door to the men's room, he saw Ram Jet leaving in a huff, followed by a dejected-looking Big Willie.

"I got word that I'm twelve points down in the polls going into the debates," Big Willie said. "Roger tried to buoy me up but, Christ, Clay, it's insurmountable. The pollsters are saying after that news conference today, public opinion is sixty-seven percent against the torture issue. That damn Ross did me in without even filing his fucking report."

Viceroy glanced around. No one was within earshot, but several people were at the end of the hall. Too many prying eyes to give his brother-in-law the sobering slap he needed. Instead, Viceroy reached out and gripped Big Willie's hand in both of his own, like a double-clasped handshake, but he bent Big Willie's thumb back in a joint lock, putting the other man on his toes.

Big Willie grunted. "Christ, that hurts. Let go."

Viceroy maintained the pressure for a moment more before easing off. "Get control of yourself, dammit!" He kept his voice low. "And don't worry. All you have to do is appear decisive and strong. Once our plan is set into motion, Harris will be exposed for the weak sister he is."

"But the polls—"

"Fuck the polls." He waited for the other man to regain his composure. "Now get back in there and start playing the part of the next president of the United States. And no more fucking booze tonight. You're starting to look like a drunk." Viceroy took out his cell phone.

"Who are you calling?" Big Willie asked.

"Never mind who I'm calling. I have a loose end I've decided to tie up."

"Clay, are you sure this plan of yours is going to work?"

"Of course." Viceroy stopped dialing and looked at him. "Remember, I am in charge."

CHAPTER 14

"Hello, Special Agent Knight," McClain said into his cell phone as he drove down the dimly lighted lanes of the Beltway. He figured using her full title sounded better. He regretted making the call when he was so tired. Exhausted, really. "This is Detective McClain. We met earlier today." He didn't know what to say next, or how to say it, but he forged on. What the hell, he was leaving a voice mail and nobody sounded good on voice mails. "I was hoping we could meet for a cup of coffee or lunch or something so we could talk. About the Fassel case, I mean. I need some help with this one. If you could please call me back." He left his office and cell numbers.

A light rain began to fall and he switched on the windshield wipers and watched his headlights reflect off the dark, slick roadway. He glanced in the rearview mirror and saw a set of headlights behind him. A truck or big SUV. He stared at the image again. It was an SUV. Perhaps an Escalade. A little closer now. Almost bordering on too close.

Asshole, thought McClain, tailgating in the rain.

His thoughts drifted to his conversation with Jen earlier. She had said, "Mom and Rex are going to some Club Med place with nude beaches." It bothered him a little. Not the part about Lynn and Rex. Divorced, he and Lynn had no claims on each other, so it was really none of his business.

Except, it *was* his business. He had the distinct impression

171

that Sexy Rexy was a bit of a freak, hardly a candidate for stepfather of the year. He didn't like his daughter exposed to Rex.

The Escalade's headlights were closer now.

What's this idiot doing? If he gets any closer he'll have to introduce himself.

The headlights swung out around McClain's Fiesta, almost hitting the bumper. The Escalade's windows were too dark to distinguish the driver. McClain heard a small blast. The wheel shook in his hands accompanied by a rhythmic thumping sound.

A blowout! One of the front tires.

He eased off the gas and scanned the road ahead, looking for a place to pull off. But he was heading into a curve and a white barrier fence was coming up fast on the right. A greenish darkness of high grass and trees loomed beyond it.

He should be able swing left and get on the shoulder, he thought, as he nudged the Fiesta over.

The Escalade, still beside him, jerked right and broadsided his Fiesta with a metallic thump. McClain swore and gripped the wheel, trying to compensate for the unanticipated contact. The Escalade swung right again, this time catching the front of McClain's Fiesta with the right rear quarter panel. The Fiesta shook and shimmied in the rain. McClain hit the brakes.

Got to get away from that barrier!

The Escalade braked too, then nosed into the left rear of the Fiesta, sending it into a quick, out-of-control spin. McClain felt the car whirling, the view through the windshield flashing with sudden changes punctuated by the sweeping motion of the wiper blades. A flash of illumination from his headlights showed a swath of high grass and trees. His Fiesta bottomed out as it smashed down hard on a gravelly hump. More high grass, more trees, the hard scrapes of branches lashing against the sides and windows of his car. Green darkness. The sound of his car hitting something hard. His airbag exploding toward him. Water sloshing over the hood and windshield. Then, darkness.

Lane poured Allison another glass of wine, then unfastened her bra strap. He figured they could afford to take the rest of the night off. With all he'd done today, he'd earned this diversion.

Allison leaned forward to give him better access. "So, what happened with your source?"

Lane tried to ignore her question as he finally got the damn bra unhooked. He reached around to grab her breasts, but she brought her hands up and held the bra in place.

"What happened?" she asked again.

Did she really think he'd give her more than she was entitled to at this juncture? "What are you talking about?"

"With your source, silly. What did they say?"

They? Her grammar was as bad as her reporting instincts, but if he wanted to get laid tonight he'd have to give her something. "They didn't say much."

"Come on."

Lane chuckled as he pushed her hands away from the front of the bra. "*She* said that Bernard had been worried about Ross's return from Guantanamo, then suddenly he wasn't worried at all."

"Do you think he heard about the accident? Is that why?"

Lane worked his hands over her breasts. "Big Willie seemed in a good mood when he came in this morning. Before the news of the accident broke. Remember when I stopped at the scene? It was early, not even nine o'clock. They didn't announce it was Paul Ross's body until the one o'clock news conference." He could feel her nipples hardening.

"Does that mean that Bernard has an inside track with the Virginia Highway Patrol?" she asked. "Or is it something more?"

He squeezed too hard and she slapped his hand. "You're hurting me."

"Sorry."

"You're not saying that Bernard had something to do with the accident, are you?"

Lane started to undo the zipper at the back of her skirt.

"Are you?" she asked.

He could feel her body tense, resisting. "We need to consider all the options, but this Ross matter is hot news for the moment. We cover it, but don't make any insinuations until we have definite proof. My source says Bernard has been planning something else."

"What?"

"She doesn't know yet, but from the sound of it, it's big." His fingers managed to tug down the zipper halfway. "Now, are we going to have some fun or what?"

She grabbed his hand and pulled the zipper the rest of the way down. "Sounds like a plan, so long as you don't leave me out of the loop."

Fat chance of that, he thought. *You're my meal ticket.* "Not to worry."

Her lips pushed into a mock pout. "Sometimes you do leave me out of things. Like with your sources."

"A reporter's sources must always be guarded and kept secret," he said. "Journalism one-oh-one." He tugged at her skirt.

She twisted her body to allow him to pull the skirt off her hips and down over her legs. "All right, but like I said, I need to be kept up on things more."

"Sure, honey, sure," he said.

Everything would work out, as long as he was the rider and she was the horse.

★ ★ ★ ★ ★

Viceroy watched his brother-in-law working the crowd as the dinner wound down and people headed out the door. He looked the part again—confident, strong, and presidential. The pep talk had apparently worked. Still, Viceroy knew he needed to keep all the balls in the air rotating smoothly. He didn't like the juggler's metaphor anymore. Back in the day, when he'd been in the field, taking an active part in the operation, yeah, then he was a juggler. But now he was directing things, still focused and in control, more like a guy keeping a table full of plates spinning on those special sticks. He'd seen a magician do that in Vegas. The guy had done a good job up until the time some idiot from the audience yelled and broke his concentration. His foot hit the table and the plates all came crashing down. He tried to fake it like it was all part of the act, but Viceroy knew the guy had committed an amateur's mistake. He'd lost his focus, failed to adapt to unexpected adversity.

Viceroy felt the vibration of his special cell—his op's phone.

"Sit-rep," he said.

"Subject one followed to his apartment where he had Red Sonja over," Lee said.

Red Sonja was their code name for the strawberry blonde, Allison Hayes. He knew Lane was fucking her, which was why he'd had both of their apartments bugged.

"They talked about the source," Lee said. "From their conversation it's clear she doesn't know who it is."

So Lane was running the show. Viceroy had figured as much. "Anything else of significance?"

"He's suspicious of last night's action. Nothing concrete."

Viceroy rubbed his temples with his thumb and forefingers. "Keep on them. Anything on Number Three?"

"Inconclusive. Baker and Lindsey reported a successful maneuver, but were unable to verify total success due to an unforeseen occurrence."

An unforeseen occurrence? What the hell had that been? He didn't want to ask on the phone, even though they were using a scrambler. But more importantly, Kevin McClain had the automobile accident as planned. Viceroy glanced over and saw Big Willie laughing and slapping the shoulder of Congressman Vernon. Would he have been notified if McClain had survived? Or if he hadn't?

"Let's wrap it up," Viceroy said. "We'll convene at zero-nine-hundred hours tomorrow at the command post."

"Roger that, sir."

As Viceroy folded his phone shut and slipped it back into his inside jacket pocket, he thought about McClain. Viceroy had felt kind of bad, ordering a former ranger taken out, but it was collateral damage. McClain had the potential to stir up too much silt from the bottom of the pond.

Ironic that I once saved his ass, only to order him terminated some nineteen years later. There was still a chance that McClain had survived tonight's mishap, although it seemed doubtful. But even if he had, Viceroy would put the brakes on any MPDC nosing into the Fassel murder until Operation Prometheus was completed. He had to accelerate the time frame. Wait until right after the debate. Tell his brother-in-law to come on strong on the terrorism and foreign-policy issues. Harris was almost certain to bring up the torture issue, even though his lapdog, Ross, and his incriminating Gitmo report were no longer factors. All Big Willie had to do was hit back, making Harris look soft on the war on terror. Then after Prometheus, Big Willie would look like a soothsayer and the public would rise to embrace the man who had been warning them all along. Harris would get the blame.

It would all go down like clockwork. When the dust settled, Joiner could "solve" the murder of Fassel by blaming it on the student radical terror cell, and none of them would be around to refute it.

McClain had no idea how long he'd lain on the gurney in the emergency room, but it seemed like hours. They'd given him something so he wasn't thinking straight. Or was that a by-product of the accident? He searched his memory. The damn Escalade had been dark blue. Or black. But it had been so dark, he wasn't even sure of that. Only that the driver had sideswiped him and caused him to lose control and veer off the road, smashing through a guard rail and ending up in a flooded marsh. As cold water engulfed him, he unfastened the seat belt and crawled out of the car, only to sink in the murky wetness up to his neck. He then managed to half swim, half crawl through the liquid blackness to the muddy expanse of high reeds and putrid-smelling grass. If a trooper hadn't arrived on the scene and shined his flashlight toward the wreck, McClain would never have been able to crawl out of the swamp. That bright pinpoint of light had saved him.

He'd cheated death once again, although this time had been a snap compared to Mogadishu.

He heard a familiar voice in the hallway. He tried to raise his head, but couldn't because of the red Styrofoam headset and neck brace that held him to the backboard.

"Kelly, in here," he said as loud as he could manage. The familiar black face pushed around the long, ceiling-to-floor curtain with a look of concern.

"Just a minute, laddie, I'm talkin' to the doc." The curtain slipped back into place.

"Drop the Father Flanagan routine and get your black-Irish ass in here," McClain said.

Kelly didn't acknowledge. Instead, McClain could hear voices talking in subdued tones, which infuriated him. As the patient, didn't he have the right to know what the hell was going on? He summoned his strength and bellowed for Kelly at the top of his voice.

Kelly's hand came around the edge of the curtain with a raised index finger. McClain said, "What the hell are you doing out there?"

"Conferring with your doctor."

"Tell him I need to get out of this damn harness and go to the bathroom."

Kelly's smiling face appeared. "In that case, I'll see if I can find a pretty nurse to put in a catheter."

"Fuck you."

Kelly raised an eyebrow. "Sounds like you ain't hurt as bad as you're letting on. I'll have to make that a male nurse now."

McClain snorted a laugh. Good old Kelly, always there looking out for him.

Chapter 15

When he woke up early the next morning, Viceroy felt a tightening in his gut. He flipped on the news and a scroll at the bottom of the screen told him what he wanted: *Off-duty MPDC Police officer hurt in I-495 traffic accident.* Damn! Hurt, but not dead. Still, McClain would no doubt be out of action for the short term. The heat would be off on the Fassel case, and Viceroy could proceed with accelerating his plan unimpeded.

The tightening in his gut increased a notch. He always got it during an operation when things started to go off kilter. But when did an op ever run smoothly? He could only think of a handful, and those weren't among his most pleasant memories. It was more satisfying to be tested before the win. To earn it. Those battles were the ones you remembered. The ones that meant something. It gave the victory more meaning.

It was time to make sure Roger Ram Jet had Big Willie primed and loaded so he could kick Harris's ass during the debate. Perhaps kicking his ass was a bit optimistic. How about holding his own? The charisma and smooth delivery of the Harvard-educated President Harris would be hard to overcome. But the beautiful thing about the plan was that Big Willie didn't have to win. He simply needed to come off sounding "tough on terror." So what if Harris won this first round? The successful op would decide things.

Viceroy made a mental note to contact Lee and West and make sure they were ready to accelerate the timetable.

Originally, he'd set it up for October, another month away, but the recent events—Fassel's identity being discovered more quickly than they'd anticipated, the torture issue hitting prime time, and now the mid-September polls showing Big Willie trailing by ten—all added up to one thing: moving up the operation.

Too bad so many people would have to die, but Viceroy returned to the Jefferson quote about the tree of liberty having to be occasionally watered with the blood of patriots.

Even unknowing patriots.

McClain limped down the steps of the bus and felt the pain shoot through his whole body. He'd felt sore before yesterday's accident. Now he felt twice as bad. He was out of sick days; too many taken for his daughter's medical issues. Today he needed one for himself, but couldn't afford to be docked paywise. And he had too much to do.

When am I going to catch a break? He saw the ZCCN News van parked by the curb in front of the station house.

Maybe it was for somebody else's case. Fassel had been a prisoner at Gitmo, but that wasn't common knowledge. The feds would keep a lid on it.

McClain couldn't quite put his finger on something else that was bothering him. Something from his past knocked on the other side of an opaque door and wanted to point something out to him. But the door wouldn't open.

He concentrated on making it up the steps. He should have accepted Kelly's offer to pick him up. He'd taken the Metro Line and then the bus to work to prove he could manage by himself. He'd arrived late for work, but they were lucky he'd made it in at all.

He'd caught a partial plate on the Escalade last night and wanted to check into that inquiry alert. He was sure there'd be right-side damage and blue paint transfer from his now-departed Fiesta. Since the Fassel homicide had obviously being shoved to the back burner, McClain figured he'd have time to look into the hit-and-run. Had the driver been drunk? He hadn't even stopped after he'd forced McClain off the road.

Felicia glanced at her watch and left her second voice mail for Detective Kevin McClain. The morning session with Joiner had been brief and to the point.

"Get ahold of that damn MPDC detective," he'd said, "and find out about him leaking Fassel's name to the press. It had to be him. We've got to keep a lid on things until we recover that second shipment of gas."

"Yes, sir."

To make matters worse, he'd ordered Bert and Ernie, who were back from their exhausting fourteen-hour-and-twenty-six-minute drive, to attend the update briefing. It was more like an ass-chewing assembly because of the press leak fiasco, but Felicia felt like she was first in the ass-to-get-chewed line. Beaumont and Johnson got less blame because they were driving back from Maine when the information somehow got leaked. Never mind that the two knuckleheads had blown their original surveillance of Fassel the night he was found murdered.

"Knight, are you listening to me?"

"Yes, sir."

Joiner shot malevolent looks toward Beaumont and Johnson. His jowls shook. "All right, here's what I want you all to do. Beau and Jack, you two trace things back. See how the hell the MPDC cops found out the murdered man was Fassel. I also want that report, which is overdue at this point, on how and when, exactly, you lost Fassel on your surveillance. Understood?"

Beaumont and Johnson exchanged a pair of sheepish looks.

Good, Felicia thought. At least he's giving them some shit, too.

"And you, Knight," Joiner said. "Your assignment is to run interference for the Bureau. Make sure you touch base with McClain. Today. As soon as possible. See what he knows, how he found out, and see if you can get him to put the brakes on his investigation. But don't tell him why."

Felicia wondered how she was going to do all that, or even if she should do it. Still, there was an awful lot at stake here. "I've put in a couple of calls to him, boss, but he hasn't returned them."

"Keep after him. Establish contact. Take the idiot to lunch or something." Joiner smacked his fist into his open palm. "And find out if he's the one who's been leaking info to the damn press. We've got to put a stop to that. In fact, I'd better see about reaching out to Allison Hayes. See if I can put a positive spin on the stuff that's been leaked thus far."

"Maybe she'll tell you who her source is," Beaumont offered.

Oh, right, Felicia thought. *Like that's gonna happen in a million years.*

"Maybe," Joiner said with a grin. "I'll have to use my charm on that."

Charm? Felicia suppressed a giggle. *The good old boy inmates are running the asylum, and one of them is my boss.*

As soon as McClain stepped off the elevator, he was met with stares and smirks. Some of the dicks asked him what happened. Others made cracks about his ex-wife beating the shit out of him. He did his best to ignore them all and made for his desk. Riley, who had a desk adjacent to his, leaned over and whispered, "Hey, Kev, the El-Tee's looking for you. And he ain't happy."

What the fuck did Beasley want? McClain thought about

how Kelly advised him to take the day off, even if they would dock him. Was it too late to admit his partner had been right?

Riley shook his head. "Christ, what the hell happened to you?"

"I got the shit slapped out of me by an airbag."

Riley took another moment to access McClain's damaged face. "Man, if I was you, I'd have called off."

"I should have. By any chance, have you seen Kelly?"

Riley grinned. "He beat feet outta here as soon as he saw Beasley was on the warpath. Said he had to go talk to some informants regarding a case."

Smart move. "He say what case?"

"Yeah. It was the *case-of-the-ass* the El-Tee's got." Riley smirked. "Anyway, Lieutenant B's been looking for you all morning. At least you got a good excuse for coming in late."

Beasley had the blinds in his office open, giving him a clear view of almost the entire squad room. But the glass windows worked both ways. McClain could see that Beasley was talking to three other men. One was Vince Peterson, who was with public relations, the other was some dorky-looking guy Mc-Clain didn't recognize, and the third was no guy at all. She was a very attractive redhead. Allison Hayes. No wonder the ZCCN van had been parked in front.

Beasley moved from behind the desk and opened the door.

"Morning, lieu," McClain said.

Beasley glanced at his watch. "Where the hell have you been?"

"Sorry, boss. The bus was late."

"The bus? You took the bus here?"

"Doctor's orders. I was in a car accident last night. No driving for forty-eight hours." He pointed to his bruised face and told Beasley all about the accident, with way more detail than he figured the man wanted to know.

"Never mind that." Beasley motioned for him to step inside the office.

McClain made a show of moving slower than he had too, emphasizing his injuries.

Peterson stood as did the dorky-looking dude with glasses. Ms. Hayes stayed seated, and McClain looked down at her and smiled.

"You're a lot prettier in person than you are on TV," he said.

She flashed him a return smile. "Thank you."

Peterson offered McClain his chair.

"No thanks, if I sit down I might not be able to get up. Car accident."

"You look terrible," Allison Hayes said. "Like you should have called in sick."

"You're the third person who's told me that, but I'm sure Lieutenant Beasley's told you how backed up we are."

"Detective McClain," the dorky guy with the glasses said, "do you have any updates on the murder investigation that occurred near the Jefferson Heights Housing Projects two days ago?"

McClain blinked twice before answering. "I'm sorry, I don't think I got your name."

Before the dude could say anything Peterson said, "Kev, this is Ted Lane. He and Ms. Hayes work for ZCCN."

"Her, I've seen," McClain said. "And no, I don't have any updates other than we're exploring several leads at this time."

"I see." Lane made a show of paging through a notebook. "The victim, Mohammed Fassel, was a prisoner at Guantanamo Bay for three years, correct? And then, under the edict from the Harris administration, he was repatriated to his native Saudi Arabia one and one-half years ago?"

McClain said nothing, taken aback. This guy had more information than Wikipedia.

Peterson cleared his throat. "As you can see, ZCCN has a substantial amount of detail about the case already. What they're looking for now is confirmation and a bit of extra information that might assist in the investigation."

"It's departmental policy not to comment on an ongoing investigation without clearance," McClain said.

"Detective, what we're looking for now is a concise statement as to the status of your investigation," Beasley said, "and anything that the press might do to further things along."

McClain wasn't about to say anything that could come back to bite him in the ass. Instead, he scratched his head. "We're working with the federal authorities right now, exploring all leads and circumstances. That's about all I can say at the moment."

Beasley's face looked relieved. "Okay, that about sizes it up, doesn't it?"

"Not quite," Lane said. "Detective Kevin McClain, is it?"

"Right."

"The same Kevin McClain who was married to Congressman Robert E. Vernon's daughter?"

McClain felt like he'd been slapped. "Yes."

"What's your father-in-law's take on all this?" Lane stared at him through thick lenses. "He's been one of William Bernard's strongest backers. Does he think there's any connection between Fassel's internment at Guantanamo and his subsequent murder?"

"I don't know," McClain said.

"Oh, come on," Lane said. "Give us something here."

"I think we've given you quite enough," Beasley said. "Now if you don't mind, we've extended every courtesy and then some to you. We do have an investigation to run here."

Lane turned back to McClain. "You were in a car accident last night? Where at?"

"On the Beltway."

Lane raised his eyebrows. "Lots of those happening. You heard about the one involving Paul Ross, didn't you?"

"Huh?"

"Paul Ross. The attorney general's bird dog, who was returning from investigating claims of systematic torture of the prisoners at Guantanamo? I'm sure your father-in-law must have mentioned him from time to time. Ross's forthcoming report was supposed to be the potential nail in Bernard's presidential-race coffin."

"My *ex*-father-in-law, pal," McClain said, turning to go. "And if you want his opinions on anything, including his politics, ask *him*."

"Tell us about your accident, Detective," Lane said.

McClain paused at the door and thought about how much he'd enjoy knocking the reporter on his ass. "Not much to tell. Go talk to the Maryland State Police. They're the ones who took the report."

"Was there alcohol involved?"

McClain was about to tell the jerk to go fuck himself when Beasley said he would not tolerate his personnel being badgered and ended with, "This interview is hereby over."

McClain made it to his desk. He watched the unceremonious departure of Hayes and Lane. The gaze of every guy in the squad room was on the strawberry blonde as she walked beside the dork.

Man, what a babe! McClain wished she'd been the one asking the questions. He probably would have been more forthcoming. But now it was time to review his lack of progress and information on this damn homicide and see if he could set up another appointment with the feds. With a little luck, they'd feed him enough to complete his preliminary report, and allow him to shuffle the murder to the lower priority stack—if Lane didn't start broadcasting a bunch of horseshit on ZCCN about it.

CHAPTER 16

Viceroy proceeded to the hangar area inside the military section of Dulles, where they normally held their briefings. It was time to start getting all his ducks in a row. He parked his car and went through the special security checkpoints to the office area of the hangar. West and Lee, both in civvies, were doing some kind of slapping sparring session. From the smiles on their faces he gathered they were just playing. Despite Lee's prowess in the cage, Viceroy wouldn't be quick to write off West in a real match-up. He'd seen the man in action. Seen him take out a lot of opponents. And in the real world, the rule book went in the toilet.

Lee saw him and stopped, coming to attention. West, his thick, muscular body leaned over in a curve, swiveled around and snapped to attention also.

"Stand at ease." Viceroy cocked his head, gesturing toward the table in the middle of the room. There were four chairs. They sat, leaving the fourth chair leaning diagonally against the tabletop.

"I've called this meeting for two reasons." Viceroy held up his index finger. "One, I need a status report from each of you, and two," he held up a second finger, "we're going to have to accelerate the timetable for Operation Prometheus."

Lee and West exchanged glances.

"How soon?" West asked.

Viceroy considered this. The next presidential debate was set for Tuesday evening. That gave them Wednesday for the press to

188

assess and comment on everything. Big Willie was set for an appearance in the Midwest—Chicago or someplace. Enemy territory. It would be good to have him heading back so the waiting reporters would be able to get his carefully rehearsed response upon arrival. He had a few more factors to assess.

"A week." Viceroy watched both men for their reactions. Neither betrayed the slightest surprise or concern. They were two of the best soldiers he'd ever served with. "But there's also the possibility that we may have to move it up even sooner." He looked at Lee first. "Status updates?"

"Baker's maintaining surveillance on Numbers One and Two," Lee said. "They spent the night together and reported to work this morning, after which they went to MPDC PD headquarters. They were in the building for one hour and fifteen minutes, exited, did some taping in front, and then returned to the studio."

"And Number Three?" Viceroy asked. He saw the skin around Lee's eyes tighten.

"He took public transportation downtown to work," Lee said. "He was walking very slow and he was late."

"Did Numbers One and Two interview him?"

Lee shrugged. "Unknown, but we have to assume that they at least talked with him. He did arrive while they were still there."

Viceroy exhaled slowly through his nostrils. McClain was more resilient than he'd thought, showing up for work even after being run off the road. Tougher too.

Should have figured on that. A white Irish kid from the South Side of Chicago, blue collar, airborne, stubborn. Perhaps Round Two would be more successful in dealing with him. He nodded and looked at West.

"I've got Dobrovits and Taylor on surveillance of the students," West said. "They've been doing their usual routines. School, eating, and going to prayers."

"Any problems with them and the Fassel matter?"

West shook his head. "They bought it hook, line, and sinker. For the most part."

Viceroy questioned that with a look.

"Fahim's being kind of an asshole," West said. "Nothing I can't handle."

Viceroy nodded. "So I assume they'll be amenable to moving up the plan?"

West smiled. It was a lips-only smile, but Viceroy knew it was also one of casual confidence. West could play those stupid student radicals like a clarinet.

"Okay," Viceroy said. "This is what we'll do. Schedule another meet with them tomorrow. It's Friday, so they'll probably be available between prayers. Give them the update that the plan has to move forward quicker than expected."

"Not a problem, sir," West said.

"Take them on a dry run Monday," Viceroy said. "And give them some mask training. They've got to think that they'll all be walking away to fight the *jihad* another day." He turned to Lee. "And your team will act as shadow. Figure how and when we're going to take these little towelheads out when we take over the op. I want them all except the two principals hit in their apartment on D-Day." He paused and reconsidered his use of the term "D-Day." It seemed almost sacrilegious, but he justified it in an instance by rechristening it "Destiny-Day"—the day his destiny, and that of the nation, took a new course on the way to victory. He caught West's sharp brown eyes. "You'll dump Hassan and Fahim in the Metro Line tunnel as evidence. Those two have to be Sarin-ills."

West nodded. "Again, not a problem, sir."

"It'll be up to both of you to complete the second phase."

Lee's eyes looked just as dark, just as steady, just as clear as West's had. His nod was almost imperceptible.

Viceroy motioned West toward the cabinets on the far side of the room. "Get us three paper cups." He took out his pocket flask, which was filled with fine Kentucky bourbon. "This calls for a pre-op celebratory toast."

West returned with the three cups and set them on the table. Viceroy poured some of the amber liquid into each one. He refastened the cap, replaced the flask in his pocket, and grabbed the cup nearest to him, raising it into the air. "Gentlemen, there is no substitute for victory."

He felt the familiar burning warmth as the bourbon went down.

She looks even prettier than she did yesterday, McClain thought as he looked at Felicia Knight from across the table. Not that she didn't always look good. It was just that the day before she'd looked really tired. Plus she'd had her hair up under some scarf. Today it was straightened and hanging down around her shoulders. *Very attractive.*

The waiter asked if they wanted some drinks or appetizers to start off as he handed them the menus. The menus were encased in fine black leather and McClain was wondering if he would be able to write this off as a business lunch. Of course, it had been her suggestion that they meet here for lunch. Did that mean she was going to be picking up the tab? Being a gentleman, he would have a hard time accepting that. No, he'd pick up the check. That was a given. Just put it on the already overstressed credit card. McClain smirked to himself as he perused the menu and looked at the prices. He'd also have to factor in taking a taxi home. No way would he wait for a bus or for someone from the department to saunter by and pick him up in a squad car. It had been hard enough to get someone to drop him off.

Aww, hell, he thought. *I might as well relax and enjoy it. How often do you get to sit across from a pretty girl in a plush D.C.*

restaurant while you're working? Might as well act rich, even though I can't even afford a rental car. "I feel like a steak. How about you?"

"It's good to see a man with a healthy appetite, Detective McClain."

Detective McClain? That sounded way too formal. "Okay, Special Agent Knight. You can call me Kevin if you want. It'll take less verbiage."

Her dark eyes swept over him. She nodded and went back to assessing the menu.

He waited a beat then asked, "And what can I call you?"

She looked up at him again. "Special Agent Knight is fine." Her smile came about four seconds later. This was a girl who had a sense of timing.

He smiled back. "Come on, we already kind of know each other."

"We do?"

"Yeah. From the gym. I've been watching you play volleyball for months."

She raised her eyebrows. "You work out there, too?"

He was mildly disappointed that she hadn't noticed him all those times. "I do. I'm usually pounding the bags in the boxing section."

"You're a boxer?"

He grinned. It still hurt a little, but it was worth it. "Can't you tell?"

She sort of chuckled at that one.

He followed up with, "Actually, these bruises aren't from boxing though. I mixed it up with an asshole on an arrest Tuesday night, then got clobbered by an airbag last night."

Her lips formed a Mona Lisa smile. They were so full and shone with some kind of pinkish lipstick that was accentuated by the darkness of her skin. "I was wondering how good you were after seeing all those bruises. I remember my father talking about Jerry Quarry and how he used to beat the other guy's gloves up with his face before knocking him out."

Irish Jerry Quarry, he thought. A girl who actually knows boxing. He couldn't believe it. "Sounds like he knew boxing pretty well."

"My dad was a professional fighter. He used to have a ring in our backyard where he trained. Sometimes I'd work out with him."

"Work out?"

"Not sparring, but I used to skip rope and punch the bags."

"Now you're going to *have* to call me Kevin. And what do people call you besides Special Agent Knight?"

She sat back. Had he asked the wrong question? Gotten too personal? He was on unfamiliar ground here. They were both in law enforcement, but she was federal and he was municipal. Plus, there was the racial thing. He'd never been out with a black girl before. This wasn't exactly a date, but it was kind of morphing in that direction. It would depend on what she said next.

She leaned forward. "Felicia."

"Felicia," he said, drawing out the pronunciation like he was savoring a delicious piece of fruit. "Pretty name. You have any nicknames?"

"Why?"

He shrugged. "Just wondering." He tried to punctuate it with another painful smile. "People call me Kev."

She studied his face. "Actually, my family calls me Cee-Cee."

"I like that, too." In fact, he was liking everything about her. He was also finding her more and more attractive, and couldn't help but wonder what she'd say if he did ask her out on a real date. But they were a long way from that point, weren't they?

She'd probably tell me she wasn't interested, he thought.

Especially with my raccoon face of late. Still, there was no harm in thinking about asking, if things worked out good with their lunch. And things were working out pretty damn good at the moment.

His cell phone intruded. McClain frowned. He'd just thought of something witty to say, but the incessant ringing continued.

Felicia canted her head. "Aren't you going to answer that?"

McClain sighed and unclipped his phone. "I almost lost the thing twice in the last couple days. Now I wish I had." He looked at the screen, saw it was Lynn, and let it ring one more time, hoping it would stop. But it didn't. He glanced at Felicia. "Sorry."

"Where are you?" Lynn's voice demanded.

She sounded upset. McClain was both mystified and angered.

"I'm having dinner with a—" He paused. Should he say friend or colleague? It didn't matter because Lynn cut him off.

"This is all your fault. I told you she needed counseling. She needed to see Dr. Moorefield, but *no*. You and your *fucking* cheap insurance." Her voice had risen to a few decibels below a scream. McClain's gaze shot toward Felicia, who was politely looking away.

"Lynn, take it easy."

"Our daughter," she said, "has been arrested."

"For what?"

"This is all your fault."

He rubbed the bridge of his nose with his thumb and forefinger and forced himself to speak calmly. "What did she get picked up for?"

"If you would act like a father—"

"Listen, if you don't shut up and tell me what's going on, I can't do anything, can I?" The contradictions in his wording hit him like a counterpunch, but it seemed to work. Lynn stopped yelling. He could hear her breathing over the phone. He rubbed his nose again. The last thing in the world he wanted Special Agent Knight to hear was him yelling at another woman, especially his ex.

"Lynn," he said in a softer voice. "Please tell me what happened."

"I got a call from a Deputy Miles in Fairfax County," she said. "Jennifer was stopped in a stolen car."

McClain exhaled slowly. *The perfect end to a perfect morning,* he thought. *I'm batting a thousand.*

CHAPTER 17

Felicia looked at the Vernons' plush, antebellum mansion. How had she ended up sitting in her three-year-old, government-issued Ford Crown Vic, waiting for her assigned target to drop off his delinquent daughter and make amends with his hostile ex and her family? As she watched the breeze rustle the leaves of a stately tree across the expansive yard, she thought that Mc-Clain wasn't really a "target" and his daughter wasn't really a "delinquent." She was a typical, mixed-up teenager looking for attention from her absentee father, who had obviously married into money and then had his middle-class butt kicked out the back door. The daughter, Jen, didn't seem too bad. Confused, a little bit spoiled, and probably looking for love in all the wrong places. Or maybe she was just looking for attention.

Back at the restaurant he'd said, "I can take a cab," as he quickly gave the waiter his credit card and told him to cash them out. She hadn't expected him to pay. But it was kind of refreshing to meet an old-fashioned gentleman these days.

"Don't be silly," she'd replied. "I'll drive you. It'll be much faster."

On the way to the station he'd gone into detail, talking a mile-a-minute about his daughter, his ex-wife, their failed marriage, and the trials and tribulations of swimming against the tide and trying to remain a part of his daughter's life.

By the time they'd reached the station, Felicia had a pretty good idea of who Kevin McClain was, and she found it not altogether unpleasant. In spite of all the drama, he seemed like a nice guy.

Jen seemed like another mixed-up kid from a broken home. She reminded Felicia of her young play-sister, Nicole, back home. She'd come from a similar background and latched on to Felicia for the guidance her battling parents couldn't provide. Luckily, Nicole had turned out all right and was now entering her third year at college, studying to be a nurse practitioner. Felicia wondered if she'd been able to reach McClain's daughter in the same way. He'd reacted in typical male, and cop, fashion once they'd arrived at the county substation, exploding and yelling at his daughter.

He'd then said he needed some air. After he'd left, Felicia studied the girl. Pretty face, nice figure, blonde hair permed and curled, way too much makeup. A child trying to pretend she was an adult. Felicia asked her if she wanted a soda. The girl's sullen expression didn't change as she shook her head.

"I do," Felicia said. She sat down across the table from the girl. "Your name's Jennifer, right?"

A quick nod.

"I'm Felicia. What do people call you? Jennifer or Jen?"

"Both. Do you know my father?"

"Not real well. We were discussing a case. I'm with the Bureau. The FBI."

The girl's eyes widened. "You're in police work? I want to go into police work like my dad. Is it hard to get in?"

"If I did it, you can. What kind of grades are you getting in school?"

From there the conversation took off and after twenty minutes they were laughing and talking about everything from what type of courses to take in college to boyfriend problems. A knock at the door interrupted them and she saw McClain standing there with a uniformed deputy and another plainclothes officer.

"You two seem like you're getting on real good," the plainclothes guy said. He'd introduced himself when they'd first arrived as the juvenile officer.

"Jen," Felicia said, "wasn't there something you wanted to say to your father?"

She looked down, bit her lower lip, then looked up with tears welling up in her eyes. "I'm sorry, daddy."

McClain looked like someone had smacked him with a belly shot.

They left the substation. Jen sat in the backseat and listened as McClain talked on his cell to her mom. Felicia eyed the girl's reactions in the rearview mirror. She looked nervous, like she knew there'd be hell to pay when she got home, but at least the tears had stopped. Felicia felt they were genuine. When they arrived at Jen's home, Felicia handed one of her cards to Jen and said, "My cell number's on the back, if you ever need to talk."

Jen's house looked like it had been transposed from *Gone With the Wind*. Quite different from where Felicia had grown up. Too bad money couldn't buy happiness.

McClain had been inside for a good forty minutes, and she tried to imagine what must be happening in there. Was he giving a rundown of the situation to his ex while Jen stood by? Felicia wondered what his ex was like. A typical Southern belle? Jen's arrest hadn't been totally egregious. The "stolen car" turned out to have merely been "taken without permission" from one of the boy's parents. Two boys and two girls, all from well-to-do families, out for a little ride in Daddy's Caddie, without his knowledge or consent. They should have been in school. The fact that none of them had a driver's license made it a bit more complicated, but certainly no criminal charges, juvenile or otherwise, were going to be pursued. Felicia had no doubt that Jen was probably hoping to get caught—a cry for attention.

McClain finally exited the house. He looked beat as he walked, like he had a heavy weight on his back. Poor guy. His face already looked like somebody had used it for a punching bag. Probably the last thing he needed was this coming down on him, too.

He opened the door and slid in, shot her an embarrassed smile, and said, "Teenagers. Fourteen going on thirty. Have you got kids?"

She shook her head.

He took a deep breath and glanced at his watch. "I want to thank you again. For everything. Especially driving me all the way out here and for talking to my daughter. I don't know what to do with that kid sometimes."

Felicia said nothing.

"It's kind of late to resume our lunch," he continued. "Why don't you let me buy you dinner to make it up to you? My treat. It's the least I can do. But only if we make a mutual promise not to talk about work stuff."

He wasn't prying into the Fassel case, and Joiner would be pleased, but why was he asking her out on some kind of a date? "You don't want to talk about Mohammed Fassel? I thought you were under the gun to investigate his murder."

"Behind the eightball is more like it," he said. "But at this point the trail's gone pretty cold, and to be honest, who gives a damn about a murdered terrorist? It's not exactly what they call a heater. All I have to do is write up a report and turn it over to the OHSCT. This one's tailor-made for what the department calls a cold case. Having exhausted all current leads, I recommend that this case be closed pending the development of new and exceptional information."

"That's interesting."

"Should work out. What do you say about dinner?"

Joiner had ordered her to get closer to McClain, gain his trust, find out exactly what he knew. Plus, he wasn't a bad-looking guy, bruises and all. "I'd like that," she said.

West held the mask in both of his hands and went over the instructions the same way he'd done a thousand times before, to a thousand different recruits. But this time he was more careful in his wording. Careful not to describe the mask with its proper military designation, an M-95. He had to tread carefully, maintain their trust. Suspicions had risen since the death of Fassel. "Keep these straps folded over the front part of your mask. It will make it easier to tighten them when you slip it on." He held the M-95 to his face and drew the straps back over his shaved head, then tightened the straps in sequence and did a seal-check. He also resisted the temptation to yell, "Gas!" as he'd been trained. He loosened the straps and pulled the mask up from the bottom, exposing his face to the air once more.

"You must immediately place your hands over the port and the canister to seal the mask to your skin after putting it on," he said as he surveyed the group. Their faces showed a curious mixture of emotions. Some were attentive, others nervous, and one angry.

"Why don't we have the same kind of mask as you and Ibriham?" Fahim asked.

West had given the only two M-95s to himself and Ibriham, the student leader. He'd given the others, Amir, Hassan, and Malik, the cheaper Israeli gas masks to use. They were harder to trace and would make the ultimate demise of this little group of subversives more plausible. M-95s were military issue and highly traceable. The Israeli masks could be bought at any flea market.

"I already explained that to you." Careful to keep his voice neutral, West hid his underlying contempt for Fahim. "Ibriham and I will be handling the actual canisters. We need the best equipment. Believe me, the masks you have will work perfectly. Now practice putting them on."

Fahim snorted. "I don't like this," he said in Arabic.

"Relax," Ibriham said, folding the straps over the front of his mask. "We need to master this skill."

"How do we know we can trust him?" Fahim said, still talking in Arabic. "I don't believe Mohammed Amir betrayed us. All we know is he is dead. It's been on the news. How do we know he is telling us the truth?"

West watched and listened, understanding every word. He moved his arms down to his sides, feeling the comfort of his Smith and Wesson. Although he didn't think he'd need it at this juncture, he knew he could take out all five of these towelheads in under ten seconds. He was going to enjoy the final session with these assholes. Perhaps he'd use his K-bar, housed in a sheath on his right calf, instead of the pistol. He mentally rehearsed the action. He'd shove Ibriham, the closest one, then bend to draw the knife. Upward stab under the ribcage hitting the heart, push him away. Kick Fahim in the balls, downward stab between collarbone and neck severing the carotid. Forward slash to Malik's neck, followed by a downward chop with his left hand. Front kick to Amir, then backslash across the throat. Pivot, deliver a back kick to Hassan, the last opponent, and deliver a pointed stab to the side of his neck. It was like running an old *kata* from his karate days. A dance of death. It would be that easy. None of them, with the exception of Ibriham, had any combat experience. Soft targets, all of them.

West listened and waited, watching Fahim. Taking him out at this juncture was tempting. Still, for the plan to move forward, he'd have to wait.

"You have more questions?" West asked in English.

Fahim's dark eyes seemed to hold nothing but hatred. He continued in Arabic. "I do not like him. Even if he is a Muslim, is he a true Muslim? I do not trust him."

"And I am convinced he is devout," Ibriham said. "If I thought otherwise, I would kill him right now."

West moved his arm fractionally closer to the Smith and Wesson.

"And I am convinced he is not," Fahim said. He threw his mask on the floor. "This is an insult. These masks were made by the Jews."

"The mask was probably made by a Palestinian worker," West said in Arabic. "Whose labor was stolen by the Israeli dogs."

Fahim's mouth twitched. West stared back, then smiled. "*La Ilaha Illa Allah.* There is no God but Allah. Pick up your mask, my brother. We have much work to do to get ready."

Viceroy and Bernard strolled along the Reflection Pool at the National Mall with the current presidential candidate's Secret Service protective detail hanging back at a respectful distance. Viceroy took in a deep breath and thought how good he felt, despite the recent unexpected setbacks and developments. But this was the part of the op that he dreaded the most: waiting while all the final pieces were set into motion. Still, it felt good to be closing in on the goal line. He pointed to the distant Washington Monument, still visible in the fading late-afternoon light.

"See that, Will? Even that damn earthquake couldn't shake it. Shows how important the cornerstone of real core values are."

Big Willie huffed, hungover from last night. Viceroy knew that he had to buoy his man up, get him ready to carry the ball. The debate was only a few days away.

"You're not still worried about those damn polls, Will, are you?"

Big Willie whispered, "Clay, this plan of yours—it's fool-proof?"

Before he could answer, Viceroy's cell phone rang. He looked at the screen. Lee. "I've got to take this," he said and strolled farther away until he was completely out of earshot of the Secret Service agents.

"Targets three and four are at a restaurant," Lee said. "Looking pretty cozy."

This caught Viceroy's attention.

"They were with the same young female as yesterday," Lee continued. "She was arrested in a stolen car earlier with three others. Pretty routine."

Viceroy listened while Lee gave him a quick rundown of Mc-Clain being driven around by Knight to pick up his daughter from the Fairfax County substation and then home. He hadn't anticipated any collusion between Knight and McClain.

"Nothing to report about one and two," Lee said. "Still in the newsroom."

Lane and Hayes were probably going over the questions she was going to throw at Big Willie during the debate. Have to get him prepared for that. "Keep on them, Lee. What about West?"

"Giving lessons," Lee said.

Everything was moving along according to his master plan except this new association between Knight and McClain. Could that be a potential problem? He needed to keep McClain out of things and the feds in. He had to manipulate Joiner into accomplishing a few more tasks before discarding him and his group. "Who's on targets three and four?"

"Muckley right now," Lee said. "Want me to pull him?"

"Negative. Have him maintain while Baker and Pomeroy do a set-up on both their hooches."

"Both?"

Viceroy could detect the uncertainty in Lee's voice. It would be dangerous to bug the apartment of an FBI agent, especially since he needed to use Joiner in the finale. What if the feds somehow found the devices? But he could offer his tech support guys for a protective sweep of all their offices and residences as a prelude to the raid. A courtesy sweep. They could remove the devices then. He'd have to keep playing Joiner like an old fiddle, but that didn't seem to be a problem. One ex-gyrene to another. With the courtesy sweep, any evidence could be quietly removed, just like it never happened. *It never happened.* The appropriate mantra for black ops. Removing the stuff from McClain's place was a different story. But that would be easy, once he'd been properly dealt with on Tuesday.

"Affirmative," Viceroy said.

"Full or ears-only?"

Viceroy considered the benefit of installing a full range of visual and listening devices against the immediate time factor. Tomorrow was Saturday, though, and neither one would be at work, so installation might be trickier. "Ears for now," he said. "We can always upgrade next week, if we have to."

"Roger that. Anything else?"

Viceroy glanced at Big Willie, engaged in a conversation with his two protectors. Everybody was laughing. The man had the gift of gab, all right. Personable, charming, and above all, malleable. The perfect candidate, the perfect means to an end. Viceroy stared at the majestic stone obelisk rising above the terrain in the distance like a huge, symbolic lance. A warrior's lance, and it soon would be his to hold in a victory march down to 1600 Pennsylvania Avenue.

"Negative," he said. "At this time."

CHAPTER 18

Ted Lane put his head in his hands and massaged his scalp. The shinny bald spot on the crown felt slick and sweaty, and it wasn't even that hot in here. He saw Allison staring down at him.

"Are you all right?" she asked.

Lane looked around. They were alone. He wondered how much to tell her.

"I was trying to review everything," he said. "What's your opinion of that McClain guy?"

"He looked like somebody'd given him a pretty rough going-over. But he did say he'd been in an accident, didn't he?"

God she was shallow. Only seeing the superficiality of things. If it wasn't for her looks, and her ass, getting him to where he wanted to be, he would drop her in a heartbeat.

His frown must have been obvious because she said, "What's wrong now?"

"Nothing. I'm just trying to figure out how all this fits together." He held up his hand, fingers extended, and started ticking off points. "One, we have a murdered Arab terrorist found in D.C., who was released from Guantanamo by the current administration. Two, we have a current presidential candidate from the opposite party, who was instrumental in using torture on that same dead terrorist when he was in Guantanamo. Three, we have the accidental death of the current administration's point man on the torture investigation. And all this on the eve of the foreign-policy debate."

"You're beginning to sound like one of those conspiracy nuts. So, let's get back to the debates. What questions should I ask Bernard about those enhanced interrogation techniques?"

Enhanced interrogation techniques? Did she have to be so fucking politically correct?

"I'm thinking it over," he said. Was it time to hit Bernard with the haymaker, or should they wait? Lane knew in his gut there was more to this. He didn't have all the pieces yet. If only Regina could tell him what the "big development" was that had Bernard in such a state of anxiety. Maybe she'd find out soon. He'd have to set up another meet with her.

"I'm still trying to figure everything out," he continued. "It's like trying to put together a jigsaw puzzle when you don't have all the pieces."

"Are you going to press your source for more then?"

"Yeah."

Allison put her hand on his shoulder, squeezing gently. "And when are you going to let me in on what's going on?"

He put his hand on top of hers and felt the stirring in his groin. "Soon," he said. "Soon."

McClain was surprised at how easily the conversation flowed between them as they ate dinner. Work didn't even enter into it. In fact, they talked about everything but, and found they had more than just a few things in common. They'd both grown up in the Midwest, him in Chicago and her in Minneapolis, and they'd both been involved in sports through high school and college. And even though she'd run track and he'd been an amateur boxer, she knew a lot about the sweet science, having watched her pro-boxer father.

"You trained with your dad?" he asked.

"I never used to spar at the gym," she said with a smile. "Daddy wouldn't let me, but I did everything else—punching the bags, using the focus mitts, jumping rope." Her dark eyes narrowed as she took a sip of wine and looked at him over the rim of her glass. "I remember seeing you jumping rope at the gym a few times."

"So does that mean you recognized me before, when we met?"

"Maybe," she said. "Or maybe I was thinking that I could skip rope twice as good as you."

"Can you punch a speedbag?"

"Of course. I can make that sucker dance."

"I'd like to see that sometime. Most people have a problem getting the rhythm down."

"I imagine my boss's face on the bag."

She smacked her right fist lightly into her open palm and McClain wondered how much the wine was affecting her. Maybe he'd have to drive her home in her car. That wouldn't be a bad thing.

"I'm sorry," Felicia said. "We promised we weren't going to talk about work tonight during dinner."

"Well, we've finished dinner." He looked over the empty plates. "Want another drink?"

Felicia said she'd better lay off the wine and have some coffee instead. McClain motioned for the waiter and ordered two coffees.

"So that guy I met, your boss. What's his name?"

"Joiner. Or, as he loves to remind everybody, Special Agent In Charge Joiner."

"Sounds like a jerk."

She leaned across to the table and whispered, "He is. Worse than a jerk. He's a prick."

McClain laughed and was struck again how pretty she was. Her mahogany skin looked creamy smooth, her lips full, and her features delicate and beautifully formed.

"Part of the requirements for being a boss," he said. "Cream and bastards always rise."

They exchanged a few more bad-boss stories and the waiter returned with their coffees. He watched as she poured in a ton of cream but no sugar. The same way he liked it.

"Did you hear about the Paul Ross accident?" Felicia asked as she stirred her coffee.

"Wasn't he that politician?"

"Inspector General's office. He was working for the Attorney General on the torture issue. Flew back from Guantanamo and was killed in a car accident."

"Yeah, I do remember that." The mention of torture set McClain thinking about Somalia. He felt an uncomfortable shiver creep up his spine.

"What's wrong?" she asked, sensing his discomfort.

"Nothing," he said. "Just visited by an old ghost."

"Well, privately the AG is convinced that Ross's accident was no accident. Seems his laptop was damaged and the AG is making the accident a Bureau case. Joiner assigned me to look into that one. And he's going to want a preliminary by Monday, too."

"I have a buddy on the state police. I could reach out to him and get you a copy of their report if it would help."

"That would be great. Save me some legwork. And I could give you enough details about your dead terrorist murder victim so you could finish your report." She smiled. "When do you want to get together?"

"I'll give my buddy a call tomorrow." Then he remembered. Tomorrow was Saturday. "Not tomorrow. This is my weekend with my daughter. I've got to take her shopping for school clothes and stuff. By the way, thanks again for talking to her today. I was getting nowhere."

"It was my pleasure," Felicia said.

"Maybe we could meet sometime tomorrow morning? Before

I pick her up?"

"How are you going to pick her up? I thought you didn't have a car."

He grimaced. "Yeah, I'll have to figure something out."

"Why don't we meet, I can show you my file on Fassel . . ." She paused. "But no copies please. I mean that. Joiner would crucify me if he found out."

He nodded.

"And then I can drive you to get Jen," she said. "I don't live that far from you. Does it sound like a plan?"

"Sure does." *Or maybe even a date,* he thought. *Sort of.*

Felicia was burning with curiosity the next morning as she drove to McClain's apartment. He lived in Prince George's County, the same as she did. Not a bad area, but certainly nothing the caliber of his ex-in-laws. She guessed his ex kept the gold mine and McClain got the shaft.

Perhaps he married for love and not money, she thought.

She parked and glanced at her watch. Eight-oh-five. Not too early, but late enough that he should be up. He'd said he had to pick up his daughter by ten.

"Custody agreements," he had said. "All the times I had to mediate those damn domestic things when I was working uniform, and now here I am being caught up in one myself."

From what she'd seen, Felicia didn't doubt that he loved his daughter very much and wanted what was best for her. It was a no-brainer that his ex, with her rich parents and Southern-style mansion, was the custodial parent. McClain couldn't even afford a temporary rental car. She took out her cell and called him. "Hi, I'm outside," she said. "Wondering if it was okay to come up?"

"I'm ready," he said. "And I hope you're hungry. I fixed a ton of eggs and pancakes."

Viceroy was doing the second mile of brisk walking on his treadmill when the special phone rang. He flipped it open and spoke while he continued walking.

"Just called with a sit-rep, sir," Baker said.

"Proceed." Viceroy was careful not to sound out of breath. To them, he was Superman and he had to maintain his image.

"Targets three and four are meeting again this morning," Baker said. "She just arrived at his apartment."

His apartment? That was interesting. "Any idea what it's in reference to?"

"On the phone she mentioned she was bringing something over and asked about his computer capabilities. Mentioned a flash drive."

A flash drive? Was she giving McClain the inside scoop on Fassel? On the operation? Viceroy felt an uneasiness grip his stomach. He'd have to listen to the recordings later.

"What about target AS?" he asked, using the code term for the Arab students. "Any problems with the double dutch?"

"Negative."

That meant that his secondary group was assisting Joiner's men, watching the students without any problems. Christ, it would have been so much simpler if he could run the whole thing with just his people. This was like playing chess on multiple boards against multiple opponents. The secret to success was to keep each game clear in your mind and address the various attacks one at a time. He hit the pause button on the treadmill and placed his feet on either side of the moving track. A couple of droplets of sweat hit the rotating rubber as it slowed to a stop. He needed to keep Joiner and his men involved, up to a certain degree. But why in the hell would Knight be bringing

McClain into it? She'd have to know that Joiner would hit the roof if he found out. Probably suspend or fire her outright. That might be the most expedient way to handle it, but then again, he was hardly in a place to explain how he'd gotten this information. He couldn't very well say he'd had his team bug both their apartments. Best to keep the tabs going on both of them and see where it led. Eventually, they were two more loose ends he'd have to deal with, but for now, he had plenty of other pieces on the board to worry about.

But starting the ball rolling early like this might be advantageous, especially where McClain was concerned. Luckily, he had plenty to play with. When they'd rebroken Fassel and gotten the passwords to the offshore accounts he was using to finance his little terrorist scheme, Viceroy had Baker move the monies into a dummy account of their own. It was always good to have a substantial amount of capital on hand, just in case. The kind that you didn't have to explain away in some report to a bunch of bureaucratic assholes whose only exposure to the real world was watching *Meet the Press* on Sunday mornings. Perhaps it was time to set his alternate plan B into motion.

He wiped his brow and asked, "Where are you now?"

"In the van outside target one's hooch."

"Call in someone to relieve you," Viceroy said. "I need you to come by here for an assignment."

"Roger that, sir."

Viceroy glanced at his watch. In about twenty-five minutes Detective Kevin McClain was going to become a very rich man, and he didn't even know it.

CHAPTER 19

McClain emitted a low whistle as he finished reading the file she'd given him. It was a PDF, so he couldn't highlight or copy parts of it. Not that he wanted to copy it. All he wanted was to find a way off this damn case.

"You see now why I can't give you too much?" she said.

"Your report says you intercepted the stuff."

"It's still ongoing," she said. "There's new intel that there were two separate deliveries. One got through."

"Is that why that army colonel was in your office the other day?"

"Right. You're familiar with *Posse Comitatus*, right? The military's not authorized to function as a law enforcement agency within our borders. That's why the Bureau has to take the lead. My boss has two men watching the new suspects right now. We've got to wait until they make their move."

"Have they got the gas?"

"We don't know yet, but the colonel's got one of his men, who speaks Arabic, on the inside." She looked at him. "So you see why I'm not supposed to be sharing this with you?"

McClain nodded, closed out the flash drive, and handed it back to her. "Thanks for sharing."

"You have enough to finish your report?"

"I don't know. Who did you say the new suspects are?"

"I didn't." Her right eyebrow raised slightly. "But they're a bunch of Arab students living in Arlington. The colonel is

212

convinced they're the ones who killed Fassel."

"Why?"

"Because they thought he betrayed them."

"Did he?"

"The colonel says they turned Fassel in Guantanamo."

So the dead terrorist was a federal snitch. No wonder they had been so closed-mouthed. "What's your take on the colonel?"

"He seems pretty impressive. Knows his stuff. My boss thinks the man walks on water."

McClain smirked. "I like him less already. You know, there's something familiar about the guy, too. What did you say his last name was again?"

"Viceroy, like the old cigarettes."

"You smoke?"

She shook her head. "My uncle did. I used to love to play with his Viceroy packs when I was little. Had an emblem with a red crown on them. He's battling lung cancer now."

"That kind of sums up how I feel about the colonel. Looks like a real pretty package, but there's bad stuff on the inside." Something else was gnawing at him about Viceroy, but it kept dancing on the edge of his memory, like a quick fighter popping a never-ending jab. "How about the students? Can I get their names and addresses to list them as known associates?"

"That'll really put me in the trick-bag," she said. "You'll have to wait until this operation has run its course. Once we pinch the students, I promise I'll call you and let you interview them regarding Fassel. And if we're going to get your daughter by ten, shouldn't we be leaving soon?"

"Will you come to lunch with me and my daughter today?"

"Lunch?" He saw the hint of a smile trace her lips. "I'm still stuffed after all those pancakes."

"We'll make it a late one."

"I don't think so." She laughed. "I'm already going to spend an extra hour on the treadmill."

"Dinner then. What do you say?"

"Let me think about it, okay?"

"Fair enough," he said.

Ted Lane glanced at his watch again. Where the hell was she? They'd agreed on one o'clock. The parking garage was practically empty. He'd been waiting for her to return his text. Waiting, then sending another one, waiting some more. When she eventually did respond it was almost eleven.

1230 the usual?

Lane quickly confirmed and thought about the questions he was going to ask her. He had to get more on Bernard's current anxiety attack. Had he seemed nervous before the accident? And what was his reaction to Paul Ross's death? But twelve-thirty had come and gone. Still no Regina.

He felt his cell vibrate with the incoming text. He flipped it open just to check.

its me. here. you?

Lane sent a quick reply saying he was on the way. As he trotted toward the stairwell, he hit the alarm button on his remote and pressed the crash-bar. Maybe he was finally going to get some answers.

Viceroy sat across from Big Willie and Roger Ram Jet in the confines of Ram Jet's hotel room and nursed his glass of bourbon. He was still on his first drink while Big Willie was on his third and showed no signs of slowing down. It was a good thing all he had to do tonight was show up at one of those pre-planned fundraisers and read his standard speech, the third one this week in the D.C. area. Hopefully, most of the booze would be worn off by tonight. Once they got through the debate on Tuesday, Big Willie was going to have to be at the top of his game, and Viceroy knew he could only do that sober.

"Will, for Christ sake," Ram Jet said, "will you put that damn drink down and listen to me?"

Big Willie paused, the glass suspended halfway between his groin and his mouth—the two things that got him in the most trouble.

Viceroy wondered again if he had picked the right horse for this race, but it wasn't as if he had much choice in that matter. And Big Willie would be totally malleable once the first part of the plan was successfully completed.

Big Willie set his glass down without taking another sip. "It's those damn polls. They sap a man's resolve."

"Tell me about it," Ram Jet said. "But that's what we were here to discuss."

Viceroy set his own drink on the coffee table and leaned forward, his elbows on his knees. "Roger's right, Will. I want to go over a few key points about the debate coming up."

"What type of things, Clay?" Ram Jet asked, then added as if to negate their importance, "I mean, we've already got our foreign-policy platform set."

Viceroy was going to personally kick this little jerk's ass all the way down the White House steps once they won this thing. But until then, he needed him. "Make sure he doesn't come off looking like he's soft on the war on terror."

Ram Jet heaved a sigh. "We've been over this already, haven't we? Harris is going to bring up the allegations of the torture issue, which was miraculously minimized by the fortuitous traffic accident that took Paul Ross out of the picture."

Fortuitous accident? This putz hasn't got a clue.

"But anyway," Ram Jet said, looking at Big Willie, "we have to move more toward the middle on this. If we come off looking too hawkish, it'll automatically make people think Harris is right about the torture stuff and we'll lose what we have of the independent voters.'"

Viceroy took in a deep breath and let it out slowly and audibly before he spoke. "Roger, as I mentioned before, I'm limited on what I can tell you about ongoing special operations. Do you remember that WMD shipment we've been tracking?"

Ram Jet's head jerked, like a dog coming to alert. "Yes."

"Now what I'm about to tell you is highly, I repeat, *highly* classified. It must not leave this room. Understood?"

"Of course."

Viceroy had the son-of-a-bitch now. A fish on the line. "Earlier in the week the FBI intercepted a shipment of Sarin nerve gas near the Maine/Canada border."

"My God." Ram Jet's face turned white. "Is that bastard Harris going to be able to use this as a trump card to show his progress in the war on terror?"

"The White House has not yet been briefed on this development. I've been working behind the scenes with the Bureau on this. It's our intel that got the location, my men who intercepted and disposed of the gas."

"And they're not working this through homeland security channels?"

"At this point we're keeping a lid on it . . ." Viceroy paused. It was time for a slight deception. "The gas wasn't the genuine article, so the current administration is in the dark."

Ram Jet stared at him. "Where are we going with this?"

Viceroy stared back, maximizing the silence before he spoke. "We're now in the process of verifying new intelligence. It indicates that the shipment of the real nerve gas did successfully make it over the border and onto U.S. soil. An attack might be imminent."

Ram Jet's jaw hung slack. After a few more seconds he leaned back and said, "Holy shit."

Viceroy did a quick glance at his brother-in-law. A crooked, lips-only smile twisted Big Willie's face. The man's eyes were on Ram Jet, watching for indications that he'd bought it, and from all indications, he had. This was all going according to the master plan.

Or, the plan of the master, Viceroy thought. His cell vibrated and he looked at the screen. Lee. He pressed the button and read the message.

I think we've found our leak.

Viceroy smiled. *This evening was turning into real windfall.*

After walking Felicia down to her car in the early evening light, McClain went back upstairs to his apartment. He felt good. They'd picked up Jen and Felicia opted to wait in her car again. Everything was running smoothly until he saw someone looking out the upstairs window. Seconds later Lynn had buzzed him on his cell phone, but he simply let it ring until it went to voice mail.

"Daddy, aren't you going to answer your phone?" Jen asked.

"Nah," he said. "I'm not going to let anything interfere with our time together today." He switched the phone to vibrate. All told, he had seven voice mails to listen to, all from Lynn.

Jen and Felicia hit it off, as they had the day before. They'd headed to the mall to finish up Jen's "school shopping," and it was obvious that Felicia had a black belt in shopping and Jen wasn't far behind. He sat and watched as his daughter modeled one new outfit after another. When all the clothes had been purchased, they went to three different shoe stores, with McClain wondering how much more his credit card could handle. He knew what his upcoming overtime check was buying.

He'd forget about getting a rental car and rattle the insurance man's cage first thing Monday morning.

When he returned home from dinner, Jen was sitting on his sofa with a Cheshire cat's grin on her face as she looked up from her iPad.

"So?" she asked.

"So?" he said.

"So, did you kiss her good-night?"

McClain rolled his eyes. "No, I didn't, not that it's any of your business."

"Why not? I think she's very pretty. And nice, too. Don't you?"

"We don't have that kind of a relationship. We're colleagues."

"You call her Felicia, and it's not like I couldn't see that you two like each other." She gave him a look so serious that it scared him. "I mean, I know what love is."

"Love? Where did that come from?"

"Oh, Daddy. I think it's totally cool."

"I told you, we're colleagues, not . . ." He searched for the words.

"Daddy, it's okay for you to be seeing somebody. I mean, look at Mom." She made some quick finger moves on her iPad and hit the screen with an emphatic touch. "Here, take a look at this. Mom and Sexy Rexy."

She handed him the iPad and McClain looked at the image on the screen, glad for the slight pause in the adult conversation. His daughter was fourteen, going on thirty. The picture caught McClain's attention. Lynn was all decked out in a black evening gown. Sexy Rexy, who looked almost dapper in a black tux, was standing alongside her. McClain's ex-father-in-law was next to Rex, also looking dapper in his tux, although a drunken simper spread across his face. But it was the face of the guy next to the distinguished congressman that piqued McClain's interest.

Colonel Viceroy.

"Where did you get this?" he asked.

"The picture? Mom posted it on her Facebook page."

"Where was it taken?"

"I don't know, Daddy. At some fundraiser last week."

"What day?"

"I don't know. Why?"

"Can you use your iPad to find out exactly when the fundraiser was? What night?"

"I already know. It was Thursday night at some fundraiser for Bernard. They all went together."

McClain's mind raced. The colonel looked familiar, but from where?

Why was Viceroy at the fundraiser? Why would he be rubbing elbows with McClain's ex-father-in-law? If it was a coincidence, it was a big one, and he didn't believe in coincidences.

CHAPTER 20

McClain thought of that old Kris Kristofferson song, "Sunday Morning Coming Down," as he and Felicia headed toward their meet with Hirum. He'd dropped Jen off ("Early, so we can all get to church," Lynn had said), and he remembered how good he'd felt walking his daughter up the decorative artificial flagstone sidewalk toward his ex's house. The good feeling hadn't lasted long. He'd been shocked to see Lynn standing there in her Sunday-go-to-meeting clothes. The flash of her glance as she told Jen to "Go upstairs and change" clued McClain in on her brimming anger. He stood in the doorway, watching as Jen went to the staircase, turned, smiled, and said, "Good-bye, Daddy. See you next week."

"Get up there now," Lynn said, her voice only a decibel lower than a low-grade scream. "We're already late." She turned back to him as soon as Jen had disappeared. "And as for you, what have you got to say for yourself?"

"About what?"

"About you setting such a bad example for my daughter."

"Hey, she's *our* daughter. How am I setting a bad—"

"You know very well what I'm talking about. You're seeing a black woman."

"First of all, she's a colleague of mine. Second, even if I was seeing a 'black woman,' it's none of your damn business."

Lynn began to rant—the same kind of rants she'd pull when they were married. Screaming, accusing, finger-shaking. Daddy

220

Vernon had certainly spared the rod and spoiled his child. Yelling back was tempting, but he knew that was what she wanted. Plus, it didn't work. He thought of merely turning and walking away, but he was half-afraid that Lynn would follow him down the walkway and then Felicia would see them. That was the absolute last thing he wanted. So he stood his ground and took it, like he'd done when they'd been husband and wife.

When she paused for breath, he asked in as calm a voice as he could muster, "You finished?"

The one-sided argument had brought reinforcements from inside the household. Daddy and Mommy Vernon, both decked out in their Sunday best, and worst of all, Jen, peering around from the top of the stairs.

"No, I'm not," Lynn said. She huffed in a breath ready for round two.

But McClain had no stomach for any more. He held his open palm up between them.

"Oh, go ahead, buster, hit me," Lynn said. "I'll have you brought up on charges so fast your fucking head will spin."

"I never hit you when we were married and I'm not about to now. I just want you to stop. You're creating a scene."

Vernon moved forward with a pained expression and put his hands on his daughter's shoulders. He pulled her back and said to McClain, "Kevin, I'm sorry for this. Perhaps it would be best if you left."

McClain thanked him and walked down the steps toward Felicia's car, hoping she hadn't heard that little vignette.

What a circus. What a pair of clowns. A hell of an ending to a perfect weekend.

"So this is our leak," Viceroy said as he and Lee leaned close over the coffee table, two cups of coffee on the space between them, as well as half a dozen large printed pictures.

"Affirmative. We dropped our tail of him to trace her back to her residence."

Viceroy studied the pictures that showed the woman's face from the side. He didn't have to ask if Lee had her name. He knew her already—Regina Griggas, his brother-in-law's personal assistant for the past several years. The woman Big Willie had stopped banging once he'd secured the nomination. Big Willie had balked at dumping her from the payroll. Regina must have figured out she was just one of his dalliances and not First Lady material. The leak was explained: a woman scorned.

"How do you want to handle it?" Lee asked. "I don't have to remind you that we're coming up on D-Day and we need to find out exactly what info she had access to and how much she's fed to Lane. Do you want me to set up a surveillance on her?"

"No. We've got enough going on right now. West's doing the dry run tomorrow, and the debate's on Tuesday. This asshole Lane is a bit of a hound dog, isn't he? He's always banging that Hayes broad, right?"

"Every chance he gets."

"Do we need to worry about her knowing about Regina?"

"I don't think so. Lane keeps her in the dark pretty much. Plus, she's as dense as a block of wood. Lane just keeps her around as a mouthpiece and for sex."

Viceroy picked up his coffee cup and took a long sip. " 'Let it work; for 'tis the sport to have the engineer hoist with his own petard.' "

"Sir?"

"A line from *Hamlet*. It's helped me figure out what to do."

Felicia noted that she was on her third cup of coffee as she and McClain sat next to each other in a booth at the restaurant, waiting for his buddy to arrive. The trouble was, she actually didn't mind the waiting. She liked being with McClain and that was beginning to bother her a little. This was moving way too fast. She was getting way too far ahead of herself. She'd had lunch with the guy one time, and that had been under orders. She'd driven him to pick up his errant daughter and helped him get her straightened out. Then, dinner. Then, a delicious breakfast. Then, spending most of the day with him and his daughter. McClain seemed like a nice guy. Easy to talk to, and fun.

She caught another surreptitious stare from another white couple. That was about all she and McClain had been doing the last half-hour—collecting stares. She laughed softly and he asked her what was so funny.

"We seem to be collecting a lot of notoriety in this restaurant," she said.

"Once you meet Hirum, you'll understand why he chose this place. And speak of the devil!"

Felicia saw an enormous man coming through the entrance-way in a gray police uniform. The campaign-style cowboy hat perched on his tiny head. It looked like a peanut atop the huge body. And it wasn't a muscular body, either. Hirum looked like a beached sea lion. He surveyed the restaurant, spotted McClain, and his mouth blossomed into a wide grin under his drooping mustache.

Felicia whispered, "He looks kind of out of shape for a cop."

"He is," McClain whispered back.

After the introductions, McClain said, "Hirum used to work investigations. That's how I know him, until he stepped on the wrong toes and was transferred back to patrol."

"Best move they ever made for me," Hirum said, settling into the opposite side of the booth. His little head swiveled around. "Kevin, you mind if'n we switch places? How does it look for a uniformed police officer to sit with his back to the dern door?"

Felicia slid over and McClain followed. Hirum managed to raise his considerable bulk out of the booth and resettled himself on the other side. The waitress sashayed over and brought a fresh carafe of coffee. She asked Hirum if he wanted "the usual."

"Sure nuff, sweetie pie. And anything my two friends here want, too. He's buying."

Hirum fished in the upper left pocket of his uniform shirt and extracted a blue flash drive. "You bring your laptop?"

"I did," Felicia said, placing her computer on the table.

"Now, considering you're a friend and associate of my good buddy Kev here, I got no objection to you copying that there report." He held the flash drive toward her. "However, I need this back. And as far as the files, you can't remember where they came from."

She nodded and plugged it into the USB port.

The waitress came with a round tray and set it up on a portable stand. One-by-one she set the various plates on the table in front of Hirum. Eggs and bacon, grits, three fresh biscuits, a stack of pancakes with a glob of melting butter on top, a side of sliced ham, orange juice, and a small bowl of mixed fruit. She beamed at Hirum, refilled everybody's cups, and asked if they wanted anything else.

"We'll have slices of coconut cream pie all the way around," Hirum said. "And wrap up one to go, too."

While Felicia waited for the file to open, Hirum shoveled a forkful of eggs into his mouth and bit off half of a stick of bacon. "I can save you a lot of reading if'n you want. Looks like a typical case of driving while impaired."

"The limo driver?" McClain asked.

Hirum nodded.

"He was drinking?" Felicia asked.

"Yeah, unless someone squirted Jim Beam down his throat. BAC was point one five. Almost double the legal limit."

"Any history of previous problems?" Felicia asked.

"Couple traffic tickets is all."

"No DWIs?"

"Nope, but that don't mean much."

"How about Ross?" Felicia asked.

"He was in the back section, behind the screen."

"What about his laptop?"

"Turned over to you guys on the scene," Hirum said. "It was pretty well ruined, being in the crash and the water and all."

Joiner must have sent the tech team to get it, Felicia thought, wondering if any of the data had been recoverable.

"Both him and Ross drowned," Hirum said.

McClain perked up. "Drowned?"

"Yeah. They ran off the road, went through a wooden fence and into a retention pond. It wasn't all that deep, maybe five, six feet." Hirum poured syrup over his pancakes and pressed his fork into the stack. "But I guess it was deep enough."

This seemed to be bothering McClain. Felicia wondered why, but figured she'd ask him later. Hopefully, she could get a good jump on her preliminary report and have it ready for Joiner tomorrow morning.

The waitress set down three saucers, each with a slice of coconut cream pie. Felicia's computer had finished copying the files and she could hardly wait to get out of the restaurant. She unplugged the flash drive and handed it back to Hirum.

"I think we've got everything we need, thanks," she said, glancing toward McClain to see if he was ready to go. But he looked deep in thought.

She wondered again what was bothering him.

CHAPTER 21

McClain's mind continued to race as he and Felicia took the elevator to his second-floor apartment. Inside, he flopped down on the couch while Felicia went into the kitchen. He heard his microwave humming. Something wasn't sitting right with him, and it had nothing to do with having watched Hirum's gluttony. It was the cause of death of Paul Ross and the limo driver.

Drowning.

The same COD as Mohammed Fassel's. Three people drowning on dry land. It could be a coincidence. After all, when he'd gone off the expressway in his accident, he'd ended up in a marshy area. The memory of the icy cold water spreading over his thighs sent a chill through him. He remembered floundering to get to the edge of the pond, his feet sinking in the mucky surface below the tall weeds, slipping as he tried for purchase. He could have easily been death number four.

He could see how Ross and his driver might have drowned, but what about Fassel? Someone had deliberately drowned him. Waterboarding? The man had been tortured. Brutally tortured. Had those student radicals done it? A memory of his own nightmare in Mogadishu flashed back. Thank God those special forces guys had found him in time.

Somalia. Torture. Fingernails being torn off. Intense pain. Despair. Rescue.

Crystal-clear images began to replace vagaries. Something else was there too, still floating on the edge, knocking on a closed door, wanting to get in. But what? He leaned back on the sofa and closed his eyes.

"You tired?" Felicia asked. "I made you a cup of tea."

That snapped him out of his reverie. He took the cup and smiled, pleased that she'd made herself at home and used his kitchen without asking. "Just searching my memory."

"You looked like something was bothering you back in the restaurant." She dipped a tea bag in and out of her own cup and sat down across from him.

"Yeah," he said. "I don't know if I told you this but our terrorist friend Fassel was tortured. It's not something we released, but somebody really worked him over. Broke off his teeth, pulled off his fingernails, mutilated him."

"The colonel said it was those Arab students."

"What else do you know about them? Are they actual students or a trained terrorist cell, or what?"

"The group I saw delivering the gas up in Maine looked hard core. Tried to take out the special forces team and got totally wasted." She grimaced. "Unofficially, of course. Officially, it never happened."

It never happened, McClain thought.

Suddenly, the door opened inside his mind and he knew who'd been knocking, wanting to get in. A man stood there in BDUs, a beret cocked on his head, bronze oak leaf insignias on the collar of his shirt. The face was heavier today, less craggy, but recognizable.

"Black ops," McClain said. "It never happened."

"What?"

"I remembered something, a strange coincidence."

It was all starting to add up. He had a bunch of new pieces, but how in the hell was he going to put them together?

★　★　★　★　★

Viceroy sat in his den, with Baker right across from him. Baker plugged a connector into a device and handed the set of earphones to Viceroy, who listened as the recorded conversation between Knight and McClain, perhaps five minutes' worth, played itself out.

Black ops, Somalia, the rescue, the similarities to Fassel, the Arab students. McClain sounded like a man on the verge of putting everything together. This wasn't going according to plan, but it wouldn't be the first time Viceroy would have to scramble in the middle of an op. He slipped off the earphones. "When was this recorded?"

"Two hours ago. I figured you'd want an immediate sit-rep and burned off a copy."

"Are they still at McClain's place?"

"Affirmative. I've got the rest of the team on surveillance. Latest sit-rep is long periods of silence and occasional snippets of innocuous conversation and computer usage. Probably writing their reports."

Not good, Viceroy thought. Having those two involved on a social level was bad enough, but if they started sharing things during pillow-talk, the plan could become prematurely exposed.

He contemplated the new developments. Would this alter anything? He still had Joiner's ear. Hell, he had a grappling hook in the man's ass. And Knight was on the outs with her boss. She would be the last person he'd listen to. Eventually, she'd have to be taken out, but it could wait until the proper time, as per the original plan. McClain was something else, though. More problematic. A wild card. The first attempt had failed. The second would have to be more effective. And more immediate.

Viceroy pondered moving things up. He'd already scheduled West's dry run with the Arabs for tomorrow. He had the matter of Ted Lane and the duplicitous Regina set for tomorrow, too. He'd run simultaneous ops before, but this one was becoming overly complicated. "Where do we stand with McClain?" he asked Baker. "Those off-shore accounts set up yet?"

"All taken care of, sir."

Viceroy took a deep breath. The periodic tightening in his chest had him concerned. Was the stress getting to him? He'd have to make a new appointment with his doctor soon, but it would have to be after the op was complete. All the different phases of it. Then and only then could he afford to relax.

"McClain has a partner," Viceroy said. "What's his name again?"

"Joseph Kelly."

Viceroy imagined he was holding a smoldering Havana between his fingers. He inhaled. The tightness eased. "Tomorrow we'll drop the hammer on a dirty cop, even though it will take some extra doing."

"Roger that, sir," Baker said. "We'll take it as far as we need to."

Viceroy smiled. Absolute, unquestioning loyalty. Damn, he loved this life. He looked down at the airborne insignia embedded in the wood of his coffee table and thought of the bond and loyalty it bred in men. Something that few understood. "How far?"

Baker smiled back. "All the way, sir."

West watched as more commuters boarded the train at each stop. This one was second from the end. Next up was Farragut North, and then McPherson Square, then downtown Metro Center station. He looked over at Ibriham who was sitting across from him, his backpack on the floor between his feet. West glanced at his watch. Zero-seven-forty-five. Fahim, Hassan, Malik, and Amir should be boarding the next train, bringing up the rear. When he and Ibriham arrived downtown, they'd simulate going to the washroom, don their masks, and connect the hose joining the two canisters. West told Ibriham they would then exit while the gas was dispersing, and drop the first canister on the platform next to the escalator. The second one was to be placed on the ascending staircase so its dispersal would rise into the main station. People would begin to drop like flies, never knowing what hit them.

Precisely six-and-one-half minutes later the next train would arrive with Fahim, Hassan, Malik, and Amir, who were supposed to don their masks and set off a bag of firecrackers to start people running toward the escalators. Today they were only carrying smaller bags, which simulated their protective masks and the fireworks.

A perfect plan. Or so the Arabs thought.

In reality, on Friday they'd all be taken out at their apartment and West and Lee would bring the bodies of Ibriham and Hassan to the main station in the truck. Once he and Lee had begun dispersing the gas, he'd set off the explosion on the arriving train with a disposable cell phone and leave it next to Ibriham's body. A deadly effective statement.

He mulled over the cost of innocent lives this statement would cause. American lives. Regrettable, but necessary, the colonel had told them. "The tree of liberty must be watered with the blood of patriots." This was going to be bloody, but that was the cost of liberty.

The train shifted and swayed. West noticed a pregnant woman standing, holding on to one of the poles. He stood and offered her his seat. She smiled and sat down. West wondered if she'd be riding the train Friday. He hoped not, but it wouldn't be the first time he'd seen, or caused, collateral damage. In Mogadishu the cowards hid behind their women while pumping out rounds with their AK-47s. He remembered the smile on one woman's face as she danced toward him, the man behind her with his rifle. Her smile had been short-lived. West cut them both down with the saw.

They were nearing the station. West shouldered his backpack, filled with hardbound books. He had insisted they all pack their bags to simulate their intended cargo. Naturally, Hassan had bristled at the suggestion they leave the masks in their apartment. "Why should we not make this simulation as realistic as possible?"

"What if some Metro line policeman stops you because you look like an Arab and finds your mask?" West continued in Arabic to add more emphasis. "If you would risk an accidental discovery before we execute our plan, you are a fool."

Hassan didn't like it, but that suited West just fine. He wanted to make sure on D-Day he'd be the one taking this little Arab prick out. The colonel had been very clear that Ibriham's and Hassan's deaths had to be from the Sarin. West had a special addition for their masks. They'd get the surprise of a lifetime. For a few seconds, anyway.

The train rolled into the station, the announcement of their arrival came over the loudspeaker, and West saw Ibriham stand up and slip his arms through the loops of his backpack. West could see a hint of a smirk hiding beneath the man's dark beard.

"This is only a few blocks from the Imperialist's White House," he whispered in Arabic to West. "The infidels will be devastated."

West grinned. *You don't know the half of it, asshole.*

CHAPTER 22

McClain felt like he was carrying a heavy weight as he bounced down the last couple steps and pulled open the passenger door of Kelly's Benz.

"You look like you had the kind of weekend I wish I'd had," Kelly said. "For a man who had the whole weekend off, you sure do look pitiful." Kelly shot out from the curb to the accompaniment of screeching brakes and a few honks.

"Christ, watch it!" McClain glanced toward the back.

"They know better than to hit a man in a Benz. It's all that German intimidation."

"I thought it was engineering?"

"That too," Kelly said. He changed lanes. "So how did it go with Jen? Did you and she spend some quality time together?"

"Some," McClain said. "But mostly I stewed about the case."

"I thought we agreed we were gonna close it and pass the ball to the OHSCT guys."

"Yeah, but I'm still the primary and a couple things have been bothering me."

"Such as?"

McClain didn't have anything solid, just a lot of hunches based on bad memories. "I want to check out a few more leads," he said. "I've got our preliminary report done."

"*Our* report?" Kelly grinned. "Like you said, you're the primary."

"Which is why I need to check out a few more things."

"Laddie," Kelly said, "I've got a feeling this is gonna be one helluva of a day."

After the weekend I had, McClain thought, *it's got to be an improvement.*

Ted Lane was driving in to work when he got the text.

meet me rite away. i got something important. real big.

It was from Regina. What the hell could she mean? He'd been pressing her to find out more from Bernard about Ross's death.

Where would Lane be without this naive little creature and her undaunted belief that Bernard would leave his wife and marry her once his presidential bid wasn't looming on the horizon anymore? It was like a complex daisy-chain, convoluted but ultimately effective.

Lane managed to text a quick reply, agreeing to meet her at the usual place. He glanced at his watch. Eight-sixteen. He could be there by eight-fifty and still make it into work on time. He hoped her news would be as big as her text said it would.

Maybe things were about to break for him.

Viceroy had already been at his office inside the Pentagon when Lee's first text came in.

targets 1-4 on move. everything as planned so far.

No capitalization. Typical Lee. It was eight-thirty and Viceroy still had at least a couple more hours before he'd know if everything had fallen into place. He was waiting to hear from West on the progress of the dry run with the Arabs. It was a three-part op today: keep the Arabs ready, deal with the reporter and the leak, and drop the hammer on McClain. If he could get those three tasks completed, they'd be halfway to 1600 Pennsylvania Avenue. Hopefully, all he'd have to worry about after today was putting the final touches on Operation

Prometheus. Then he'd sit back and watch his brother-in-law sail to the White House on the winds of outraged popular opinion. Big Willie could fulfill his ultimate goal of being president, and Viceroy was sure the man would make a fine president.

So long as he doesn't realize that he'll just be keeping it warm for me!

McClain had listened to and dismissed ten of the fifteen tip-messages he'd gotten over the weekend about the murder of Mohammed Fassel. Most of them were crank calls.

Until he got to the last one.

"Detective McClain," a Mideastern-sounding voice said. "I have important information regarding the death of Mohammed Fassel. I wish to share this information with you. Call me."

Something about the tone set it apart from the other ones. McClain did some checks on the number and found out it was a throwaway cell.

Interesting. Why all the precautions?

He dialed the number. "This is Detective McClain. You called me."

"How do I know who you say you are?" The voice sounded the same as the one on the message.

"How else would I have gotten your message?"

"That proves nothing. How do I know that you are actually McClain? Are you the same man whose name and picture were on the news?"

Good old ZCCN broadcasting his baby blues all over the airwaves. "Look, I don't have time for games or twenty questions. If you've got information about the case, I'll be glad to listen. Otherwise, I'll hang up."

"Where are you now?"

"I'm in my office. Where are you?"

"That is not important. What is your cell phone number?"

McClain gave it to him.

"I shall call you back shortly."

McClain blew out a slow breath and glanced over at Kelly. "What's up?"

"I might have a live one," McClain said. His cell phone rang. Unknown caller.

The same voice said, "We can meet and I will tell you. But this information is not cheap."

"What do you mean by that? This isn't like TV, where I can pay you a lot of money."

"Money is not part of it," the voice said. "If I talk to you, my life is in danger. Grave danger. I will need protection. A new identity."

"Okay," McClain said. "Let's agree on a place."

"It must be a place of my choosing. And I must make certain you are not bringing other policemen to arrest me."

"That won't happen, I assure you. If you want to talk, I'd like to listen."

"Get in your car and start driving east. I will contact you on your cell phone once I have verified that you are alone."

The call ended.

"What was that all about?" Kelly asked.

"Maybe something, maybe nothing." McClain smiled. "Feel like going for a drive?"

Ted Lane pulled in to the parking garage and steered toward the up ramp to the third level. Pulling into the spot nearest the stairwell, he took out his cell phone and thumbed in his text.

I'm here. Where r u?

The reply came back almost immediately. Hardly enough time to bounce off the repeating towers.

ok. me 2. Come up.

She was already here. That's a first, he thought as he got out of his car and jogged to the stairwell. Up half-a-dozen stairs each way and he'd see what it was she had for him. He felt lucky this morning, like he was on the cusp of something big. Some real answers.

As he grabbed the U-shaped handrail and swung around to ascend the second set of steps, a shadow moved up on the next landing. Regina?

No, a man. Some Oriental guy with a misshapen nose, like he was a boxer or something.

Lane trotted up the last few steps. The guy didn't move.

"Mr. Lane," the Oriental said.

"Yes. Do I know you?"

"No, but you're about to." His left fist shot out and Lane felt it smack into his solar plexus. The wind whooshed out of him and he sank to his knees. He heard the guy say, "Pull up," into some kind of radio.

Lane struggled to catch his breath, each one hosting an accompanying wave of pain.

Sounds of an engine, a screech of brakes. The Oriental guy opened the door to the next level of the parking garage. He wore skin-tight black leather gloves. A dark van was on the other side of the crash bar, its side door open.

Oriental Guy grabbed Lane under the arms, lifting him like he weighed no more than a sack of groceries, and walked Lane toward the open door of the van.

Lane's feet dragged with each step. He still ached with every breath. He saw something inside the van as he got closer. Legs. Bare legs. A woman's bare legs. Shoes. Two more halting steps and he saw the woman's face.

Regina. Some big white guy behind her, holding her arms.

She looked terrified.

"No," Lane managed to say. "You can't do this."

"Get in," Oriental Guy said. His voice had a flat sound to it.

Lane tried to resist but felt himself swept along, like he was caught in a riptide.

"People know where I am. You can't do this."

Lane tumbled forward onto the van's hard metallic floor. Oriental Guy got in after him.

"Somebody will see this on surveillance video and you'll get caught," Lane said.

"Shut up." Oriental Guy shoved a gun in Lane's face. "That's one thing you liked about this place. No video cameras inside."

Chapter 23

McClain was getting tired of waiting when his cell phone finally rang. He glanced over at Kelly. "Looks like our boy."

"Are you in your car?" said the Mideastern-sounding voice.

"I am. Where are you?" McClain put the call on speaker.

"That is not important. Are you alone?"

"Are you?"

"Very well. I see you do not wish to talk with me. You do not wish to hear the information I have."

McClain spent a few moments cajoling the caller, who finally agreed to a meet and gave him the address of a parking garage.

"Come inside the structure," the voice said. "Go to level four. I will instruct you from there."

McClain glanced over at Kelly. "What do you think?"

"Could be something. Could be nothing. Could be a set-up, too."

"I've thought about that. You got your vest?"

"Shit, no. I don't wear that thing unless I really have to."

"You have to." McClain patted his chest. "I got mine."

"Good, I'll stand behind you. Mine's in my locker at the station."

McClain swore. "We can go back for it."

Kelly shook his head. "I ain't gonna wear it. Anyway, why we even going through all these changes? Ain't this one just one step away from a cold case hand-off?"

"Yeah, but a couple of things have been bothering me. I

wonder if the military or the CIA is involved."

"Spook stuff? Why do you think that?"

"Nothing concrete. Just a hunch." McClain rubbed his thumb over his fingernails, remembering how it felt to have them torn off. "We'd better pull over so you can get in the back seat, just in case somebody's watching when we go into that garage."

"Good thing I brought the snake," Kelly said, patting the big chrome Colt Python in his shoulder holster.

"You forget your vest but bring that unauthorized cannon?"

"The vest don't shoot back. The snake will. I can hit a fly on the White House wall from Constitution Avenue."

"I'm sure the president would appreciate that." McClain pulled over to the curb. "But let's hope that this time you can keep the snake in your pants."

The text buzzed on Viceroy's cell.

phase 1 complete. phase 2 in progress.

Viceroy sent an acknowledgment: *Give me a sit-rep when completed.*

He looked at his watch. Nine-fifteen. He wished he could personally supervise the interrogation of Lane. And Regina. Find out what they knew, what she'd told him. But he'd have to leave that to the others. Besides, it could be awkward if his brother-in-law found out that his paramour had been interrogated. Viceroy didn't want him thrown off his game. Not with the foreign policy and homeland security debate coming up tomorrow. Let him think she died in a car accident with Lane.

Hopefully, Ram Jet was getting Big Willie ready.

McClain and Kelly set their police radios on a "talk-around" band so they could communicate inside the parking garage without interference from the main channel. Plus, it would give them an edge until they found out exactly who they were dealing with. The caller told McClain to pull up to the fourth level and park.

"I'll leave it unlocked," McClain said to Kelly, who was crouching on the floor behind the front seats and holding his Glock.

"Okay. Don't take too long or I'll fall asleep back here."

McClain grinned. If the snitch was legit and he led McClain to Fassel's killer, like maybe that group of Arab students Felicia had mentioned, he could go to Beasley with a legitimate link that wouldn't put her in the trick-bag with her boss, and allow the case to be closed. The Colonel Viceroy connection still bothered him, though. He owed the man for saving his life, but something gnawed at McClain. He hoped this meeting might clear things up.

He rounded the last curve to the fourth level and stopped in the middle of the aisle, his eyes darting back and forth, ready to shove his car into reverse, if necessary. His cell phone rang. The throwaway number.

"I told you to park," the voice said.

"Yeah, well, I'm not gonna do that till I see where you are."

"Are you alone?"

"Of course," McClain said. "Are you? And give me a name. I like to know who I'm talking to."

"My name is Saddam."

"Okay. Now show me where you are. Step out into the aisle."

"And how do I know you will not shoot me?"

"You called me, remember? I don't even know you."

"You will leave your gun on the top of your car."

"No way, pal. Let's cut the shit. Either you want to talk to me or you don't. I'm through playing games. Step out into the aisle so I can see you."

"And then you will do the same?"

"Yeah." McClain scanned the area. Scattered cars, all parked perpendicular to the wall on the sloping ramp that led to the next adjacent level. A sturdy-looking barrier of metal posts and steel cables ran along the wall as a safety barrier.

About fifty feet away McClain saw a car door open and a man get out. He wore a baseball cap, a black hoodie, and a dark jacket with the collar pulled up. McClain couldn't see his face.

"Get ready, partner," McClain whispered. "I'm not liking the looks of this."

"Got your back," Kelly whispered.

McClain shifted the car into park and parked it in the center of the aisle. It would give him and Kelly a modicum of cover if the shit hit the fan. McClain thought about taking out his own piece and keeping it by his leg, but that might spook the guy. He slipped his radio into his jacket pocket. Saddam moved forward, his hands at his sides, empty for the moment. He kept his face down, staring at the concrete floor.

McClain tried to see the other man's face, but the brim of the baseball cap blocked the view. Scanning the man's body, he saw a bulge on the right side. He keyed his mic. "This fucker's packing."

Kelly keyed his in acknowledgment.

"Hold it right there," McClain said, grabbing his own weapon. "Keep your hands where I can see them."

The guy stopped, but kept his face down.

"Look at me," McClain said, his hand on the butt of his weapon. "I like to see who I'm talking to." The guy still kept his head down, but McClain could see he was no Arab. "Who are you? And don't try to tell me your name's Saddam."

The guy didn't move.

McClain's foot hit an old, discarded pop bottle and it went skittering across the floor. The suddenness of the sound caused McClain to reflexively crouch. As he did, he felt the whining rush of a round shooting by his head with the accompanying roar of a gunshot. The other guy pulled his coat back reaching for his piece.

McClain drew his weapon and brought it up just as a second shot rang out. This one struck him squarely in the chest. The impact felt like he'd been hit with a brick shot out of a cannon.

He fell to his knees, then went all the way down, rolling toward the parked car to his right. His arm felt asleep. As his shoulder struck the ground, his Glock slipped from his numb fingers. In a slow-motion roll, he watched the gun strike the solid floor and bounce. He continued to roll, feeling the chips of concrete spraying over him. He was weaponless and in a nar-row kill-zone between two cars. At the end of one of the cars, an open space loomed beyond the metal fence. He scrambled toward it as fast as he could.

Suddenly, he heard another boom from the other direction.

Kelly was returning fire.

"Sit-rep." McClain heard someone say.

"You get him?"

"Negative," the guy said. "But he lost his weapon."

"Secure it."

Shit, McClain thought. *They must have radios. Who are these guys?*

He'd reached the concrete curb and the edge of the fence. He pulled himself under the steel cable, rolled off the edge, and searched for a grip on the curb to lower himself down to the next level. His fingers still tingled with numbness. They scraped over the hard surface as he felt another bullet smack into the concrete next to him. Shoving himself through the opening, he freefell, landed feet first onto the hood of a parked car, then fell back hard into the windshield. The glass buckled under him and the car alarm screeched and then settled into a rhythmic beeping. Above him, he caught a flash of "Saddam's" face.

Arab my ass, he thought as the man's pistol extended down

through the opening. McClain rolled off the car. More rounds zipped by him as he managed to run across the aisle.

Up above, he heard the reports of several weapons.

Christ, he was disarmed and Kelly was up there by himself. McClain's side ached and each breath felt like a stabbing knife. Had he broken some ribs? No time to worry about that. He had to get to Kelly, get his back-up piece, and return fire. With as much speed as he could muster, he ran up the ramp to the fourth level, his chest aching, his hand fishing for his radio.

Another gunshot, then two more rapid ones. The slamming of a car door, the squeal of tires, the crunch of metal striking metal. Out of the corner of his eye, he saw a black SUV, its left front fender ripped with a fresh tear, barreling around the corner. He threw himself between two parked cars and rolled under the one on his left. The speeding SUV sailed by him without slowing.

Between the systematic beeping of the car alarm, he heard something else: a siren.

Was it the cavalry? God, he hoped so.

He crawled out from under the car and spoke into his radio. "Kelly, you okay?"

No response.

McClain ran up the ramp and switched the channel to police main-band frequency.

"Officers need assistance," he shouted into the radio, giving the address and ending with, "Shots fired."

He heard the dispatcher's confirmation as he rounded the curve to the fourth level and saw the unmarked, still sitting in the center of the aisle, its left side caved in. He kept searching for Kelly.

"Joe Kelly!" he yelled.

He scanned the aisle. No sign of the bad guys.

"Joe," he called again. Then he saw Kelly, face down between two cars, his hand extended outward, his Glock still in his fingers, a red puddle under his chest.

"Oh, God." McClain knelt beside his partner and checked his pulse. It was there, but weak. McClain yelled into his radio that they needed an ambulance. "Officer down! Officer down!"

He dropped the radio and lifted Kelly up, gently turning him so he could cradle his head. A bloody stain soaked through his shirt. McClain applied pressure to the wound with one hand while the other held Kelly's head.

"Joe, Joe, can you hear me?"

Kelly's eyes flickered. His lips twitched. His voice came out in a reedy gasp. "Fuckers got me good." His face had the graying look of a man about to die.

"Hold on, Joe, hold on. Help's on the way."

Kelly's eyes flickered again and McClain thought he detected a trace of a smile grace his partner's lips. "Guess we shoulda gone back . . . for my vest."

"Don't talk. It's going to be all right." McClain shifted his leg under Kelly's and applied more pressure. "Just hold on."

He heard a whelping siren approach.

Oh, God, he prayed, *please don't let it be too late.*

Ram Jet was putting Big Willie through the paces. *Good,* Viceroy thought. Big Willie had to appear tough on terror and ready, willing, and able to pick up the gauntlet. Ram Jet had two of his aides role-playing and they were asking all the right questions. One was acting as the debate coordinator and the other as President Harris.

"Mr. Vice President," the aide acting as the debate coordinator said, "much has been said about the use of enhanced interrogation techniques against prisoners of war during your tenure in the previous administration. What is your opinion of the use of these techniques and do you believe they constitute torture?"

Big Willie took a deep breath before he started, his face already flushed. His fingers brushed at his nose. "First of all, let me say this. I have never endorsed the use of—"

"No, no, no," Ram Jet interrupted. "Will, your body language is off. You're crouching. Like you're trying to duck. Don't dignify the question. And quit touching your face. It looks like a sign of guilt. Okay, let's start over. Bob, hit him again."

"Mr. Vice President, much has been said about the use of enhanced interrogation techniques . . ."

Viceroy's cell phone vibrated. A text from Lee: *problem phase two*

Viceroy sent a text: *How bad?*

can u call?

Roger that. Stand by.

"And how can you justify endorsing the circumvention of our Constitution?" the aide playing Harris asked. "How can America stand up and be an example to the rest of the world if we stoop to that level?"

"In principle, I agree with your sentiments, Mr. President," Big Willie replied, "but my *experience*—"

Viceroy had to trust that the rehearsal would enable his brother-in-law to rise to the occasion. Right now he had to assess the latest problem. He slipped out the door as unobtrusively as possible and pressed the speed-dial for Lee's cell as he walked.

"How bad?" he asked as soon as Lee answered.

"Bad enough. They failed to neutralize the target. His partner was hit, unknown status."

So McClain was not only tough, he was lucky too. It would have been better if he'd been killed, but he was effectively neutralized for the moment. With the back-up plan already in motion, McClain would be forced into a corner, making it totally believable that the soon-to-be "disgraced cop" would commit suicide in a few days.

"Sir," Lee said, "Bravo team recovered the target's weapon."

Now that's interesting. Perhaps it can be worked into the alternate plan. "What type?"

"Glock, forty caliber."

Better and better. "The same as Bravo was using?"

"Affirmative."

"Hold both of them. I'll call you in fifteen with further instructions."

"Roger that," Lee said.

Viceroy terminated the call. McClain's weapon was the same caliber as the one his partner was shot with. So it would be a simple manner of switching the barrels of the two weapons and the ballistics would trace it back to McClain's gun. If they recovered an identifiable projectile. Plus, he would have to figure some way to get McClain's weapon into the hands of the proper authorities. It was time to call Joiner.

Felicia wasn't sure what to think as she headed into the office. Joiner had sent out a message for the team to "meet immediately. Urgent matter." Knowing him, that could mean anything. Either way, it gave her a sense of purpose to get moving. As she drove she mulled over the past weekend and thought about how much of it she'd spent with Kevin McClain.

He was a unique man, thoughtful and serious. He came with some baggage—a bitch of an ex and a confused teenage daughter. And there was the race thing. She'd never dated a white man before, not that their spending so much time together constituted dating, but once or twice it had seemed like a good fit. Fun, too. It had been so long since she'd experienced anything like that.

Her cell rang. Damn! Joiner's ringtone.

She pulled over to the side of the road and glanced down to look for her phone.

When she finally flipped it open, Joiner's voice came through loud and clear.

"Knight, where are you?"

"On the Beltway, heading in."

She heard an exasperated sigh. "How soon before you get here?"

"Hard to say. Traffic's a nightmare. What's up?"

"Not over the phone." His chastising tone made her flush with irritation. "Just get here ASAP."

CHAPTER 24

McClain lay on the gurney, the blood pressure cuff attached to his arm doing its periodic tightening and measuring. The second time in a hospital emergency room in a week, he reflected. How much abuse was he going to have to take before his luck changed? But it could have been worse. Other than being naked under his gown and the extreme sensitivity of the right side of his chest—a hematoma, the doctor had called it—no broken ribs. Only bruises from the fall. He was okay. Physically, anyway. Emotionally, he was a wreck from worrying about Kelly. Why hadn't they gone back for his vest?

Shoulda, woulda, coulda. Too late now. Way too late.

He reached down and made sure his shoes were covering the plastic bag containing Kelly's Colt Python. Luckily, he'd known one of the uniforms who'd accompanied the ambulance to the ER and collared the guy and said he needed to get Kelly's shoulder rig and snake for safekeeping. The patrolman knew that the wounded Kelly didn't need the added grief of having to explain why he'd had an unauthorized handgun on his person. The patrolman left and returned moments later with a solemn expression and two plastic bags. He handed the one with the Python in it to McClain, who said, "How's my partner?"

"They took him into surgery." The patrolman held up the other bag. "I got his piece and his personal stuff. I'll turn it over to the dicks when they get here."

McClain thanked him.

That seemed like an eternity ago.

The curtain ripped back and two guys he didn't know pushed their way through. They identified themselves as Baron and Walker.

"We're going to need a preliminary statement," Walker said. He stood with his pen and notepad poised.

McClain ran it down for them exactly as it had happened.

"Where's your weapon?" Baron asked. He reached under the gurney to grab McClain's personal items.

McClain grabbed the man's arm. "Hey, that's my stuff."

Baron stopped and glared at him. "You know the drill. We'll need to take your gun, your vest and your clothes." He tried to pull his arm out of McClain's grasp but couldn't.

"And I'll give them to you," McClain said, "as soon as I get my wallet out of my pants."

"Suit yourself."

McClain released the man's arm and moved his legs off the gurney. The tiled floor felt cold on his feet even through his socks, and he wished he'd kept his damn underwear on. He bent down, knowing he was exposing his bare ass to the detectives, and carefully sorted out his vest, jacket, shirt, and pants. The Python was still safely tucked under his shoes. Straightening up, he fished in his pants' pocket and removed his wallet and ID badgecase. He gave the other items to Baron, who'd opened a big brown paper bag.

"Where's your weapon at?" Walker asked.

"I lost it during the firefight. I heard one of the offenders say he had it."

"How'd you hear that?"

"The offenders had radios," McClain said. "I dropped my gun as I fell through the space along the edge of the wall. I landed on a car on the next level down. Up above I heard one guy say to grab my gun."

Walker said nothing for a few moments. "So it's your statement that you lost your weapon during the incident?"

"Yes."

"What about your partner? Where's his weapon?"

"The uniform said he had it bagged for you."

"Any idea who these shooters were?" Baron asked.

"No."

"You got a cell phone number for the leader?"

McClain located his cell and scrolled down to "Saddam's" number. He read it off to them, then added, "But it's a throwaway. I already checked."

"Can you describe them?" Walker asked.

"The guy who called himself Saddam was faking a Mideastern accent. He's a white guy, maybe early to mid thirties. About six-one, six-two, a buck ninety. Wearing a dark jacket and pants. Some kind of gym shoes."

Walker scribbled the description down. "Remember anything else?"

"Yeah," McClain said. "Like I told you, there were at least two of them and they had radios. I think they were military."

"Military? What the hell does that mean?"

"It means what I said. Their speech, the way they moved, it all points to them being military guys."

"And you know this how?"

"I was in the Army."

Baron smirked. "I was in the Marines."

McClain watched their reactions. It was clear they were humoring him. Great. The only lead he had and they were ready to put it in the circular file.

After a few more questions they said McClain would have to appear downtown in the morning for the review board inquiry and left him alone.

McClain tore the blood pressure cuff off his arm. It hurt to walk and he felt every step. One of the nurses saw him and stopped him.

"I need to check on my partner," he said. "He was shot."

He felt her gentle but firm touch as she guided him back to his cubicle.

"As soon as I hear anything, I'll let you know," she said. "In the meantime, is there anyone you'd like to call on your behalf?"

McClain flipped open his cell and scrolled down to Felicia's number. Before he could press the button, the nurse steered him back to the gurney and told him to lie down.

"Your cell won't work in here," she said. "I'll get you a phone."

"Sounds like a plan," he said, wondering what Felicia would say.

Dumbfounded would be an understatement, thought Felicia. She sat in Joiner's office as her boss expounded upon the "latest development." The man across from her, Tom Greeley, was from the financial crimes unit. Appropriately, he looked more like an accountant than an FBI agent. She felt her cell phone vibrate on her belt, but didn't dare look to see who was calling. Not with Joiner on a tear.

"This off-shore account information was recently brought to our attention and I've directed Special Agent Greeley to assist in our investigation," Joiner said. "Since you were assigned as liaison agent to the perpetrator, I want you to work on this as well."

"Perpetrator?" Felicia said. "Have we verified this information yet? And where did it come from?"

Joiner pursed his lips. It really irritated her when he did that. Like he was demonstrating his distaste being in the same room with her. "Let's just say that it came from a reliable source."

Which probably meant Viceroy, she thought.

"We'll need you both to coordinate with MPDC's internal

affairs division," Joiner continued. "They need to know they've got a dirty cop in their midst."

"Aren't we being a bit premature?"

"Premature?" Joiner's jaw hung slack and the bags under his eyes bulged slightly. "Need I remind you what all is at stake here?" His gaze shot toward Greeley.

Felicia wondered how much he'd told the other man.

"I don't want us to make a rush to judgment before we have—"

"Rush to judgment?" Joiner's voice rose a few decibels. "I want McClain dealt with immediately. At best he's a loose cannon gumming up the works. Most likely, he's some kind of dirty cop. Now, get over to MPDC headquarters tomorrow and start the ball rolling."

As Felicia stood up, she felt her cell phone vibrate again.

Joiner's allegations couldn't be true. She couldn't have misjudged McClain so totally. She wondered what he'd say.

"I really appreciate you coming to get me," McClain said, as he stretched out inside her car. "I didn't know who else to call."

The evening darkness was settling over everything and a light rain had begun to fall. The flashes of oncoming headlights were starred by the drops on the windshield until they were obliterated by the moving wiper blade. On the floor by his feet he could feel the bag containing Kelly's snake and shoulder rig. At least he'd managed to get that out of the hospital.

"I'm glad you did," Felicia said.

She was great, saying she'd be there immediately, after he finally got through to her. That had taken most of the afternoon. Now it was almost eight and he was starving. But he knew stopping at a restaurant was totally out of the question. Not with him in hospital scrubs instead of clothes. At least they let him keep his underwear. He wanted to get home, take a hot shower, and try to unwind. Kelly had come through the surgery okay, but was totally out of it. The doctor said it was still touch and go. McClain made a silent vow to get back to the hospital first thing tomorrow, then remembered he'd have to appear downtown to answer questions. He turned to Felicia.

"Ever notice how sometimes the whole world seems to be stacked up against you?"

Her smile looked nervous, uncertain. She said nothing.

"I mean, there I was, all set to hand off this Mohammed Fassel case to the OHSCT with a cold case clearance, and out of the blue an anonymous informant calls me, based on that stupid news report that somehow got leaked, and the next thing I know my partner and best friend is lying there shot and I've lost my damn gun."

"How's your partner doing?"

"Collapsed lung, but thank God the bullet missed his heart." McClain shook his head. "If only we'd taken the time to go back for his damn vest."

"Don't leave home without it."

"Yeah, right." He looked over at her profile as she drove. Her face was intense. "I don't suppose I could convince you stop off at one of these fast-food places on the way and get an order for two, could I?"

"Kevin, I don't think that would be such a good idea tonight."

"Yeah, it figures. I haven't had a good idea all day. It's just—"

"Just what?"

"I almost bought the farm today. And my partner is still not out of the woods. I don't feel like being alone tonight."

He felt her hand on his arm and a warm squeeze.

"What have you got a taste for?" she asked.

Felicia rolled over and looked at the illuminated digital clock beside McClain's bed. Ten-forty-seven. Had they really been in

253

bed for over two hours? She felt his naked body move against her hip and leg. His backside. He'd dozed off after their heated lovemaking session, but he'd given her some cuddling first. His breathing was sonorous. The only other light was the ambient glow of the streetlights. Not that his apartment had much of a view, which made the idea that he was on the take even more ridiculous. But how could she explain that to Joiner and Greeley? By all rights, she shouldn't even be here. This whole thing was one big mistake. A career-ending mistake, if she wasn't careful.

She reviewed the evening in her mind. *How did we end up in bed together?*

It had started innocently enough—the ride from the hospital. She got the impression that he didn't even have enough money for a taxi. And no one else to call. That alone would have been enough to convince her to go get him, but deep down she knew she had a growing attraction to him. The way he treated her—professionally but also respectfully.

Their fast-food dinner had spilled into laughter, as they watched TV and he told dumb jokes. She was glad that the conversation hadn't turned to law enforcement until he began talking about how sore he was. His recounting of the shooting, his suspicions about the assailants being military or ex-military, his concern for his wounded partner. There were a lot of unanswered questions. And a lot he didn't know yet. But it was bearing down on him like a runaway train. It was all she could do to keep from warning him, even though she was totally convinced that these latest allegations about him being on the take were ludicrous.

She'd offered to give him a back massage in order to change the subject. They'd strayed too close to the pending investigation. Greeley had probably already dug into McClain's financial records, but she wanted to do more research herself.

When her fingers began to knead the tense muscles of his back she was surprised at how muscular and solid he felt. Not that she'd thought of him as soft. She remembered seeing him working out at the gym, but up close he felt like a rock. He winced when she hit a tender spot. She suggested he take off his shirt so she could see the bruises.

Yeah, right.

It was a prelude to foreplay. After the shirt came off, he rolled onto his side, looked up at her, cupped his hand behind her neck, and pulled her face down toward his. The kiss was gentle at first, their closed lips just brushing together once, twice, then coming together again with the flicking of tongues. The next thing she knew they were entwined in each other's arms and frantically pulling at zippers, buttons, and snaps.

It had been a long time for her. So long that she didn't want to think about it. She only wanted to think about now. The here and now.

He moved at half-speed, caressing, seemingly more intent on satisfying her than himself. His lips gazed over her neck, down to her breasts, his tongue flicking over her nipples. His big hands moved over her stomach, her hips, and his touch felt so soft.

It was a uniquely wonderful experience.

But she also wondered if it would happen again, once he found out that she and Greeley were supposed to be investigating him.

God, she dreaded telling him. Slowly, she tried to untangle their legs so she could slip out of bed and silently leave. But as she moved, he stirred, opened his eyes, and smiled.

"Hey, beautiful. Where are you going?"

"Nowhere," she said, leaning forward to kiss him. "I'm right here for you."

★ ★ ★ ★ ★

As Viceroy sat in the darkness of his den and fingered one of the Havanas, the text update from Baker came: *Targets spending night together at his apartment.*

Any conversation?

Just pillow talk.

So McClain was dicking her, eh? Interesting turn of events. He calculated how this would affect the overall plan.

If anything, it might work out for the better. An illicit romance would call Knight's investigative abilities into question, but he didn't want her out of the picture yet. He needed her to stay on the case long enough to participate in the ill-fated raid on the student radicals' apartment so he could wipe her and the rest of the FBI team out in one fell swoop. And this had already set in motion.

Let the two lovebirds enjoy the moment. Let them have tonight. Tomorrow, when McClain went in for the shooting review, he'd get the surprise of his life.

He'll be the one getting fucked. More movements to plan on the chessboard.

Viceroy lifted the lid of the humidor and replaced the Havana.

Victory would make it taste sweeter.

CHAPTER 25

Felicia was gone when McClain woke the next morning. He brought his face to her pillow, trying to gather a remnant of her scent, but that was gone too. The apartment was silent as well.

A bit of role reversal, he thought as he got out of bed and headed for the shower. It was supposed to be the guy who made a Lone Ranger exit in the morning.

Beasley's call surprised him, coming at seven-forty and telling him they wanted him to report in at nine-thirty sharp.

"I still haven't gotten my car back, Lieu," McClain said. "I'll have to take the train and the bus."

"I'll send a car for you," Beasley said. "Just be ready."

The terseness of the lieutenant's tone gave McClain pause. He hoped it didn't mean that Kelly had taken a turn for the worse. As soon as Beasley had hung up McClain called the hospital and asked for the nurse's station in intensive care. He was told that Mr. Kelly was "resting comfortably but still under sedation."

The car Beasley sent turned out to be a marked unit and McClain had to ride in the back, the plastic seat hard and unforgiving and the floor smelling of regurgitated booze, piss, and pepper spray. By the time they got to headquarters he was irritated. He hoped they hadn't learned about Kelly's unauthorized gun.

As he walked toward Beasley's office, he noticed that the lieutenant's blinds had been closed, effectively blocking the view inside and out. Several of the other dicks eyed him. Two of them offered a thumb's-up.

Inside the office he saw Elliott Zook, Internal Affairs, some geeky guy in a suit, and—he couldn't believe it—Felicia.

Beasley's face looked drawn. He motioned McClain to the chair in front of his desk.

What the hell's going on?

"McClain," Beasley said, "let me make the introductions. This is Special Agents Greeley and Knight from the FBI. You know Lieutenant Zook from IAD."

What are the feds doing here? And Felicia?

"We need to get a preliminary statement from you concerning yesterday's incident during which Detective Kelly was shot," Zook said.

"I gave my statement and my report at the hospital."

"I know. I read it. I have a few more questions."

"How is this an IAD matter? Shouldn't it be reviewed by the shooting board?"

"Like he said, we just have a couple of questions." Beasley cleared his throat. "As well as another matter we need to address."

McClain looked around. Felicia's face looked as tight as an overwound clock. "My report says it all."

"It also says you lost your weapon," Zook said.

"That's right."

"How'd you do that?"

McClain didn't like the IAD man's tone, and silently counted to ten before answering. "I thought you said you read my report."

"I'd like to hear it from you."

McClain took another ten count, then related the entire incident.

"Did you fire your weapon at any time?" Zook asked.

McClain thought back. Had he fired? "I don't believe so."

"You don't *believe* so?"

"That's right," McClain felt his anger rising. "I didn't fire my weapon because I got hit *before* I could shoot."

He glanced at Felicia. Her face looked even more pained. Why the hell was she here?

"What would you say if I told you the sleeves of your jacket came back positive for GSR?" Zook said.

"I assisted Detective Kelly after he was hit. He fired his weapon. Some residue must have rubbed off on me."

"How did you lose your gun again?" Zook asked.

"I told you. I dropped it when I got hit."

"Yeah, in the vest. Very fortuitous."

"What's that supposed to mean?"

Zook shrugged. "I was wondering how come you had your vest on, but Kelly wasn't wearing his."

McClain stared at the man. He tried to figure what they were insinuating. "Detective Kelly left his vest here. We should have gone back for it."

"To say the least."

"What are you insinuating, Zook?"

"Are you sure you didn't fire your weapon?" Zook's tone had the resonance of a gunshot.

"Yeah, I'm sure."

"We recovered your weapon from the scene early this morning."

"Where was it?"

"Under a trashcan in the parking garage. An anonymous citizen notified a security guard when he saw it."

"Anonymous citizen—what kind of bullshit is that?"

"Listen to the man, McClain," Beasley said.

"A cop got shot," Zook said. "We rushed the ballistics on this one."

Michael A. Black

"So?"

"So, we managed to recover a projectile from the driver's-side headrest of your unmarked. A forty-caliber round. It matches your gun, pal. The round that hit Kelly was a through and through, but we're still hoping to recover it, too. In the meantime, how do you explain a bullet from your weapon being lodged in the headrest of the squad car your partner was standing next to when he was shot?"

McClain felt stunned. "I can't."

"Especially when you *say* you didn't fire your gun. We'd also like to give you a chance to tell us what you know about this account at the Royal Bank of the Cayman Islands."

"The Cayman Islands?" His gaze shot toward Felicia again. Was she a part of this? And what about last night? Had she known about this then?

"We can do this the easy way, or the hard way," Zook said. "Regardless, at this point I'm obliged to make you aware of your rights."

"I know my fucking rights."

"McClain," Beasley said, "watch your mouth."

"Do you want to cooperate or what?" Zook asked.

"You don't want to know what I want to do." McClain got to his feet.

Zook stood up. "You want to take a swing at me?"

McClain stared at the man's face. Zook was a whole head shorter than he was. Was he hoping to provoke a physical confrontation?

"No," McClain said, barely able to contain his disgust for the man. "But I'm not answering any more of your questions until I speak to an attorney."

"That figures," Zook said.

McClain regained a modicum of control, and although he still felt like he'd been sucker-punched, he managed to turn to

260

Beasley and ask, "Is there anything else?"

"Sit down, McClain," Beasley said. His eyes looked like two glaring headlights.

McClain returned the stare for a few seconds, then sat. Zook hovered over him. McClain pointed to the IAD man. "Get that asshole out of here."

"You're not making the rules here," Beasley said. "Your partner's in the hospital with a hole in his chest, apparently shot with your gun, with no witnesses to the shooting, and now the feds found some heavy off-shore accounts that trace back to you."

McClain felt like he was starring in a nightmare.

Beasley read him a formal complaint. It stated that he was being stripped of his police powers, effective immediately, and suspended with pay pending the outcome of the investigation. Beasley ended with, "We've already got your gun, so give me your badge and commission card."

McClain swallowed hard. He'd been set up. Totally set up. But by whom? He reached into his pocket, removed his badge-case, and tossed it on Beasley's desk.

"All right," Beasley said, "if you don't want to answer any questions, get the hell out of here. You're stripped."

McClain looked at each of their faces, ending with Felicia's. He thought he detected a hint of compassion in her eyes.

Was last night a fucking dream, he wondered, or had Felicia been trying to see if he'd talk in his sleep, maybe say something about the Cayman Islands?

Felicia made sure all the stalls in the ladies' room were empty before she pressed the button to make the call. It rang twice and then went to voice mail.

Felicia debated whether or not to say anything as the record-ing beeped. Did she really want to leave traceable voice evidence that she'd contacted McClain during an ongoing investigation? But hell, they'd slept together last night. What if that came out? She'd been backed into a corner, just like McClain.

"Kevin, it's Felicia," she said. "We need to talk. Unofficially. I need you to know I am *not* the enemy. I'm on *your* side. Call me. Please."

She heard the door to the washroom open and a female officer came in and went to one of the stalls.

I've said it all anyway, Felicia thought as she terminated the call. *And probably said way too much.*

McClain stopped when he got outside and took a couple of deep breaths. The air felt cool. He brought his hand up and massaged his temples. His cell phone vibrated in his pocket with a message.

Fuck it, he thought. *I don't want to talk to anybody.*

He tried to figure out his next move. What was open to him? And how in the hell had all this happened so quickly? It was like he'd been suddenly recast as Job in some weird stage play. Only this was real life. His fucking life.

He put all the pieces in front of him as he walked. Maybe if he arranged them in order, they'd make sense. *The Fassel murder, the anonymous tip, the meeting in the parking garage, the set-up, the firefight, Felicia. Had she been part of it all along?*

No, there's no way she would have gone to bed with me if that were the case.

And what about his gun? He reviewed the incident in his mind. Had he fired his weapon? No. So somebody else had.

The bad guys had picked up his gun after he'd dropped it. Because they were trying to set him up.

What about the offenders? Radios, military lingo, escape plan. They were organized. Like they'd done it before. And they'd vanished into thin air, just like they were never there.

Never there, never happened, who did that sound like?

It was the slimmest of leads, tenuous and probably unprovable, but it was all he had. He was tired of getting punched without being able to punch back. He saw a cab.

"Take me to the Pentagon," he told the driver. It was time to hit back.

CHAPTER 26

Viceroy saw the button on his office line light up but ignored it. On the other side of the desk Lee held the flash drive toward him. "I thought you'd like to know Bravo team successfully entered Lane's apartment and recovered his laptop, sir."

Viceroy smiled as he took the flash drive. "And this?"

"He backed up the files," Lee said.

The light on his phone continued to blink. Viceroy still ignored it.

"I'm assuming the announcement of the discovery of the wreck will be forthcoming shortly," Viceroy said. "The cover story is in place?"

"Reservations were made in his name, with his credit card yesterday." As usual, Lee's face showed no emotion, part of what made him so formidable both in and out of the ring.

With Lane's predisposition as a hound dog, having reservations at a hotel for him and a guest in Bethesda would look like another little recreational diversion. So what if the girl turned out to be an administrative assistant to Big Willie? Shit happens. People fall in love. Or lust. It happened a lot in Washington, D.C.

He thought about how he needed to break the news to his brother-in-law about Regina's "accident" before it hit the news. It would be hard because the idiot had been getting sentimental lately. He'd have to put it behind him before the debate tonight. Ram Jet could handle the brief press statement expressing their condolences.

Viceroy saw two men stop in front of his closed office door. Through the glass window portion he saw that one was in uniform. Sergeant Barry. The other was in civvies, but he looked familiar.

McClain.

What the hell was he doing here?

Sergeant Barry grabbed McClain's arm, but he shook it off and banged against the door.

Lee jumped to his feet as the door was thrust open.

"I'm sorry, sir," Barry said. "He came in the main office wanting to see you and I told him to wait. He snuck in here when someone else went out."

Viceroy raised his eyebrows. "Is that so?"

McClain's face twisted into a snarl. "We need to talk. Now."

"Security's on the way, sir," Barry said. He tried to grab hold of McClain's arm again but the cop balled up his fist and drew his arm back.

"Hey, there's no need for that." Viceroy raised his hand. "Who the hell are you?"

"You know damn well who I am." McClain kept his arm cocked, fist clenched.

"Have we met?" Viceroy waited for a few beats, then said, "Oh, yeah, we did meet at Special Agent Joiner's office, didn't we? You're that MPDC detective."

"Not anymore, thanks to you."

Viceroy feigned surprise. "I'm afraid I don't understand."

"You want me to escort him out of here, sir?" Lee said.

Viceroy shook his head. "I don't think so. You've obviously got some issues, Detective, but I don't see how I'm involved with them. After all, we hardly know each other."

"We know each other all right," McClain shot back, keeping his gaze on Lee. "Back in ninety-three in Somalia."

"Somalia?" Viceroy again feigned surprise.

"I was a prisoner. Your team rescued me."

Viceroy clucked sympathetically. "Sorry, can't say that I recall. But that was a lot of missions ago."

"Black ops," McClain said. "It never happened."

Viceroy remembered the field hospital on the other side of the world, but he only smiled and shook his head.

Two uniformed MPs pushed through the door and grabbed McClain's arms.

McClain glared at Viceroy.

"I don't know how all this ties together," he said. "But I know you're behind it. And I'm gonna find out if it's the last thing I do."

"You want him charged, sir?" one of the MPs asked.

"No. Just document everything and escort him off the premises." He glared back at McClain. "But if you come back or come anywhere near me, it'll be a big mistake."

"You're the one making the mistake," McClain said over his shoulder as the MPs were escorting him out of the room. "Considering how many times you've tried to take me out and failed, I figured you'd know that."

"That was the troop we rescued in Mogadishu?" Lee asked after McClain had been escorted from the room.

"Yeah. Ironic, isn't it? You remember him?"

"I remember the mission is all. What now, sir?"

With his partner shot and his reputation called into question, Viceroy had assumed the detective would crawl into a corner and stay there until he could be properly dealt with. But he was stubborn, like a pesky horsefly—a swatable horsefly.

"Maintain the full-time surveillance on him, Lee. Have Baker and his group give me periodic sit-reps." Viceroy blew out a slow breath. The debate was scheduled for tonight, after which he'd planned to let things settle for a day or two before executing Prometheus on Friday, but perhaps it was time to move things up again.

After putting the two taxi rides on his already overextended credit card, McClain scavenged his apartment for something to take the edge off, found a bottle of scotch, and splashed some into a glass of ice as the television voice piqued his interest.

"There are further details emerging regarding the shooting incident at the Jefferson Heights parking garage facility yesterday involving two MPDC detectives," the announcer said. "Police released the names of the officers involved: Detectives Kevin McClain and Joseph Kelly, who was seriously wounded. Sources within the police department stated that the detectives were in the garage investigating a recent homicide and came under fire.

"Officer Kelly is reported to be recovering after surgery," the newscaster continued, "and is listed as critical but stable at this time."

Thank God for that, McClain thought. At the hospital, a few hours ago, the doctors had told him Joe had made it through the surgery all right but was being kept sedated. McClain managed to give Joe's hand a quick squeeze. He hadn't stirred, but McClain hoped he'd somehow felt it. Joe's son and daughter had arrived from upstate New York and McClain had felt uneasy staying there. What if the department persisted with the horseshit accusation that Joe had been hit by friendly fire? At least that hadn't made the news.

Yet.

Both the newspapers and the TV channels were broadcasting his and Kelly's names. But they were also showing photos. That certainly wasn't standard procedure. Had the department brass released that info in order to set the stage for something else? To ward off the bad publicity they anticipated if that bullshit charge about some kind of secret Cayman Island bank account was true?

I wish I did have a secret bank account. Shit, all they have to do is take a look at my real bank balance and they'll see I'm living just above the poverty level.

His cell phone vibrated again. He glanced at the screen, hoping it was Jen, but saw it was Felicia.

He'd tried several times to get through to Jen after the story with his name hit the news. He wanted her to hear about it from him first. But Lynn had put the kibosh on that, refusing to let him talk to her and screening her calls. Even her cell went to voice mail, which the service said was full.

"Well, will you at least tell her I'm all right?" he'd asked his ex.

"She already knows," Lynn said before hanging up.

His cell was about ready to go to his voice mail. He answered.

Silence, then, "I wasn't sure if you'd pick up. I've been calling you all day." She paused then said, "How are you doing?"

"Just great."

"I can't say I'm surprised at how you're talking to me now, but I'd like a chance to clear the air."

"Fine."

"Do you want to meet for coffee or something?"

"How would that look? You being seen with the suspect of your investigation."

"Look, Kevin, I'd like a chance to explain things." Her voice sounded tight, like she was ready to cry. Or explode. "What happened and how it went down was as big a surprise to me as it was to you."

"Do you believe it?"

"We don't need to be talking like this on the phone, do we?"

She was right. Suppose they'd initiated a wire tap on him? The feds just needed one party consent to get a warrant, and no warrant if it was connected to some homeland security issue, even if it was based on a bunch of bullshit.

"Come on by if you want," he said. "I still don't have a car."

"I'll be there shortly."

When she'd hung up he slowly set his cell phone down and went back to watching the news. Maybe now he'd be able to get a few more answers.

CHAPTER 27

Viceroy was knotting his tie when his cell chimed with the incoming text.

Lovebirds getting together. His place. Baker texted.

Lovebirds. Knight and McClain. For a special agent with the Bureau she was showing exceptionally poor judgment by seeing the target of a special corruption investigation.

Baker sent another text. *Any special orders?*

Negative, Viceroy texted back. *Maintain surveillance and notify me of anything untoward.* Untoward. He liked that word. Very Shakespearian. He tried to recall which play this most recent series of events reminded him of, and kept coming back to the histories. *Henry IV,* Parts *One* and *Two* to be exact. Prince Hal setting the stage for the ultimate triumph over his enemies, all the while letting others, like Falstaff, take the credit and the glory. For the moment. And when the time was right, he too would "break through the foul and ugly mists."

Roger that, Baker texted back. *Targets 1 and 2 on news channel.*

Viceroy picked up the remote and clicked on the TV. The scroll beneath a Breaking News banner said: *ZCCN reporter and friend killed in traffic accident.*

Good, it was perceived exactly the way he wanted. And from the looks of it, they were withholding Regina's name and her association to BigWillie's office, for the moment. And by tomorrow, it would be shuffled to the bottom of the news deck.

Everything looks good, he texted. *Maintain surveillance.*

Roger that, sir. Out.

Viceroy set the phone down and finished touching up the knot on his tie. He knew his presence at the debate tonight would be crucial to Big Willie being able to perform. *Prince Hal propping up another of his lackies, until the mists were burned through.*

"You knew it was coming and you didn't even tell me?" Mc-Clain said. "Even after we'd—"

"That made it harder, believe me." Her eyes welled up with tears as she put her hands over his. "But I want you to know that I never believed it. Not for a second."

He stared at her, wanting so much to trust what she was saying. Did she really believe in him? It mattered to him that she did. It mattered a lot.

"And I won't rest until I've cleared you of this stuff," she said. "I promise."

Something in the way she said it buoyed his inner spirit. Here was a beautiful woman, a professional colleague, someone inside the investigation, saying that she knew he was innocent. But was that going to be enough? He canted his head toward her.

Her gaze stayed on his face. "What?"

"It would mean a lot to me if you stayed with me tonight."

"I'd love to stay, but I can't."

"Why?"

"Remember those radical students I told you about? The ones who are suspected of murdering Fassel?"

He nodded.

"We're working on a search warrant for a raid on their apartment. We have to get the complaint worked up and ready. Joiner wants us to follow the tactical team in."

"He wants you on the raid?"

"Yes."

"Make sure you wear your vest," he said. "How much longer

271

can you stay tonight?"

"Long enough."

He leaned forward and kissed her softly on the lips. "I guess we won't be watching the debate after all, but that's all right. I've heard enough double talk in the last couple of days to suit me. My bullshit gauge is on extra-full."

She kissed him back, then added, "President Harris is going to win, anyway." She unbuttoned her blouse.

"I hope so," McClain said, starting to get undressed.

The applause was substantial. Big Willie waited until it had all but faded before he struck back with, "In principle, I agree with your sentiments, Mr. President, but my *exper-i-ence*—" he drew out the word "—tells me a different story, from a different perspective. For one thing, I doubt that the Founding Fathers ever intended that our Constitution would be used to protect our enemies in a time of war."

The other side of the audience applauded. *Our side,* Viceroy thought. Good. His brother-in-law was playing the role perfectly. Every move was exactly as they'd practiced it.

The man was a spin-artist.

Viceroy had molded Big Willie into the perfect model of the patriotic conservative—the kind of leader the country needed after the next major terrorist attack on American soil. The burgeoning public disapproval of the torture issue would evaporate by this time tomorrow night, and Harris would be relegated to the role of the president who was soft on terror, dropped his guard, and let it happen on his watch.

The perfect foil to set it off. And it was only hours until it would all unfold. Viceroy flipped open his phone. It was time to yank Joiner's chain.

★　★　★　★　★

Her breathing felt slow and regular and he wondered if she'd dozed off. She felt warm and comfortable, lying partially on top of him, her head resting on his shoulder. They'd been moving in that special rhythm together that brought both of them to the brink numerous times, only to mutually slow and back away, until, inevitably, they'd both tumbled pell-mell down that slippery slope into ecstasy and bliss.

Remembering it, he thought about how enamored he was with her, and wondered if she felt the same way. But even the lingering ecstasy of their interlude couldn't erase the pervasive gloom.

Her steady breathing continued as he turned on the TV. A pair of newscasters discussed the recently concluded presidential debate. "Certainly the most contentious issue that came up tonight was the one of the use of torture during Vice President Bernard's tenure."

The picture shifted back to the two men standing behind lecterns on the stage: Bernard looked broad-shouldered and burly compared to the lean President Harris. "Mr. Vice President," the moderator stated, "much has been said about the use of what has been referred to as 'enhanced interrogation techniques' against prisoners of war during your tenure in the previous administration. What is your opinion of the use of these techniques and do you believe they constitute torture?"

The camera shifted to Vice President Bernard. "First of all, let me say this. I have never endorsed the use of torture on prisoners of war or captured enemy combatants. However, there is a clearly defined line between torture and enhanced interrogation techniques, such as waterboarding. Such techniques do not, in my opinion, constitute cruel and unusual forms of interrogation and have been shown to be effective in gathering information that helped safeguard our shores."

Bernard's side of the audience applauded. It sounded weak.

The debate moderator asked President Harris to respond. He said, "It's unfortunate that this issue has become a game of semantics and such euphemisms as enhanced interrogation techniques has become a stand-in for the word 'torture.' Endorsing that type of brutality is inimical to our Constitution and to the very ideals upon which this great country was based." He paused for a hearty round of applause from the audience. "How can America stand proud and be an example to the rest of the world if we stoop to that level?"

The applause came again. Bernard's face looked stoic and movie-star handsome. "In principle, I agree with your sentiments, Mr. President, but my *exper-i-ence,*" he said, drawing out the word, "tells me a different story, and from a very different perspective. For one thing, I doubt the Founding Fathers ever intended that our Constitution would be used to protect our enemies in a time of war."

McClain hit the mute button as Felicia's cell chimed.

"You're not going to answer that, are you?" he said.

"I have to, Kevin. It's Joiner's ringtone."

He rolled on his side so he could watch her.

"Yes, sir," she said. "No, sir, I'm in bed."

He chuckled. Her dark eyes flashed angrily at him. "Now?" she said. "Has it been started?"

McClain felt a twinge in his gut. What was this about?

"All right," she said. "I understand." Another pause. "It has? What time?" Pause. "Oh, my God." Pause. "Okay, I'll be there shortly."

She leaned down and kissed him, said, "I have to go, Kevin," then began collecting her clothes. "The raid's been moved up. Seven-fifty tomorrow morning. Joiner wants me to help finalize the warrant. That alone will probably take me a couple of hours. Then it'll have to be reviewed and authorized."

"It's what, nine-thirty now? Are they going to wake up a federal judge at midnight?"

"For something like this," she said, "the U.S. Attorney has the judge on speed dial."

"Where is this raid?"

She slipped on her thong and looped her arms through the straps of her bra. "You know I can't tell you that."

"Come on."

She fastened the bra hooks. "It's in Arlington, on Whipple Street. But that's all I'm saying."

"I guess I'll see it on the news tomorrow to find out the rest." He flipped off the TV. "You were right about the debate. Harris kicked his ass."

CHAPTER 28

In and out under the cover of darkness. Those were the colonel's instructions. West, Lee, and two other Alpha team members, Taylor and Dobrovits, stopped at the building adjacent to the target site. West looked at Lee, who pulled out his cell phone and thumbed out a quick text. Their faces were tiger-striped. Just like old times.

They waited. It was four-thirty in the morning. They were in an alley. West watched a rat scavenge through some trash, the cans carelessly left on their sides.

Pathetic. The area was next to the nation's capitol and it had turned into a ghetto. Maybe the colonel would be able to straighten things out, once his plan went into effect.

He heard Lee's phone vibrate.

Lee read the text and nodded. That meant that Baker, who was manning the surveillance van with his FBI helper, had made the switch that would mask all the audible sounds coming from the listening devices inside the students' apartment. On the playback it would be all static. Their movements would be totally indistinct.

West did a quick peek around the corner. It was clear. He motioned as the others lined up next to him. They all did a simultaneous quick-step to the cover of the adjacent building.

West was already intimately familiar with the rear door. He used his master key to open it and held it as the others slipped inside. They crept up the stairs to the second landing. Noise control. No loose equipment on their belts, no hurried steps.

West came up the stairs last. The others were on each side of the back door of the apartment. In and out, under the cover of darkness. So far, so good.

West inserted his key into the deadbolt lock first and twisted it slowly. He felt the bolt retracting. He slipped the key out and worked it slowly into the doorknob lock. That opened just as easily.

It had been the plan to hit the towelheads early, before they got up for morning prayers. They had no idea D-Day had been moved up.

Just another bad assumption in their history of stupidity.

West entered the apartment first.

He grinned. This time he didn't have to take off his shoes. He flipped down his night-vision goggles and gestured with three fingers as he passed the first bedroom. He pointed toward the farthest room. Ibriham and Fahim would be sleeping in that one. The other three of lesser status, Amir, Hassan, and Malik, were in the first bedroom. West, Lee, and Dobrovits moved into that one. Taylor stood ready in the hall, holding his Sig Sauer at chest level. The colonel wanted them to do this silently and without gunplay.

And why wouldn't they be able to do that? They were a trained special forces team taking out five stupid Saudi exchange students who had been recruited for their devout gullibility, not members of the Iranian Quds Force. Not even Al-Qaeda wannabes. No, these punk-asses were nothing more than some foreign-grown low-grade terrorist pawns that the mad mullahs had originally recruited for early martyrdom.

It was time to send them looking for their seventy-two virgins.

West moved into the first bedroom, his goggles illuminating the scene. Two slumbering men, Amir and Hassan, lay next to each other on the bed. The third, Malik, was on a mattress on the floor. He took Malik as Lee and Dobrovits went on either side of the bed. When they were all in position, each man waited for three seconds, then reached down and secured the proper strangling holds on each of the three slumbering Arab's necks. Their fingers made the proper grabbing and ripping motions that they knew would spell death quickly and quietly.

Malik squirmed a little, his eyes opening in terror as West used a knee to pin him down. The eyes stayed wide open as West crushed the man's larynx.

Allah a akbar, West thought. God is great.

After Malik had stopped moving, West used his free forefinger to poke one of Malik's open eyes. No twitch, no movement. It was done.

He stood and glanced over at the other team members. They were doing the eye-checks on Amir and Hassan. Lee nodded at West: Two more in eternal slumber.

West took a deep breath in anticipation of phase two. He'd been relishing the thought of taking these next two out, especially Fahim. He wished he could have beaten the man first, but the colonel had been explicit: These two had to be gassed. When their bodies were later found in the tunnel, it would look like they screwed up and succumbed to their nefarious plot.

West thought again about the innocent civilians who would die in a little under four hours. Civilians inevitably got killed in a war. Collateral damage. There was nothing he could do about it. The good of the country versus the deaths of the few. In the long run, he told himself as he moved past Taylor to the next bedroom, they were actually saving innocent lives by preventing future terrorist killings.

He checked his watch: four-forty-two. Right on schedule. Maybe a little ahead. Stopping outside the door, he slipped off his backpack. Two M-95 gas masks, straps folded back over the faceplate, each hooked up with the special gas cylinder connected to the drinking tube. The tube had been doubly sealed with duct tape to prevent even the slightest chance of a leak. West then took out the nylon rope, the folded body bags, the duct tape, and his own gas mask. They'd rehearsed it numerous times. Subdue and secure them. Once they had been tied up, one man would hold while the other slipped the gas mask over the target's head. Tighten all straps, check the seal, open the valve on the canister to release the small but lethal dose of the gas. Seal them with the garbage bags and then inside the body bags for transportation by him and Lee while Taylor and Dobrovits remained behind to open the gas line and set the IED. Not overly complicated, but intricate enough to require total focus, total concentration. West was looking forward to seeing Fahim's face as he squirmed right before the mask was forced over his head. The little prick was finally going to get to try on his M-95, not the Israeli model he so much despised. Too bad the Israeli model didn't have the drinking tube to attach the gas canister. It would have been as nice an irony.

West flashed the others a thumb's-up and slipped into the room. Ibriham was lying on the right side of the bed, Fahim on the left.

West cocked his head for the others to follow as he moved to the right side. He waited to put on his own M-95 so he could look down into Fahim's face when he was awakened for the deadly kiss.

The kiss of death.

Viceroy had never been able to sleep during an op, even after he'd stopped going into the field with his men. Despite being miles away, it was like he was right there, smelling the sweat, feeling the adrenaline surges of the actual execution. Fingering the Havana, he stood on his balcony in the darkness and looked at the lights of the city. In the distance he could see the Washington Monument. He wondered what the view would be like from the White House.

Viceroy looked at the text message.

Like clockwork. Going to point 2.

Good. Lee and West had the bodies of Ibriham and Fahim in the van and were heading to get the Metro Transit Line maintenance service truck they'd "borrowed" earlier. It would allow them easy access along the railroad tracks so that the two bodies could be placed appropriately while it was still dark. Then Lee and West would return the truck and board their respective trains. Once they'd arrived at the station, they'd set the two suitcases down at each end of the platform, next to the ventilation ducts, then don their masks and twist the valves.

Viceroy pictured the chaos. He'd seen firsthand what nerve gas could do, back when old Saddam had used it against the Kurds. Not a pretty sight—people dropping, bleeding from every orifice, coughing and dying in the wave of odorless, color-less, tasteless death. This would take place just a few blocks from the White House, with ZCCN news showing the aftermath.

It would be Harris's demise. There was no way he could recover, especially after looking soft on terrorists in the debates last night.

The images of the dying flashed through Viceroy's mind again. *Regrettable, but necessary. To be a well-favored man is the gift of fortune.*

He couldn't remember which play that was from. Later, after it was all over, he'd allow himself the luxury of looking it up. So much was left to unfold, so much left to do.

The pink tincture of the sky to the east told him dawn was coming.

The prelude to a new dawn.

Keep me posted, he texted back.

When Felicia felt her cell vibrate with an incoming call, she wondered if it was McClain, but didn't dare answer it. She didn't even risk looking at the screen. It was six-oh-three and she and Joiner were in an abandoned gas station a few blocks away from the target site—the final briefing in the staging area before deployment. Joiner stood behind her, decked out in his black ninja outfit, looking like a fat clown in spandex. Ill-fitting spandex stretched way too far around his substantial girth. But she didn't look much better. She wore black BDUs, the same kind she wore for tactical training exercises. She'd covered her hair with a camouflage scarf and a baseball cap.

The tactical team leader from the FBI's SWAT team, Special Agent Dahlstrom, went over the raid plan, placing his marker on each section of the oversized diagram of the apartment building. "Team one will approach the front door after team two has assembled in back. We have observers and surveillance personnel on scene, waiting. They will not participate in the raid and will remain outside the building as the raid is executed."

Felicia felt her phone vibrate again. Maybe she'd get a chance to listen after the briefing. She sensed it was nearing an end.

"Once both teams have assembled, we will simultaneously breach both the front and rear doors," Dahlstrom said, his marker dotting both exits. "Remember, you still have to go up one flight of stairs and then do a second breach. Move quickly, but pace yourselves." He paused and glanced around the room. "Agents Beaumont and Johnson will follow team one in the front. Agent Knight will follow team two in the rear."

Move to the back of the bus, Felicia thought. She also thought of how ironic it was that she'd been the one up all night, writing the damn complaint, reviewing it with the U.S. Attorney, answering all the questions from the magistrate, and then slipping into her BDUs to play Rambo. Or should that be Rambette? Regardless, she felt crusty. She hadn't even had time to shower.

"Questions?" Dahlstrom asked.

Felicia could feel Joiner's close proximity. Why did he have to stand right behind her? The man's breath was God-awful.

"All right," Dahlstrom said. "Take five and smoke 'em if you got 'em. We'll do some vehicular-exiting rehearsals and then be ready to move out in fifteen."

The vehicles were all dark-colored vans. Inside, they had two long seats running along each side with nothing in the middle, allowing for a quick exit.

She thought about her voice mail. Joiner had gone up front to converse with the team leader. Felicia glanced at the last incoming number. Not McClain's. It was totally unfamiliar. She hit the voice mail designation and held the phone to her ear.

"Ah, hi, Felicia, this is Jennifer McClain. We met last week, remember?"

The girl's voice sounded hushed, nervous.

"I'm sorry to call you like this, but I'm so worried about my dad and my mom won't let me call him. He was involved in a shooting. She took away my cell phone, even." The girl's speech sounded like she was running instead of talking. "Anyway, I'm here at the train station. I snuck out early this morning and walked all the way over here. I'm going to take the Orange line downtown and wait in the Metro Center Station until my dad comes. I need you to call him and tell him to meet me there. I should get there by eight-ten. I don't have his number because my mom took my cell, but I got yours from your card. Thanks. I really need you to help me on this. I absolutely have to see my dad. Please. And please tell him not tell Mom, okay? Thanks."

What a time for teenage angst, Felicia thought, pressing the button to disengage the call. But was there ever a good time?

She had to get hold of McClain. She couldn't let Jen sit alone in the train station, waiting for her dad. Jen was no street-smart city kid. Felicia had to call McClain now, but Joiner watched her with his prying eyes. Had he seen her on the phone?

Felicia slipped the phone into her pocket and started for the door.

"Knight," Joiner called out. "Where do you think you're going?"

She returned his stare. "To the bathroom."

"What? Absolutely not." Joiner's face twisted into a frown. "I forbid it."

"You forbid me to use the bathroom?" She let just the right bit of outrage creep into her voice.

"What if somebody sees you dressed like that? We can't afford to jeopardize this operation. You should've gone before."

"I've been up all night, remember?"

"Agent Joiner, let her go," Dahlstrom said. "The last thing we need is someone going on a raid with a full bladder." He turned to Felicia. "The water's been turned off in this place, and there's nothing else open along this strip. The best I can offer is the alley out back."

"There's a couple of dumpsters down about fifty feet," Beaumont said.

"Yeah, that's what the rest of us been using," Johnson chimed in. "Go ahead. We won't tell."

"Just watch where you squat," Beaumont added. His idiot partner snickered along with him.

"Fine," Felicia said, "and I won't tell anybody about the helicopter ride up north."

That silenced both of them. She held their gaze for a few moments, then said, "I'll be back in a minute."

"Don't let anybody see you," Joiner yelled.

I'm not planning to, she thought.

CHAPTER 29

The ringing woke McClain. Six-oh-eight. Rays of early morning sunlight were beginning to filter between the slits of the blinds. *Christ, who was calling at this hour?*

Then he thought about Kelly.

His cell phone was across the room, on his dresser. As his feet hit the floor, he heard something—felt it, too. Cold air. The back door of his apartment opening. He heard footsteps. Rapid footsteps.

McClain pulled open the drawer where he'd put Kelly's shoulder rig and Python. The gun was coiled inside the holster rig. As he grabbed it, a dark-clad figure came through the door with a semi-auto. The Python and shoulder holster slipped from McClain's hands as he whirled.

"Don't move," the figure said.

The holstered Python bounced on the rug, the speed-loaders spilling out of the smaller leather cases. McClain figured even if he dived for the gun, he'd never get it unholstered in time. Something about the way this guy moved smacked of professionalism, like he was law enforcement. But there were no visible insignias, and the guy had on a black face mask with slits for his eyes, a pair of night-vision goggles flipped up on top of his head.

Not law enforcement. McClain raised his hands. *Military.*

A second man, similarly clad, appeared, also holding a pistol. He stepped into the room, carefully avoiding the line of fire from the first man's weapon, and kicked the Python off to the side.

"On the floor now," the man said. "Face down."

McClain lowered himself to the floor and put his hands down. He stayed on all fours, mentally calculating the distance to the Python and his chances of making it.

"All the way down," the first guy said.

The second man kicked McClain in the side. It wasn't a hard kick, but enough to knock some of the wind out of him. The guy's foot then pressed down on McClain's back. "I said all the way down."

McClain felt himself being flattened. The second guy knelt on top of him and pressed the barrel of the Glock against his temple. "Make a move and you're dead."

The man on top of him twisted McClain's arms behind him and ratcheted handcuffs over his wrists.

"If you guys are looking for money," McClain said, "you're shit outta luck."

"Shut up," the guy on his back said.

"Let the man talk," the first guy said. "The more he co-operates the easier this whole thing'll be."

The second guy got up.

"See now," the first guy said. "That wasn't too bad, was it?"

"What do you guys want?"

"In due time." First Guy holstered his weapon and keyed the microphone on the radio attached to his belt. "How do things look down there?" Pause. "Roger that. We're secure. Stand by."

McClain rotated his head and saw the errant speed-loader lying a few feet away on the rug, and next to it the small handcuff key. It must have fallen out of Kelly's shoulder rig when Second Guy kicked it.

First Guy pulled out a cell phone. "I'm going to notify command. You go locate his computer and get started on that."

Second Guy nodded and left.

My computer? What the fuck's going on?

The two teams practiced getting in and out of the vans four times, starting in slow motion and then gradually doing it faster and faster. Felicia was feeling the strain. She'd been up all night and was dog-tired. This Dahlstrom guy was thorough, she'd give him that. About the only pleasure she got was watching Beaumont and Johnson struggling to get in and out of the van's doors each time. Good thing they were bringing up the rear.

She wondered if McClain had gotten her voice message. She figured he'd text her back to let her know. Maybe he was in the shower. She glanced at her watch. Six-twenty. Not much time left.

Dahlstrom whistled. "All right, line up in proper order and get back in. We're shoving off." He keyed the microphone on his radio and said, "T-one to t-two. Are the snipers set?"

Felicia couldn't hear the reply, but saw Dahlstrom waving his arm to speed them back into the vans. It was getting close to crunch time. She tried to push all thoughts of McClain out of her mind.

Can't think of anything else until this is done.

Viceroy read the incoming text message: *target one secure*

That meant they had McClain in custody. It was just a matter of them typing out his "suicide note" on his computer and persuading him to sign it.

Computer? Viceroy texted back.

In progress.

Hard drive removal and substitution too?

Roger that.

Womack and Thomas were two of his best Bravo team members. He didn't doubt they'd be able to get McClain to sign the note without leaving any discernible injuries, even thought they'd dropped the ball in the parking garage. But McClain had been lucky during that one. Plus, Viceroy had given them instructions to forge a scribble if McClain wouldn't cooperate. With the planted evidence and bank account investigation on the new hard drive, they only had to make it look feasible that McClain had taken his own life. The customary, cursory investigation would avoid any embarrassing scandal, and McClain would be quickly forgotten, brushed under the rug, scraped from the bottom of their departmental shoes.

The listening devices had to be removed. Viceroy sent another text: *Ears recovered?*

Working on it, sir.

Maintain proper time control, he texted. *Advise when plan execution completed.*

Roger that.

Viceroy felt the tension start to lessen. It wasn't over yet, and a few more crucial pieces had to fall into place as phases three and four were executed. It was like being fifteen yards from the goal line. They were on the cusp of scoring. After that, victory would be inevitable.

Chapter 30

While First Guy texted, McClain had rolled onto his side and tried to inch closer to the handcuff key, but First Guy flipped his phone shut and looked down at McClain. "Going somewhere?"

"Just want to take the pressure off my arm." McClain grunted, as if in pain.

"Sit tight. We'll be with you shortly." First Guy turned and spoke to his partner, whom McClain could hear moving in the other rooms. "Howie, don't forget Command wants the hard drive removed and substituted with the one we brought. Get the ears while you're in there. And bring me a chair so I can get this one."

Ears?

First Guy caught McClain's perplexed reaction because he laughed and said, "It'll all be crystal clear in a little bit."

"I'll bet."

The slitted eyes stared down at him. "Don't recognize me?" First Guy pulled off his mask, then grinned. "How about now?"

McClain scanned his face. White guy, dark hair, about thirty. Face unfamiliar, except for the jawline. That did strike a chord of recognition. McClain couldn't place where. The guy's grin remained wide, showing a set of oversized teeth.

"Give up? Okay, one more clue." He lowered his chin to his chest and said in an altered, Mideastern-sounding voice, "How do I know you will not shoot me?" He looked up, his big teeth flashing. "Remember now?"

Saddam, McClain thought. From the parking garage.

"Yeah, go ahead," First Guy said, keying his mic. "Roger that. Keep me advised. I'll contact command." He glanced down at McClain and grinned again as he pulled out his cell phone and typed in a text message.

The way he'd talked convinced McClain more than ever that these guys were part of Viceroy's crew. That's who "command" was. "Giving the colonel another update on me?"

"You're smarter than you look, but then again, right now you're looking pretty damn pathetic."

From the other room, Second Guy said, "I got the ears. Waiting on his computer to boot-up. Want me to get the one in there?"

First Guy glanced up at the ceiling. "Nah, I can get this one. Give me something to do. He ain't going nowhere."

McClain followed the man's gaze toward the mounted light fixture. *Ears. The fuckers had wire-tapped his apartment.*

He rolled onto his side again, moving with slow deliberation, and managed to brush his fingers over the key on the carpet. He picked it up and began trying to fit the end into the rounded slot in the handcuffs.

Second Guy set a chair in the middle of the room, directly under the ceiling light fixture. He looked at McClain and said to his partner, "You gonna be okay here?"

"Sure. He ain't no problem. Besides, this'll just take a minute. You get that note written on his computer?"

Note? Computer? The key kept tracing over the smooth surface of the metal instead of the slot. McClain moved his fingers over the edge of the handcuffs, trying to reorient himself. It was so damn hard when you couldn't see what you were doing.

Second Guy returned to the other room while First Guy—

"Saddam"—holstered his gun and adjusted the chair. McClain was probably four feet away from it.

"I got to admit," Saddam said, placing one foot on the chair and testing its stability, "listening to you snore and sing in the shower was pretty dull duty." He stepped up with his other foot and reached both hands toward the fixture, unscrewing the decorative nut that held the glass shield in place. "But when you were getting it on with your girlfriend, well, that was interesting. She's quite the moaner, ain't she?"

McClain kept trying to work the key into the tiny hole, but kept missing.

Saddam guffawed and looked up at the light fixture. "Don't worry, she'll be well taken care of shortly."

The base-nut was almost unscrewed. Now or never, thought McClain as he felt the key slip inside. He twisted the key, the ratchet released, and his left hand slipped free, his right still cuffed. Saddam held the light fixture in one hand now as he fished in the glass bowl with the other. When he glanced downward, McClain curled into a ball, drew his knees to his chest, and thrust his legs toward the leg of the chair.

Wood splintered. Saddam hit the floor with a heavy slam. McClain, his right hand still manacled, slid over and delivered two elbow strikes to Saddam's left temple. His eyes rolled back.

McClain heard someone scurrying in the other room. He reached for the shoulder rig and got his right hand around the grip, the handcuff dangling from his wrist. He tore off the holster with his left and raised the big revolver just as Second Guy came through the doorway, his pistol at chest level.

McClain squeezed the trigger and the Python exploded. The roar was deafening, the recoil jolting. Smoke burst from the barrel and hung suspended in the air. Second Guy grabbed his chest and stumbled backward.

No blood. Maybe the guy wore body armor. McClain aimed

at the man's face and pulled the trigger again.

This time the roar seemed less startling. As his vision shifted from the sights to the figure beyond them, McClain saw the man's head jerk back like he'd been hit with a sledgehammer. He bounced off the doorjamb and fell, face first, onto the floor, a widening red puddle flowing outward from the left side of his head. McClain moved forward, grabbed the fallen man's gun, and tossed it away. He checked the man's pulse. Nothing.

McClain whipped the Python back toward Saddam, who was still flat on his back but beginning to stir. McClain moved over and clamped his left hand over Saddam's right wrist. He put the barrel of the Python against the man's face and cocked the hammer. "Give me a fucking reason I should let you live, asshole."

Saddam blinked twice but didn't say anything.

McClain took the man's pistol, a Glock forty, out of its holster and tossed the weapon away. Then he used the key to remove the remaining handcuff.

"Single action takes the slightest trigger pull," McClain said. "You move, even a little bit, your brains will be splattered out the back of your head. Now, I want some answers. What's the plan?"

"Plan?"

McClain remembered the man's radio and saw the ear mic.

"Open your fucking mouth," McClain said. He kept the barrel of the Python pressed against the guy's face until The Grinner opened up. Then McClain jammed the barrel into The Grinner's mouth and used his other hand to pull out the ear mic. He tossed it aside, then stripped off The Grinner's radio and patted him down. The Grinner had a pair of handcuffs in his pocket. McClain removed the barrel from the man's mouth, rolled him over, forced the guy's arms behind his back, and slipped the cuffs over his wrists.

"Now." McClain prodded The Grinner's cheek with the Python. "Tell me your plan."

"No plan."

McClain slapped The Grinner's face. "I ain't playing with you, asshole."

"No plan."

McClain slapped him again, harder. "How many men have you got downstairs?"

"None."

McClain punched him, then grabbed The Grinner's cell phone and reviewed the text messages, trying to put the snippets together with the parts of the conversation he'd overheard. He saw several recent texts from COMMAND.

McClain assumed he was target one, but who was two? Then it struck him. Felicia.

"Who's target two?" McClain asked. "Tell me."

"What you gonna do, hit me again?" The Grinner's teeth were streaked with blood, but he still managed a smile. "Go fuck yourself."

McClain's fist slammed down onto the man's face.

The Grinner flashed bloody teeth. "Shit, that the best you can do? I'm special forces. I'm tougher than you could ever imagine."

McClain knew the other parts of Viceroy's plan were unfolding as they spoke. He took a deep breath and moved the Python down against the back of The Grinner's right leg.

"Okay, I'm through playing," McClain said. "Either tell me everything I want to know, or I'm going to start blowing away some of your body parts. Understand?"

"You ain't got the balls."

McClain thought about Felicia and squeezed the trigger. The Python recoiled in his hand as The Grinner's leg jerked spasmodically. The man screamed, then settled into a keening

293

moan. A red stain poured outward from the man's thigh.

McClain felt sickened by what he'd just done, but remembered Mogadishu. People would do anything when they had no other choice. The die was cast. He moved the Python to The Grinner's left leg. "Want to try for two?"

The Grinner's words came through clenched teeth. "I'll tell you. I'll tell you. We were supposed to do a suicide note, make you sign it, make it look like you killed yourself."

"What's the rest of it? What's phase two?"

"The raid. Your FBI girlfriend."

"What about her?"

"Christ almighty, call me an ambulance."

"Shut up. Give me the rest of it or I'll shoot you again."

"Arab apartment's rigged to explode. IED. Gas line left open."

Shit, McClain thought. His head swiveled back toward the clock. Seven-oh-five.

Felicia said the raid was set for what? Seven-forty? Seven thirty? Seven-fifteen?

"How they gonna set off the IED?"

"We got a man on the back. He's got a cell phone."

"What street is it on?"

The man recited the address.

McClain knew he had to move fast. Plus, he had more hostiles to deal with outside.

"What's phase three?"

"Ambulance, please."

McClain jammed the barrel of the Python against The Grinner's back. "Want to be a paraplegic shitting in a bag for the rest of your life?"

"They're gonna hit the Metro Center Station downtown."

"Who?"

"Sergeant West and Captain Lee."

"How? With what?"

"Sarin."

"When?"

The Grinner moaned.

"When?" McClain roared.

"Eight-ten train."

McClain picked up The Grinner's phone and dialed nine-one-one. Before he hit the send button, he said, "How many of your personnel are downstairs and what are they driving?" He punctuated the question with another nudge of the Python against the small of The Grinner's back.

"Two more men, black Chevy van."

"Where's it parked?"

"In back."

McClain drew his fist back and punched The Grinner in the face. He hoped the blow would knock the man out, but it didn't. Instead, his head bounced off the carpet and he writhed in pain. The thought of punching the man again sickened McClain. He used the guy's pistol belt as a tourniquet, then stood up. Ripping the sheets and light blanket from his bed, he spread them on the floor, then rolled The Grinner into the folds several times, securing him. McClain slipped on pants and a sweatshirt and stuck the Python and the handcuffs into his beltline. He put on his gym shoes and a jacket before hitting the send button on The Grinner's phone.

"Metropolitan Police, what is your emergency?" the dispatcher asked.

"This is Detective McClain, MPDC Police. I've got two home invaders inside my house. One is dead, the other wounded. There may be more invaders outside." He gave his address.

"Hold on, sir, I'll dispatch police units and an ambulance. I'll need to—"

McClain dropped the phone on the bed. He figured the

telemetry of the dispatch center would hone in on the signal. Right now he had to warn Felicia. He grabbed his own cell phone as he headed out the door. Felicia's cell went into her voice mail. McClain hit the end button. He'd have to call her again, after he'd taken care of the other hostiles.

He swung around the stairs, holding the Python out in front of him. Outside, in the distance, he heard a siren. *Shit!* He'd never be able to explain everything to the responding units in time to stop Felicia from going on that raid. He ran to the next apartment building over, cut around the corner, and went to the rear. A quick peek showed a man in black standing at the back door. He spoke into a radio. A black van sat idling next to him. McClain could see one man behind the wheel. There were a half dozen cars between him and the two hostiles. He skipped across the expanse to the first car, then crouched and went around to the back. A rickety cyclone fence separated the apartment parking lots from an abandoned strip mall. McClain found an opening in the worn fence and slipped through. Moving up parallel to the rear of the van, he stuck the barrel of the Python through the fence and zeroed in on the man behind the wheel.

The guy at the back door raised his radio and said something. He shook his head and turned back toward the van, at which time he made eye contact with McClain. A look of shock spread across the man's face as he reached inside his coat.

McClain fired at the man in the van, then rotated and fired at the other guy. The big Python roared in his grip. The outside guy was back against the building, holding his chest. The side window in the van was shattered, the occupant not visible.

The sirens were growing louder. He had maybe sixty or seventy more seconds to act. McClain stuck the Python back into his beltline and grabbed the wires of the fence, scrambling upward. The fence had been inverted, with the barbed bottom on the top. The sharp edges cut into his hands and leg as he went over. He dropped to the other side and ran to the van, ripping open the door. The second outside man was on his side, slumped over the passenger seat, a neat hole in his left temple, his face covered with tiny shards of shattered glass. McClain pulled him out of the van and jumped in. He jammed it into gear and felt the sickening rise and fall as he drove over the dead man's body.

His mind raced as he dialed Felicia's cell again. *Where had she said the raid was going to be?*

He saw the flash of approaching squad car lights, so he cranked the steering wheel to the right and drove through an adjacent parking lot, bouncing hard over a railroad tie and a low stone barrier that separated the two areas. He curled around the building to get on the street.

Felicia's voice mail kicked in and he waited frantically while the automated voice spelled out the options. When the tone sounded, he practically yelled into the phone, "Felicia, it's a trap. The apartment's rigged to blow. Gas line open. Don't go in." He hung up, then redialed nine-one-one.

When the dispatcher came on the line McClain reidentified himself and stated he'd just called about a pair of home invaders at his address.

"Yes, sir, we have units responding. Please give me your current location."

"No time for that," he said. "Listen carefully. The FBI is doing a raid in Arlington." He recited the address twice. "I need you to contact them immediately and have them cancel. It's a trap. It's rigged to explode."

"All right, sir, but I'll need more information. Please stay on the line with me."

McClain hung up. He didn't have time to play twenty questions. Hopefully, the dispatcher would notify the feds. But how long would it take for the info to filter down? Too fucking long!

He glanced at his watch. Seven forty-five. And what about the Sarin at the Metro station?

He was running out of time.

He came to an intersection with heavy traffic and a red light. Cranking the wheel, he shot around the line of cars. He honked his horn and swerved into the lanes of oncoming traffic to a cacophony of blasting horns. The van sideswiped an oncoming car. McClain didn't even slow down. Cars darted out of his way. He continued until he got to the intersection and wormed across the street to the screeching of brakes and more blaring horns. Once across, he dialed the mobile operator and asked for the Arlington emergency dispatch center. After several questions and a few more delays, a woman asked him what his emergency was.

"Apartment building on Whipple," he said. "Big gas leak. It's going to explode."

"What's the address, sir?"

He gave the address, added "A bunch of students live there," and searched for something else to say that would narrow it down. "The police or FBI is doing a raid there this morning. Right now. Send the fire department. Gas leak."

He couldn't waste any more time and hung up. He had to figure out a way to get there in time. He glanced at his watch. Seven-forty-eight. He'd never make it, but he had to try. He pressed his foot down on the accelerator and his hand on the horn.

The vehicle sat idling, no movement, no communication, nothing. Felicia sweated inside the cramped van. It seemed like they hadn't moved for an hour, but she knew it had to be more like fifteen minutes. They were supposed to go at seven-fifty. It was already past that. Something was up with the raid. They'd been deployed down the street, waiting for the snipers to get set up, just in case they were needed. The smell of perspiration was oppressive inside the van. Nerves. Her cell kept vibrating with incoming messages, but she couldn't look at it.

The vehicle moved forward slightly, then stopped.

Now what?

In the distance she heard something. A pair of sirens. Loud sirens. Blaring fog horn. It sounded like a fire truck.

One of the team members asked for an update on his radio, then turned to the group. "What the fuck?"

"What's happening?" she asked.

"I wish I knew. The fire department's showing up."

"Fire department?" another team member said. "This is turning into a cluster fuck."

Dahlstrom, who was in the other van, came over the radio. "This is t-one. We've got some kind of mix-up at the target building. The fire department's here. Move up and exit the vans, but do not execute the raid until my command."

Felicia felt the van move forward. By the time it stopped and her group had filed out, she saw Joiner in animated conversation with one of the firemen, whose helmet and long, sallow overcoat made him look like Darth Vader. Joiner's looked like a Will Farrell clone of Rambo. Dahlstrom stood on the side, his MP-5 hanging from his shoulder strap.

"And I'm telling *you* we got a call of a major gas leak from this building," the fireman yelled. "You want the whole block to go up?"

Joiner's face was bright red. "Listen, buster, I'm the Special Agent In Charge with the FBI, and I'm giving you and your men a direct order to cease and desist immediately."

"Not till we verify the gas readings," the fireman shot back.

Joiner looked ready to explode. Dahlstrom pressed his mic. "Tac-One to team. Deploy covertly on each side of the building. We'll go in as part of this diversion on my command."

The group moved out. Felicia began to follow her group when she heard the screeching of brakes from the street. She looked and saw a black van drive over the parkway. It stopped abruptly and McClain jumped out.

Joiner withdrew his Glock and leveled it at McClain.

McClain raised his hands. "Agents, hold on," he yelled. "It's a trap!"

"Stop where you are!" Joiner shouted. "Get on the ground."

Felicia ran up next to Joiner and said, "Don't shoot him, he's a cop."

"I know who he is." He looked at McClain. "Last chance. Get on the ground now."

McClain slowed to a stutter step, his hands still raised. "Listen to me, there's a gas main open inside that apartment and it's set to blow as soon as you enter."

"On the ground!" Joiner's face was as red as the fire engine.

"Hey, Lieu," one of the firemen said, running up to them and addressing the fireman who'd been arguing with Joiner. "Smitty's getting heavy concentration readings, coming from inside. We need to do a shut-off immediately."

The fireman turned to Joiner. "You hear that, Mr. FBI?"

Joiner still had his Glock trained on McClain who was getting into a push-up position.

"Knight, see if he's got a gun," Joiner said.

Felicia moved toward the now prone McClain.

"Will you listen to me?" McClain said from the ground. "This whole place is about to blow."

"Shut-off's complete," one of the firemen said. "We need to get inside."

"Execute the raid!" Joiner shouted.

"No!" McClain yelled.

"T-one," Felicia heard one of the SWAT team members say in her ear mic. "One of the military surveillance guys is using his cell phone."

Seconds later, a concussive wave from one floor above them lashed outward with an accompanying sea of broken glass, smoke, and other debris. Its force knocked Felicia off balance. Joiner, too, who discharged his weapon, narrowly missing McClain. Yellow flames billowed outward from the shattered windows like an enormous burp, then sucked back inside the apartment. Firemen began directing a water stream up at the second floor landing.

"Stand down and let fire enter," Dahlstrom said on the tactical frequency. "Be ready."

Felicia knelt beside McClain who looked up at her.

"Don't ask," he said. "We've got to alert MPDC and have them evacuate Metro Center Station right away."

"Metro Center Station?"

"Viceroy's gone rogue." He began getting to his feet. "They tried to take me out this morning. That's how I found out you were walking into a trap."

"You!" Joiner ran toward them. "You're responsible for this?"

"If you mean saving your ass," McClain said, "I am."

Joiner raised his Glock and pointed it at McClain's face. "You're under arrest."

"Put the gun down," Felicia said. "He just saved us all."

Joiner's oversized head swiveled toward her. "You shut the fuck up."

McClain's left hand swept up and knocked Joiner's gun off to the side. His right snapped down on the top of the weapon, stripping it from Joiner's grasp. McClain stepped back and held the Glock down by his side. "How about I give this back to you when you're mature enough to handle it?"

Joiner lurched forward. McClain put his left hand on Joiner's chest. "Take it easy, pal. You almost shot me a few seconds ago. I'm assuming that was an A.D. instead of a bad aim."

"Kevin." Felicia tugged his arm.

"That was not an accidental discharge," Joiner said. "It was a warning shot."

McClain laughed.

"Kevin," Felicia said again, the urgency creeping into her voice. "Did you get my message before about Jen? She's taking the Orange line downtown. She'll be at Metro Center Station on the eight-fifteen."

McClain turned and ran toward the black van. Felicia ran after him.

"Knight, where are you going?" Joiner's voice cracked behind her.

She kept running toward the van.

"Knight!"

She reached out and grabbed the door handle.

"Knight, get back here."

McClain was already in the driver's seat and shifting the van into gear.

"Knight, you get back over here or I'll have you brought up on—"

Joiner's voice was cut off as she jumped into the passenger's seat and slammed the door. As they bounced over the curb and onto the street, Felicia couldn't help but think that she was leaving her career back at the burning building. She took out her cell phone.

"I'll see if I can get them to stop the trains," she said.

"What time is it?" McClain asked as he accelerated down the street, blowing his horn.

"Eight-oh-four," she said, while wondering if they were going to make it in time.

CHAPTER 31

West held the handrail in the last car, the suitcase containing his mask and the two canisters of the binary gas in front of him. *Standing room only. Busy commute.*

Lee was in the first car with his suitcase and mask. The bodies of Ibriham and Fahim were in position, underneath the cement platform. And their Metro Transit Line maintenance truck was parked at the edge of the station, waiting to take them away from the carnage once they'd dispersed the gas. It was a simple matter of waiting until this train arrived, getting out with the crowd, and setting their suitcases in the preplanned positions.

West would set his right by the wall's intake system, at the far end of the station, and Lee would deploy his by the front. The air-circulation system would do the rest. West's little IED was already set up on the floor of the train. A quick cell phone signal and the chaos would begin. Then they'd rendezvous back at the truck—and escape.

The crowd of people huddled inside undulating with the train's rhythmic movement.

Eight-oh-six. The train was running a little behind schedule. But in a few more minutes the vast majority of these people will be dead. It's almost over except for the crying.

"We'll be there in two," McClain said, gritting his teeth as he wheeled the van up onto a patch of sidewalk and then back out onto the street, sideswiping a few parked cars as he went.

"What's the story? They stopping the trains?"

Felicia smacked her leg in frustration. "They're looking into it. They can't decide to do shit. Everything's got to go through *channels.*"

McClain swerved around another group of cars, banging into one that stopped in front of him. Felicia grunted and braced herself as they impacted. He kept on driving.

"I think Metro's on scene," she said. "Maybe we can coordinate with them."

"I need to find Jen, and that's what I'm going to be doing."

Felicia grabbed the dashboard as they bounced over a median strip, scraped against two more stopped cars, and wobbled sideways as they took the corner.

"Station's right up there," she said.

McClain saw a sea of red and blue lights flashing, a uniformed officer halting traffic on the street in front of him. No place to go. He stopped, backed up, struck the car behind him, accelerated until the wheels spun, then drove up onto the sidewalk. He hit the horn as people began scattering. The uniformed cop ran toward them, his weapon out.

"Show him your badge," he yelled to Felicia.

She held up her open badgecase. McClain hoped it would be enough as he advanced toward the corner and the huge, hooded opening over the escalators that led to the underground station beneath the streets.

He'd tossed Joiner's Glock in the back of the van, but now wished he'd kept it as he realized the Python was low on ammo. How many shots had he fired? His mind couldn't focus. His only thought was to find Jen and get her out safely. He skidded to a stop and was pulling open the door when he saw several uniformed men approaching. Felicia had already jumped out, dressed in her black tactical outfit with a big FBI insignia on the front and back. She held up her badgecase and yelled instructions to the men. McClain ran past them to the stairs and took them two at a time, pushing ascending people out of the way.

Suddenly, miraculously, Felicia was right next to him as he rounded a corner, and they both ran down the lengthy tunnel that led to the ticket gates and the train tracks.

"You don't need to do this," he gasped.

"Yes, I do," she said, equally breathless. "I'm with you."

Another group of uniformed officers were standing by the gates, holding them open and waving people through. McClain and Felicia stopped next to the cop.

"FBI," Felicia said. "We have to get through."

The cop stopped a few exiting people and ushered McClain and Felicia past the gate. McClain turned to her. It wasn't fair for her to risk her life.

"Go back," he said, "I'll look for her myself."

Felicia pointed. "You go that way. I'll check down here." She held up her cell. "Call me if you find her."

Then she was gone, before he could even say thanks.

The train had come to a full stop and the conductor made the announcement over the loudspeaker system. People bristled with anticipation of imminent release. West mixed with the departing crowd as he wheeled his suitcase onto the platform. The people began moving toward the up escalators. West walked in the opposite direction, toward the big ascending wall with the slatted vents of the cooling and heating systems. It was about thirty feet away and he kept his walk at an unhurried pace. No sense drawing undue attention to himself. He was already going against the flow, and he still had to open the suitcase, put on his mask, and adjust the dials on the two canisters to allow the combination and release of the gases.

He reached the wall, looked around, smiled, and took out his phone.

He and Lee were doing direct talk down here. He pressed the button and said, "You in position?"

"Almost. Lots of people. Hard to move."

"Roger that. I'm setting up now. Advise when you're ready." West replaced the phone in his pocket, set the suitcase next to the ventilation shaft, and unzipped it. Holding his palm next to the row of metallic slats, he felt the firm tug of the air being sucked through the openings.

His M-95 mask was in the black nylon haversack on top of the canisters. He removed it, knelt by the suitcase, and began pulling apart the Velcro thatch that secured the top of the mask's carrying case. It made a crackling sound. His fingers felt the smooth rubber of the mask, the straps looped over the front to aid in quick facial application. He still hadn't gotten confirmation from Lee. He couldn't start the dispersal until he was sure Lee was masked up.

West held the mask down, blocking it from view, and looked toward the crowd. Most were still ascending those long escalators. The huge, arched cement ceiling would be an effective container for the circulation of the gas. By the time the group in the middle got up top, the ones at the bottom would be dropping dead or at least drooping over the sides in their initial death throes. The platform was about a hundred yards long and Lee was at the other end. Lee should be set up soon. Then they would both jump down and—

A lone figure came down the bank of escalators. A sister. A pretty sister dressed in some kind of dark tactical gear with big gold letters on the front. A black baseball cap covered her hair. More gold letters on that.

Suddenly, a flicker of recognition clicked. The FBI chick. He fished in his pocket for his phone, found it, and brought it up to his mouth.

"You set yet?" he asked Lee.

"Negative."

"We got trouble. The feds are here."

"Give me thirty more seconds."

West replaced the phone in his pocket and gripped the handle of the Smith & Wesson in the holster under his sweatshirt. It wasn't a pretty thought, shooting a sister, but if she was here, she was gonna die anyway, and West figured he was doing her a favor.

Who wants to die choking and gagging and bleeding out from Sarin gas?

As McClain ran down the metallic steps, he scanned the sea of faces going up the other side.

No Jen.

He called her name, collecting a few errant glances from the ascending crowd.

Nothing.

Dammit, she has to be here somewhere.

He looked around for Viceroy's assholes, too. If he could stop them it would save Jen, and Felicia and the others. But he had no idea where they would be. Which meant he had to find Jen. Now!

He continued his slow descent down the escalator, to the subterranean chamber of the train tracks. He scanned more faces, hoping to see her.

Something else caught his eye: a man walking away from the bustling crowd, going toward the far wall of the lower section. A man towing a suitcase.

McClain dashed down a few more steps, slowed a bit as he stumbled, then caught his balance and again zeroed in on the guy with the suitcase. The man was talking on a phone. His head swiveled toward the escalators briefly and McClain caught a glimpse. High cheekbones, black hair clipped military-short, slanted eyes. An Asian. A familiar-looking Asian.

The guy he'd seen in Viceroy's office. What was his name?

Lee!

It had to be him, and his suitcase probably contained the gas.

No probably about it, McClain thought. As he began running down the rest of the stairs, he pulled Kelly's big pistol out of his beltline.

Felicia was holding her Glock down next to her right thigh as the escalator continued its downward movement. Still no Jen, but in the meantime she'd seen something else. The man who'd been moving in the opposite direction of everybody else was rolling a suitcase behind him. He stopped now and looked up at her. They were about thirty-five yards apart. She was on a slightly elevated plane, due to the escalator. Their eyes locked and a switch flipped inside her head. His bald head, the powerful sweep of his shoulders. The flicker of recognition dawned on her as she saw him raising his arm, something dark in his hand. She saw the flare of a muzzle blast as the round hit her square in the chest. She fell back, struggled to keep her balance, her gun dropping from her fingers as she hit the stairs behind her.

Her tactical vest stopped the bullet, but it still stung. Her fingers slipped over the hard rubber of the handrail and she curled into a ball.

Where's my gun? The words echoed in her mind.

She saw the Glock a few steps below her and she scrambled toward it, cutting her knees on the sharp edges of the angled metal stairs. It hurt to breathe. Three feet more. Her hand reached out, her fingertips brushing the hard handle of the

Glock. She edged forward, pushing with her feet, and grabbed the gun.

Attain target acquisition, she heard the voice of her range training officer telling her. Long ago and far away. She longed to be back there, paying more attention. She longed to be anywhere but here.

She crouched along the side of the escalator, suddenly cognizant of the throngs of people screaming as they pushed over each other and tried to get up the ascending escalator. She gripped her right hand, her shooting hand, with her left, then took another deep breath. Painful, but renewing. She looked over at her assailant—Sergeant West, she remembered—and raised up, acquiring the sight picture as she rose. He'd put on a gas mask now and his hands were doing something inside the suitcase.

Oh, God. I can't miss and hit that.

She aligned the front sight with its beveled rear twins and centered on West's chest. Then she squeezed the trigger.

West jerked back like he'd been punched hard, then leaned forward again, his arms reaching back toward the suitcase.

Felicia sighted and pulled the trigger again and again, the Glock recoiling upward with each shot, as she concentrated on putting each round into her target.

McClain ran full speed as he brought the big Python up and tried to get a bouncing sight picture on Lee. The Asian was by the ventilation ducts, bending over and unzipping the suitcase. McClain squeezed back on the trigger, then watched as the hammer jerked back, fell forward, and clicked.

Empty. He'd used up all six shots and hadn't reloaded. *Stupid, stupid, stupid.*

Gunshots sounded from farther away. McClain hoped Felicia was okay.

Lee looked up as he ripped open a black haversack and pulled a gas mask over his face, flipped the straps back over his head, and began pulling each one back, tightening the mask.

The gas has to be in the suitcase. He's getting ready to deploy it.

McClain did a stutter-step and cocked his arm back, then threw the Python with everything he had. It sailed forward, wobbling end over end, but miraculously clipped the top of Lee's head.

Lee jerked back, giving McClain enough time to surge forward, jump over the upright suitcase, knock it over—and collide with Lee.

The momentum sent both men backward, then down hard on the solid cement floor with McClain on top. He saw the overturned suitcase. The gas hadn't been released yet, or he'd be dead.

Lee pulled McClain forward and butted his face, but the mask muffled the impact. McClain responded with two quick body blows. They rolled and McClain felt Lee going for something on his right side. *A gun.*

Both groped, searching, scratching, tearing. McClain managed to get his fingers around the grip. The gun came out of the holster but he couldn't secure his grip. They rolled over again. Lee's almond-colored eyes flashed from behind the glass goggles of his mask.

McClain wedged his thumb behind the trigger so the gun wouldn't fire. But Lee's left fist shot up and slammed into McClain's cheek again and again.

The blows weren't hard, just arm punches, but they hurt. McClain concentrated on using his two hands to get control of the gun. He and Lee half-rolled on their sides, McClain on the left, Lee on his right. Lee kicked McClain's shins several times. Somehow they struggled to their knees, still fighting for control of the gun—a Smith & Wesson M&P 9. Designed specifically for military and police usage.

The irony flashed in McClain's mind. So did something else.

Lee's breathing was ragged behind the mask. That gave Mc-Clain a cardio advantage. If he could keep him dancing, maybe he'd wear himself out. McClain noticed a trail of blood seeping from a gash on top of Lee's head. Another advantage, albeit a small one. This guy was as tough as they come. Strong and quick.

Both of them struggled to an upright stance. Lee's right knee slammed into McClain's side once, twice. McClain brought his elbow down to block the third strike and almost lost his grip on the gun.

Like fighting an electric fan.

He shifted his weight forward and made an all-out effort to gain full control of the weapon. Lee shifted too, and they both went down again, slamming onto the hard smoothness of the floor, their arms moving upward, the gun slipping out of their hands. It bounced twice and skidded five feet away. McClain scrambled for it. Lee grabbed his leg and pulled him back.

McClain kicked, felt a connection, and then reached down and grabbed for the mask. His fingers curled around the air filter and he ripped upward, tearing the mask off Lee.

He won't set the gas off without it, McClain thought. *It'll give Jen and the others a chance to get out of here.* He wondered if Felicia had managed to find Jen in all the confusion.

Lee got to his feet first, going for the gun. McClain seized the man's legs and pulled him back. They both stood and Lee turned toward him, his hands raised in a fighting stance.

Just like being back in the ring, McClain thought. He raised his hands as well.

Lee tossed out a quick left jab and followed it up with a paralyzing kick to McClain's left thigh. A jolt of pain shot up his leg. He tried to dance back but Lee pivoted, his left leg

311

shooting outward and catching McClain's gut.

Rolling with the blow, McClain managed to stumble to his right, circling to stay between Lee and the gun. Time was on his side. The longer he could hold out, the more people could escape. Plus, the cavalry had to be around the corner.

Lee sent a front kick into McClain's chest. The blow felt like a knife. McClain threw a left hook that missed. Lee peppered him with two short rights, his face intense.

McClain's left shot out with a jab that hit Lee's nose. Trying to follow up, McClain threw another jab, then tossed a right. Lee slipped the punch and came up with an uppercut that staggered McClain.

What am I doing, getting hit with a punch like that? McClain shook his head.

He threw another combination, but missed as Lee danced nimbly out of the way.

I'm punching nothing but air. This guy's a ghost. McClain heard his old boxing coach yelling, "Move your head, move your head," but Lee caught him with a straight right that rocked him to his toes. He stepped back, but Lee's foot shot up in an arcing motion and the instep smacked into McClain's face. Black dots swarmed in front of his eyes and his knees buckled.

Clinch and recover. He reached out and grabbed Lee, who twisted him to the ground.

McClain felt the jolt of hitting the concrete platform with his right shoulder, the pain shooting through his arm. Lee ran for something. The gun? No, the mask. McClain jumped to his feet and sprinted after him, catching Lee around the legs. Both of them went down about three feet from the suitcase. Lee's legs fluttered in a series of kicks and McClain had to let go. He tried to grab the other man's foot, but Lee scrambled away, the mask in his hand. He was at the suitcase now, slipping the mask on and twisting one of the valves.

McClain lurched forward, tackling him and knocking him away. He tried to hold his breath in case the gas had leaked out, but Lee's elbow caught him in the solar plexus. The air whooshed out of McClain's lungs and he took a breath, wondering if he'd inhaled the deadly gas.

They rolled on the ground and McClain lashed out with a right hand, striking the mask twice before lowering it to Lee's chest, stomach, then down to his groin.

Lee recoiled momentarily, then smashed McClain's jaw shut with an upward palm strike. He started to scramble away, back toward the gas. McClain flipped over. He tried to push himself up. His hand brushed against something. The gun. He grabbed it just as Lee reached the suitcase.

McClain aimed at the side of Lee's head and fired. Lee jerked like he'd been hit with an electric jolt. He slumped forward and fell on his left side, his right eye visible through the elliptical lens of the mask. McClain fired two more rounds into him as he advanced. He could hear a hissing sound from the suitcase. The valve on one of the canisters was turned to a horizontal position. The other one was still vertical.

How come I'm not dead? McClain took two more steps toward the suitcase, knelt beside it, and stared at the two side-by-side canisters that contained certain death. His military training came back to him. *Must contain a binary gas. Need to be combined to become lethal. One was open, one still closed. But which is which?*

He blinked trying to clear his head, then put his fingers on the valves. If only he knew which one Lee had turned.

Time to guess, he thought. *Maybe I should get his mask first.*

He glanced down at Lee. He hadn't moved but the blood had pooled behind the glass of the left goggle.

McClain heard an amplified voice yelling, "Don't move! Police!"

He raised his hands. Hopefully, somebody would know which

valve to twist. And which way.

"Drop the weapon!"

McClain hadn't realized he was still holding it. He let it slip from his fingers. Still holding his hands up, he started to rise.

Another command, this one closer, advised him to stay down. Then he heard a muffled but familiar voice say, "It's all right. He's MPDC Police."

Felicia stood next to two SWAT guys clad in tactical vests and gas masks. She had a mask on, too.

McClain pointed to the suitcase. "He twisted one of those valves. Not sure which one."

"Move away from it," one of the SWAT guys said. "We got a haz-mat specialist to take a look at it."

McClain felt himself slide backwards, falling to the hard floor. Felicia, next to him, cradled his head. He smiled up at her beautiful eyes, visible behind the lenses of the mask.

"Jen?" he managed to say.

"She's safe. I found her."

McClain felt a flood of relief. He pointed toward Lee's body. "Get me his cell phone."

Viceroy watched the news, waiting for the inevitable breaking story about the attack, but so far the newscasters were recycling the same, tired headlines of the night before. No news of the op.

He sent a text for a sit-rep—got nothing. None from Lee or West. None from Bravo team. None from Taylor or Dobrovits.

Then: *you lose asshole. coming for you just like i said i would.*

The text came through on Lee's phone, but it was McClain.

It was over. They'd be coming for him. He'd be doing some kind of media-perp-walk on the five o'clock news, the lights shining on him in total disgrace.

No, that wasn't going to happen.

He took his time, putting on his dress uniform, replacing the eagles with the stars he'd never gotten but knew he deserved. Then he picked up the Havana. When he inhaled, he felt his heart speed up in a silent warning protest.

He exhaled. Smoke hung in the air. He opened the wooden box containing the chrome-plated Vietnam Commemorative Edition Colt Commander, 1911 Model. He inserted the chrome magazine, racked back the slide, and set it down in the green felt impression of the open box.

Cocked and locked and ready for action. His path was clear. The only path left for him now. Enjoy the Havana and then exercise the warrior's option.

Wearing his General's stars.

Should he leave a farewell note? A sonnet or a haiku?

No.

In the end, he returned to Shakespeare. *Henry V.*

Men of few words are the best men.

EPILOGUE

McClain thought Kelly looked frail and weak as he lay in the hospital bed with the tubes running from his side, an oxygen line under his flaring nostrils, and the IVs still hooked up. But it was good to see him grinning.

"So you mean I can quit pretending to be out of it when IAD comes back asking me questions?" Kelly looked from McClain to Felicia. "Now I see why you ain't been by to visit me."

"Give me a break, will you? The debrief for this thing took two solid days."

"And the report took another one," Felicia said. They exchanged quick smiles.

"Looks like they are still in the process of rounding up the usual suspects, too." Kelly pointed to the television set on the opposite wall.

The replay of former Vice President William Bernard expressing deep sadness at the reported suicide of his brother-in-law, Colonel Clayton Viceroy, was playing for the umpteenth time that morning. The newscaster came on, adding that Bernard had "declined to comment on rumors that he intends to pull out of the presidential race, leaving the nomination to the vice-presidential candidate."

Kelly laughed, which turned into a coughing spasm. Then he grinned again. "Politicians. Who you think they gonna run against Harris now?"

McClain shrugged. "At this point, they could choose Ronald

316

Reagan's clone and it wouldn't make any difference. But who gives a shit?"

Kelly chuckled. "If getting shot don't get me promoted, I might look into taking a desk job. Maybe something in public relations."

"Talk about putting a bull in a china shop," McClain said.

Kelly tapped his index finger against his hair. "Make that a *buffalo* in a china shop. You heard of the buffalo soldiers, ain't you?"

Felicia laughed.

"We better get going," McClain said. "We'll miss our plane. You ready?"

Felicia looked at him for a moment. "Yeah."

It was such a delicious-sounding "yeah," McClain felt a shiver of anticipatory pleasure run up his spine.

Kelly said, "Plane?"

McClain nodded. "Technically, I'm still on administrative leave, and she's the new FBI section chief. That means she can take time off whenever she wants."

Felicia grabbed his hand and held it in both of hers. "So we're taking a little trip."

"Oh? Where?"

"We're going to Disneyworld," McClain said. "Jen's coming with us. It'll be a good, get-acquainted trip."

Kelly raised his eyebrows. "Sounds interesting."

"We really should wish Ex-Special-Agent-In-Charge Joiner well in his new assignment," McClain said.

"No thanks," Felicia said. "I'm ready to blow this town for Space Mountain."

Yeah, McClain thought. *Me too.*

ABOUT THE AUTHOR

Michael A. Black is the author of 19 books and over 100 short stories and articles. He has a BA in English from Northern Illinois University and a MFA in Fiction Writing from Columbia College Chicago. He is an army veteran and was a police officer in the south suburbs of Chicago for over thirty years and worked in various capacities in police work including patrol supervisor, SWAT team leader, investigations, and tactical operations supervisor. His Ron Shade series, featuring the Chicago-based kickboxing private eye, has won several awards, as has his police procedural series. He has also written two novels with television star Richard Belzer of *Law & Order SVU*. His most recent books are *Sacrificial Offerings, Pope's Last Case and Other Stories,* and *Sleeping Dragons* in the Donald Pendleton's Executioner series.